A PETAL AND A THORN

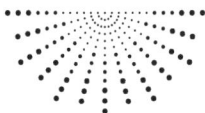

SALLY BRYAN

First Printing, 2015

ISBN: 9781688016613

CONTENTS

For the beautiful English County of Yorkshire,
My birthplace.
I hope this story is suitably crazy.

EPIGRAPH

After a lifetime of disappointment, I'd given up on writing, given up on life, given up especially on women. But then came help, sort of, in the most unlikely form imaginable.

Call it providence, divine intervention, or a visit from the angels, if you wish.

What would I call it?

In the years since I've had time to consider that very question. And the most likely explanation is that maybe I'm just bat shit crazy.

TROUBLED

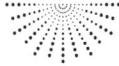

nother group of undesirables, much like the last lot, squeezed through the small gap between my desk and the long line that gathered around the table opposite. They didn't stop for me though, just like the others hadn't, and instead gave me pitying looks not unlike so many I'd received over the last few hours.

A pattern was emerging. They'd inspect my name on the laminated sign taped to the table and, if they were young, narrow their eyes whilst silently asking themselves, 'who the fuck is she?' If they were older and knew my identity, as many still did, I'd receive an altogether different reaction that was only compounded once they saw the title of the book I was promoting.

I leaned back as my seat creaked and for the fifth time counted the squares on the ceiling pattern above but gave up when they started moving. The untouched books piled atop my desk obscured me from the woman beyond - The one with the crowd of fans. Occasionally, I'd peek around my stack of masterpieces and cringe if we made eye contact.

That used to be me; popular and well-liked, though only in a literary sense.

Her line was no longer stretching outside the store, as it had throughout most of the morning when I could only occasionally catch sight of her blurry form, though admittedly, that was not due to the quantity of fans, but rather the sheer size of them.

Take for example the hippo closest to me. His black *Megadeath* t-shirt bulged out from the belly, his faded jeans stretched in equal measure, the black belt buckled with spikes and extra holes punched at its limit, the long black hair, unwashed like the rest and skin pale as one of Dracula's victims. He was the reason I'd leaned back in the first place. And they were all like him. Seriously, what kind of author was this?

I reached down inside my bag, rustled about for the good stuff and pulled out the bottle of Scotch before taking another satisfying nip and not caring whether the huge stack of books obscured my little foible or not.

Another Goth, almighty grin etched upon face, plodded toward the checkout to make the purchase of his signed copy and now her line had diminished to the extent we were again making eye contact. At least, I thought we were. She wiped her forehead in an annoyingly exaggerated way and mimed what was probably the word "phew." Worse, she was now approaching, and if there was one thing I hated more than anything else, it was the pity.

She stopped a pace from my desk and scanned the tabletop just long enough to see what I was promoting but quickly returned her polite eye to meet my sceptical glare. Clearly, she wanted information on me, we authors are nosey like that and people watchers to a fault but all thanks to my squiggly Victorian font she was still busy guessing. "How's it going?"

Was that sarcasm? I moved out my arms to encompass the barren wasteland to my fore. "Absolutely great, as you can see, I'll soon be in need of a long respite."

The damned Scotch taunted me from my bag on the floor, its neck and cap protruding temptingly from between the zips and I could still taste the sweet nectar on the inside of my mouth, its delicious burn still teasingly present.

Her eyes were drawn to some of the neglected promotional material to my rear. "Why do you have a cardboard cutout of Kiera Knightly?" If she thought my setup tacky she didn't say but the woman was now becoming borderline impertinent and I'd never asked for any of it.

I spoke in monotone, so she knew I wasn't joking. "Why do your readers slash fans all look like they were dredged from the River Ouse?"

The woman took a small step back but her face betrayed no sign of offence.

Now, taking the opportunity to properly appraise the pest up close, I was surprised to find she wasn't quite as much an eyesore as what I might have come to expect; slender, black blouse with the occasional red tat on the arms, long dark hair with tints of red styled in a grungy way, the type of dangerous lunatic you might expect to see jump on a motorcycle with the local Hells Angel, except something about this one screamed dyke. Truthfully, she looked like one of her own fans, but by far the pick of them, a photogenic face with nothing out of place and probably a bit younger than my thirty-six years.

Though through her sheer front and boldness, she'd already tested and irritated me to the limit and it had absolutely nothing to do with her having fans while I didn't -

Honest. I'd been happy in my melancholy before she'd sauntered over to chat and so my upcoming iciness would be doing her a favour. I wasn't friend material. Mostly because I had zero patience and acceptance for other people's nuances, so stay away. A lesbian, I was, but welcoming of other people, I most certainly wasn't.

At least, not anymore.

She held up her hands in a playful, yet over exaggerated mock gesture of surrender. "Ok, you win, you got me. I'm G. T. Giles. Zombie author." Well, that explained it. She held out her hand with only the slightest sign of trepidation at my callousness.

I shrugged at her name but took her hand anyway.

She lingered, "sorry, my hand's a bit clammy from holding that bloody pen for a hundred and twenty minutes straight." See how she did it? Without even realising, she was rubbing it in. And how did she know I wasn't the sensitive sort? She let go and squinted again at my name, cogs grinding inside her head, like she knew and was bothered by it, but it hadn't yet clicked. "Look, I know what it's like."

I blinked as her face came in and out of clarity. "You do?"

"Mmm, this used to be me," she gestured to the stack of untouched books, "sitting in Waterstones, despairing as people pass you by, wondering just who the bloody hell you are." The incredible thing was that she truly wasn't intending to be condescending but instead, in her own way, conciliatory.

I did not stifle the yawn and made her wait until I finished before replying. "It's the life we chose." Oh, what a moron. To be talking to me this long and not know. But, as I'd learned, she was not unlike so many others. People forget you so easily in this day and age.

She frowned and half turned away but then glanced back

with a hand covering her chin. "You know, maybe you should work on your social media. That's my advice to you. If you build a Facebook following then one quick message can alert all your readers you're in their town doing a signing. It can make a world of difference." She smiled as though pleased she'd given me her little tidbit of unwanted advice.

I twisted over my shoulder, to where 'Dan,' according to his name tag, the store manager, was clamping a phone to his ear with an expression that betrayed he was dealing with a complaint. He'd have another in a minute. I gave my attention back to my interrupter and gestured to Dan by jerking my head. "Look, they stuffed up, there's only ever meant to be one author at a time signing books, otherwise things like *this* can happen."

The skin at the top of her nose scrunched up. "Things like what?"

I sighed and decided to give it to her straight, which was the only way I knew. "My readers don't have quite the same, shall we say, level of *sophistication* as that lot," I nodded toward some of the exceptionally large hazy blobs in black awaiting her return as they plucked a book from each of her stacks, "and I hazard that if one of mine saw one of yours they'd question whether they were in the right era, never mind the right bloody bookstore."

She shook her head, disbelieving of what she was hearing, though still managed to remain infuriatingly professional. "You're blaming me for your quiet day?"

"All I'm saying, dear, is that you're hardly helping," I held up an anticipative hand to block her protest and made to stand, "but don't worry, you can have this one, I'm wasting my fucking time here anyway." As always, but despite my overt hostility, I was dismayed to find I'd barely nabbed a flinch from Miss Teflon and her eyes were again squinting at my squiggly font.

"Wait," she placed a hand on my arm, which was the most action I'd got in about as long as I could remember, and she glanced again at Miss Knightly before staring wide-eyed at me, "you're Clara Buckingham."

I rolled my eyes. "Tell me, genius, did you recognise me or did the name on the book cover give it away?" Great, now I'd have the usual questions to bat away; where have you been? Are the rumours true? Are you really as reclusive as they say?

She again brushed off the spitefulness, my lack of ability at getting a rise annoying me to the point it was impressive, "yes, you are." She stared again at Knightly, who'd hardly been my preferred choice to play Tilly, but then none of the actresses they'd carted in had come close to my ideal. "What the bloody hell are you doing *here*?"

I shook my head in exasperation. "You've been sitting opposite me for the last two hours. You know damn well what the *bloody hell* I'm doing here."

She flapped a hand. "No, I mean here in York. Shouldn't you be in LA or somewhere? And why do you need to spend your days sitting here signing books anyway?" She'd meant it as a compliment, surely, though from the genuine look of confusion it was hard to tell. Her skin turned suddenly red and she cupped her face in embarrassment. "Oh, my God, and there was me giving you social media advice, I am so stupid."

I exhaled and did not disagree, "I suppose I must be here for the love of meeting and speaking with my multitude of readers, listening to their stories about how they cried when Tilly and Elspeth finally came together on Whitby beach… yawn…and most of them have that certain glare of insanity behind the eyes. Still, it might be worse, they could be zombie fans, right?"

"Right," she dismissed nonchalantly. Oh, the girl could not be offended no matter how hard I poked and the thought occurred that by now she was needlessly starstruck by my former fame, which would only make provoking her for my own amusement infinitely harder. Though, I wasn't out of tricks yet.

"So what's your latest release?" Without asking she excitedly plunged forward with an impossibly long arm and whipped a copy from the untouched pile on my desk before taking a good look at the cover. "Oh, I see." She made a sad smile and slowly replaced the copy of *A Petal And A Thorn* as though my masterpiece was somehow fragile. And then, much to my resentment, she made the now familiar look of pity, the same dopey expression 'Dan' the store manager had bestowed upon me earlier. Though where he'd stopped at soothing words, she now absolutely gave my forearm a little squeeze. I'd be taking her back home at this rate. "You hang in there, ok? I believe in you," she said with a sympathetic tilt of the head.

I'd been willing to let her have this one, I thought, as my jaw clenched, but was now reconsidering my prior good-natured conciliatory gesture to leave and let her have the place to herself.

She glanced back at her desk, where more freaks had now gathered. "Well, duty calls. I'm Gemma, by the way. You don't have to refer to me as *G.T.*" As though I ever would, and she skipped back, finally, as my fist began to shake, either out of sheer anger and frustration, or because I was in another bad need of a serious nip of the good stuff.

I yanked the bottle free, not giving a shit that I was drinking whilst supposedly on the job and tipped it home, allowing the fluid to burn my throat in its usual delicious way.

My eyes went glassy at the stack of books before me. I'd written *A Petal And A Thorn* twenty before, aged only sixteen, in a sudden burst of inspiration and a fit of rebellion aimed at pissing off my parents, most notably my mother. Somehow, it had become a best-seller across the world. Unfortunately for me, however, *Clara Buckingham* had burnt herself out far too early and I'd been unable to produce anything of value ever since. I was a one book wonder once compared to Emily Bronte, though at least she'd had the luxury of dying early whereas I'd tried and failed miserably at reproducing anything that didn't completely stink. And twenty years was a long time to be a failure. She'd written *Wuthering Heights* and died a legend. I'd written *A Petal And A Thorn* and had to live with pity and sympathy of the likes I'd just received.

I scowled at the unworthy Kiera Knightly, who'd received an Academy Award nomination for her part as Tilly, despite sucking big time.

A flash brought my attention back to Gemma, the zombie woman, who was posing for photos between two creatures of the River Ouse, shaking hands, having the time of her life with adoring fans. I saw genuine happiness. She was loved. At least within a very small and disgusting demographic.

That used to be me, minus the disgusting bit.

And in the moment, I knew I had to do something about it - Not my own happiness, mind, but hers.

I snapped the pen I'd been holding and approached Dan at the cash register. He was staring at something on his screen before seeing and heeding to me immediately. "Hi, how're you getting on?"

I pointed at Gemma, or whoever she said she was and raised my eyebrows at him. "Tell me what you see, Dan."

He made the mistake of leaning too close and blanched, though he tried to hide it, and smiled apologetically. "Yes, I know what you're thinking, it was a genuine mix-up. We have a new admin girl." He shrugged as though it was out of his hands but he was wrong if he thought I'd drop it there.

"A new admin girl, indeed. What are you going to do about it?"

He made a long, strange sound while his brain tried to decide which word to begin with. "Ho…iiis…eee…is it really such a problem?"

I made a show of folding my arms for his benefit. "It is when she leaves her desk to bother me and anyway, that's beside the bloody point. If I knew you'd double-booked, I wouldn't be here. It's disrespectful and embarrassing for you, Dan."

"Well, I can't remove her now. She's making a killing and would you just look at that line…it's been like that most of the day as well…all paying customers." He made a feeble pointing gesture but I didn't turn around to look.

Instead, I decided to play my ace card. "Did you know that when Tim Waterstone was made redundant by WH Smith and set up his fledgeling bookstore as a penniless loser, that it was I…me, who turned up at his Kensington store opening, all gullible idealistic teen, to carry out a signing?" His mouth began to gape. "And the rest, as they say, is history."

He looked beyond my shoulder to where more camera flashes and laughter were grating against my sensibilities, in two minds over what action to take. I'd help him arrive at the right decision.

"Look, how about I ring Tim, we're still on pretty good terms," we weren't but he didn't need to know that, "and let slip that his York store manager, Dan, made a double booking the very same day Clara Buckingham was in store to do a book signing?" I had him and he knew it, and he adapted a submitting posture. "It would be pretty embarrassing for you, right, Dan?"

I'd also suspected since my arrival that he was a little starstruck by me. They didn't often go as far out of their way to ensure my comfort, offering tea and biscuits as Dan had, at least not anymore. He'd also given me the prime location facing the front door, while the zombie girl was opposite and somewhat off to the side, obscured by a badly placed support column. Just to clarify - My seeking to have her turfed out the store had absolutely nothing to do with her having a successful day while I wasn't - No, it went far beyond that, honest.

He made that pained, caught in two minds expression again and looked between myself and her. "Is there any other way? Perhaps I could book you in for any Friday or Saturday you would wish. They're our busiest days. We have Michael Crichton here in three weeks, but any other day, just name it."

I held my default stern expression. "Oh, Dan, it's really not about being here on a busy day. It's not about shifting books either, you see, and it's certainly not about the money. Heavens, I have more than enough of that already."

He waited for me to finish and after a while took his cue. "Then what is it about?"

The truth was, I was pretty much done with this, with everything. "It's about winning, Dan. I'd like her removed with haste, if you wouldn't mind." I didn't wait for him to reply and stomped back to my quiet desk.

He didn't approach her right away but spent the next two minutes pacing between the cookery section and new adult novels scratching the back of his head. Finally, he slinked around the crowd of zombie weirdos, hunched over Gemma's side and whispered in her ear. She stopped mid squiggle, pen in hand, and shook her head, glared at him, shook her head again then whipped back to look straight at me with a mouth so wide I saw three fillings. Oh, no, had he just told the girl I'd asked for her to be moved along?

She made placatory hand gestures and said something appeasing to her readers, which I didn't catch over the audible grumblings of a dozen demons of the Ouse. Then the girl stood, her gathering fanned out, and she began stomping over toward me with an angry mob in tow. For a moment, I feared she'd barge straight through my desk, but she stopped a foot in front to loom down upon me.

"I held my tongue before but I can hold it no more," she began as she clutched the desk's edge, "but *you*, Clara, or whatever your real name is, are the bitterest, most hate-filled little woman I've ever encountered in my entire life ... No, no, don't interrupt when I'm speaking ... You may have money and success, everything I dream of, but in you, I see nothing else to be proud of. You are the iciest most unfriendly human being I've ever encountered." She alternated between arms crossed, arms akimbo and pointy fingers, which was quite comical to watch and it was a struggle not to laugh. She could not do anger with conviction, not at all, and for brief flashes even looked extremely hot, which really wasn't the effect she was trying to give. She was impressing her crowd though and one particular hardcore Goth was extra fervent with the fist shaking.

"You're repeating yourself."

"What harm was I doing, huh? Some of these people have travelled all the way from Newcastle to meet me. Do you have no conscience?" She sounded less angry for the last part and seemed to ask with genuine interest.

I laughed, "conscience? You've lost me now." I chuckled some more, which hardly ingratiated me. "No…no, I don't have a bloody conscience. Not anymore. A conscience is for people who've yet to learn the reality of human nature. Give it another ten years, love, and you'll lose yours too." Oh, how the grim looks and hostility were thick within the air. "When you too realise that every single person you ever meet is nothing but a disappointment then you too will stop giving a shit about hurting others." I was able to say the last part with a straight face because unfortunately, I'd found it to be too true. "Oh, you'll learn. Why, I'm sure one day you'll even enjoy it, as I just have."

She gasped but quickly brought herself under control, turned sharp on her heel as though I was already past tense and erased from mind and quite theatrically, opened out her arms, book in hand, "sod it and sod Waterstones," before throwing it over her shoulder, from where it came to land somewhere behind Kiera. "Let's go to the pub."

There was a cheer, and a younger female fan even placed an arm around her shoulder in a gesture of support while others were giving me hostile looks, pointing fingers and laughing in a way that sounded mocking and then she was marching out the store somewhere in the middle of a cheering crowd of adoring fans.

"What's one more enemy?" I muttered, somewhat flustered, and was about to delve for the bottle when…

"Are you happy now?" Dan. Where the bloody hell had he been standing?

I composed myself and told the truth. "Oh, yeah." I gestured with my head to the giant cardboard cutout. Knightly could never have hoped to compare to the real thing, the image of perfection I held in my mind. Nobody ever came close to Tilly, not by a long way, and that's the one true tragedy of my life. People, women especially, have been nothing but a long line of disappointments, which is pretty much why I gave up on them years ago.

I grabbed my belongings from the floor. "I told them not to cast her, you know, but they didn't listen. I mean, who am I? Only the damned author, after all." His face softened and I nodded again to the cutout. "You can keep her...something to jerk off to tonight."

I left the store and didn't look back.

2

A VISITOR

I don't know what vibe I was emitting as I walked through The Shambles, the medieval cobbled street of York where the rooves of opposing shops almost touched as the buildings slanted into the street's centre, enshrouding all in near darkness. Tourists and shoppers all seemed to turn away as I approached and even the early Friday drinkers avoided my eye.

One man was standing outside Ye Old Shambles Tavern, taking some fresh air and resting his ears from the singing that resounded out from within. It was because of the din that I stopped to press my curious face against the window and peer inside because we Yorkshire folk didn't often sing, unless drunk, but the song was recognisable from my childhood.

> *Tha's been a cooartin' Mary Jane.*
> *Tha's bahn' to catch thy deeath o' cowd.*
> *Then us'll ha' to bury thee.*
> *Then t'worms'll come an' eyt thee up.*
> *Then t'ducks'll come an' eyt up t'worms.*

Then us'll go an' eyt up t'ducks.
Then us'll all ha' etten thee.
That's wheear we get us ooan back.

With a sleeve, I wiped away the window fog caused by my breath in preparation for the chorus, not because I wanted a clear view of them singing any more than I wanted to hear it, but it reminded me of a time I was happy, carefree and would occasionally get drunk with friends and be free to do such things. I wasn't always such a misery and this would be the closest I'd get to human contact this weekend.

Inside, a large group stood gathered around the fire, swaying from side to side, arms about each others' shoulders and I silently mouthed along to the words with them.

On Ilkla Mooar baht 'at
On Ilkla Mooar baht 'at
On Ilkla Mooar baht 'at

Ah yes, the legend of Mary Jane who ventured upon Ilkley moor without a hat and died of exposure.

Upon completion, there were shouts and whoops, stamps of feet on wood, a loud chink of glass and one woman, who was the centre of everybody's affections, twisted around to embrace one of the others.

It was the woman from the bookstore, half drunk and merry, surrounded by love and admiration.

And I couldn't even remember her name.

I stepped back from the window and tried to recall a time I'd ever had a drink with a fan. The answer was *never*. In fact, I could barely remember the last time I'd had drinks with anybody. Hunching my shoulders, I continued the journey home.

Through The Shambles it was a short walk to my flat inside the former Saint Williams College. The college was built in 1465 but hadn't been used as such since the Civil War, when it had been utilised as a printing press. Today the building was used as a restaurant, conference room, banqueting hall and an extremely hard fought for flat occupied by one of York's most reclusive residents. It was a beautiful half-timber framed building situated behind York Minster, the second largest building of its type in Europe and I didn't wish to speculate as to its increase in worth since I made the purchase. Of course, with this being York, like every other building in the city, my home was rumoured to possess a ghost, a seventeenth-century murderer who liked to roam the corridors and there was at least one ghost tour company that held its meeting point right outside my front door. It made a fine story, of course, but wasn't the reason I never had visitors. I may be a bitch but at least I'm an honest one.

I pushed through a small knot of tourists to access my front door, entered and closed it behind me before staring up the bare wooden steps and exhaling. Friday night; same old, same old.

The second step creaked as I transferred my weight, causing my parrot Percy to commence his insane shrieking as I continued upwards. The stairs were about four hundred years old and even if I could attain planning permission to have them removed and replaced, which would be unlikely, I could never bring myself to have them demolished anyway. Besides, my place would look weird with a modern set of stairs when everything else was so old.

As soon as he saw me, Percy chirped with contentment and I tapped his cage and smiled as his stunning red, blue and green plumage flapped to life. "Mummy's home, my darling.

Who's been a hungry bird? Yes, you have." I refilled his feeder before heading to the kitchen, switched on the light, stood, exhaled and leaned against the wall. What to do?

It must have been ten minutes later when I finally decided on a cup of tea, filled the kettle with water and threw a few pieces of wood into the stove. After a few minutes, of which I spent leaning against the wall, the kettle began to whistle. I hovered with the spout over the cup, stared at the tea bag and then threw it out.

"Much better idea." A fresh bottle of Talisker, the real and genuine Scotch, distilled on the Isle of Skye, peeped down from the top shelf. I grabbed it, unscrewed the cap and tipped a quantity into the teacup.

I must have spent the next hour pottering about the flat with its insanely high ceilings making me feel small, the squeaky floorboards and original oak timbers as I sipped on the whisky and the familiar welcome inebriation began to take effect.

I poured more into the cup, gave it a swirl for no particular reason, and perched against the living room wall as the faces opposite glared back. The people I'd met, long ago, when I was somebody, before the interest and phone calls slowed to nothing. Now, all I had were my memories and plenty of lessons learned. Oh, and a wall covered in framed photos; prime ministers, presidents and royalty. The many with movie stars were kept in another room as the lounge wall was only so big.

I collapsed into my genuine late Victorian red velvet two-seater divan, the material fading and worn where I sat, the velvet on the other side quite untouched. The grandfather clock opposite made its usual steady rhythmical sounds that I found so relaxing. Much time past as I continued sipping my drink and thinking of nothing in particular.

The TV set was out of place with the rest of my decor, but like every other idiot, I needed distracting from the more important things from time to time and so I'd settled on a piece of trash from the sixties. But now the analogue signal had been switched off by the government, I owned a large piece of clutter that I'd been meaning to throw out. It was too big for me to carry and it wasn't like there was a wife to help with the heavy lifting. Regardless, I switched it on and stared at the fuzzy black and white dots. Ten, fifteen, twenty minutes? It was all the same.

I reached for the small round mirrored glass table beside the divan where I'd set my latest sketch attempt. I was no artist with a pencil but I'd become at least mediocre at drawing this particular subject. Even with my limited skill, she was beautiful, although I'd never managed to get her quite like I intended. I was no good at the fine details that gave these things life and there was never any soul in the eyes. She was supposed to have soul in abundance but I only ever failed her. I caressed my fingers over her smooth clear cheekbones as though the paper was somehow real before smudging it with a tear.

I replaced the sketch on the whisky, tea and coffee ring stained table which had once belonged to Robert Louis Stevenson, took another sip of liquor and set the cup atop the sketch. I'd do a better job next time.

The whisky bottle had somehow slipped down the crack at the back of the divan, so I pulled it out, unscrewed the cap and again refilled the cup before setting the half-empty bottle beside it.

Resuming my pottering, I stopped during the fifth or sixth lap of the living room after spotting the scrap of paper upon the mantelpiece, on which was written my mother's telephone number. Beside it, I turned back to face outwards the last photo we'd taken together, from my university graduation. I smiled at the memory, which hadn't been altogether unpleasant, for a change. She actually had her arm around me here and I felt the heat rising within me. I fanned at my face with the small scrap of paper, finding insufficient relief and, in a fit of insanity, pulled out my mobile phone and began to dial. I made it through the first five digits before pausing to grab a clump of hair at the back of my head. Finally, seeing sense, I cancelled the call and turned the photo back to face the wall, stuffing the paper behind it.

My vision was swirling now as the walls moved backwards and forwards. The wavy pattern on the divan spiralled like a visual vibration and I turned away, heading to the corridor and, ignoring Percy's cries for attention, opened the closet. The washboard ribs played silly tricks with my eyes so I blinked hard several times, pushed aside the flat irons and placed my hands around the wooden step ladders. I held them firm for a while, the only sound that of the strutting clock in the other room. I shook the fog from my head, let go of the ladders, closed the closet door and wobbled back to the living room, collecting my latest manuscript from the bottom of the birdcage on the way before crashing hard on the divan. Percy squawked from the disturbance but quieted after a few seconds.

I flicked through the pages, all thirty of which I'd managed to write and for whatever ungodly reason, sniffed at the paper, blanched and tore the sheets in two, four and eight before scattering the shreds over the sketch on the table.

Draining the remaining whisky from the mug, I then stared blindly at the clock as its rhythm and swinging pendulum again took me away. It was half eleven when I finally snapped out of the trance.

"Wow," was it really that time already? "Where did it all go?"

I stood and stumbled again into the corridor, acknowledging Percy's protestations by sprinkling a full box of feed inside his cage, over a nearby bookcase and on the floor before opening the kitchen window followed by his cage door. He twitched with uncertainty so I scooped him up, brushed my hand against his feathers and kissed him on the head before placing him on the bannister. "It's your choice, my sweet."

Opening the closet door, I pulled out the stepladders and rope. I don't know why I'd kept the latter after it was last used to haul up a Victorian cabinet through the window. "You know, Ikea furniture comes in bits," the delivery man had remarked after almost giving himself a hernia. Funny I should be thinking of that at a time like this.

Now, I threw one end of the rope up toward my Victorian styled chandelier, aiming for one of its decorative branches, missed and sent the rope flapping uselessly across the floorboards. I tried and missed again, this time, in my inebriated state smashing two of the chandelier's hanging glass bowls, popping out three bulbs in the process and plunging one corner of the room into near darkness. For my next attempt, I aimed more carefully and this time the rope flew over the branch to dangle over it.

To ensure the setup was sturdy enough, I gave the rope a hearty tug and was *lucky* not to be killed when the whole thing crashed to the floorboards.

In shards of glass and sparks, I jumped back a little too late, but untouched and laughed, "and that's why the stupid council wouldn't allow you a proper one with real candles."

The room was dimmer now without its principle lighting apparatus and only the wall lanterns remained. I pulled the rope out from beneath the heap of shattered glass and bent metal, kicking the thing as I did. What a calamity, but it wasn't like I was practiced at this. The crossbeam, the original, strong and sturdy exposed wooden support for the ceiling loomed down from wall to wall above, and I'm sure it would have laughed at my drunken stupidity if only it could and I threw the rope over the joist sans trouble. Why I hadn't tried this first was beyond my incapable mind although it wasn't like I still required a functioning faux Victorian chandelier, expensive as it had been.

I didn't know how to tie a genuine noose or if it differed much from a lasso knot, which I did know how to tie, but after a quantity of fiddling, one end was knotted and the other wound several times about the beam until I was satisfied it wouldn't unravel. After all, it wasn't like I'd tried this before, or would ever do so again.

Evidence of this soon followed when I realised I'd been stood holding the noose whilst wondering what to do next. "A bloody stool." And I had just the thing, a four-legged appliance that had once belonged to Oscar Wilde, which I dragged in from the bathroom. Having originally bought the thing for the guest bedroom, and having never once used it for its intended purpose, it was now my *waiting for the bath to draw water* seat. Meanwhile, the guest bedroom itself had become a large store cupboard for various hoardings.

I held the rope and judged the slack, assuming there was ample enough so I wouldn't choke to death miserably, but not too much that my damned feet would hit the floor before the rope reached full tension.

So, with a shaky leg, a throbbing head and a pulse beating in my neck, I stepped up and slipped the bloody noose over my head as my glassy eyes managed to half focus on the step ladders I'd earlier brought in for this very purpose. "You bloody fool." I rolled my eyes inwardly as my foot tapped an involuntary jig on the spongey part where the arse went, which made one of the uneven legs vibrate against the wooden boards.

My breathing descended into heaving motions, blood swirled around my head making me dizzier than before yet conversely, I felt a strange clarity at the same time. The main sensation, however, was the odd concoction of sounds that came from within my throat to resonate in my ears, the thudding beat of pulses, blood gushing so fast it sounded like waves were crashing in my brain and Percy began shrieking uncontrollably from beyond the door.

I lost balance as two stool legs tipped off the floor, which I was only able to regain control over by tightening my abdominals and bending my knees to lower my centre of gravity. My heart leapt into my throat and remained there, beating, hammering so hard it hurt as sweat poured down my face and I tasted salt on my lips. "Concentrate, you bloody fool." These were my final moments and I wanted to be thinking happy thoughts when I took the step rather than the mental and physical trauma of the moment. No easy task under the circumstances.

"I forgive you, mother," I stuttered as the tears streamed down my face. I wouldn't forgive the others, however, Fiona especially, the rest could screw it for all I cared. My final thoughts? It was my childhood. Times of innocence, of before I knew what the world was, of what people were and of what I'd become. Christmas at home.

I readied myself, raised a foot and tilted forward…

…The clock struck midnight.

"Christ." It was the only sound in all existence, and it shattered my happy thoughts. Percy now also made his contribution. Three, four, five chimes…

Fucking interruption, and after I'd managed to build up the necessary courage too. Hurry up and finish, dammit. Eight, nine, ten… The room became suddenly claustrophobic, as though it had shrunk to a fraction of its original size. It was all in my head, of course; I was fully tanked on Scotch with a rope restricting the airflow to my brain. Eleven, twelve, silence…

A draft blew in through an opened window and I carefully turned my head to look outside. In my stupor, I'd neglected to close the curtains, not that it mattered, but strangely there were no street lights that usually illuminated the small courtyard between my flat and the minster. The reason soon became apparent.

A mist seeped in through the crack, thick and grey, which lingered and hung, no pun intended, around the window and concealed everything outside.

The claustrophobic sensation heightened further yet at the same time, I felt at peace. I sniffed, wiped my eye and tipped forward. This was it…

…Knock, knock, knock.

"What the bloody…?"

Was that the door knocker? It certainly sounded like brass on brass.

Impossible!

I waited as my thumping heart screamed inside its ribcage.

It was nothing, my damned former author's imagination.

Knock, knock, knock.

"Ok, that one really happened." I don't know why, but I scanned the room as though doing so might provide answers, and all the while the rope chafed against my neck. In the moment, I was rather somewhat preoccupied to bother dealing with some drunken midnight straggler who'd come calling for no conceivable reason. "What do you want?" I croaked, doubtful my voice had carried.

Knock, knock, knock.

How long had it been since I'd even heard the sound of that knocker? There was that piece of fan mail sent last year that required a signature and a few months ago I ordered a pizza, but that was about it.

"Who the fuck are you? It's midnight. Piss off!"

Knock, knock, knock.

The persistent swine.

"I'm busy. Call back in ten minutes."

Bloody hell. Why didn't whoever it was just shout up through the opened window and state their business? It was hardly like they had a sudden care for social etiquette and the whole street would've heard that brass door knocker anyway, so why not just shout and announce their need for spare change or some drugs?

Knock, knock, knock.

It's human nature and curiosity that often makes us act. It's the reason my readers continue turning the pages to see how the story will end, or why explorers persist with pushing into the dangerous unknown before discovering new lands. Not that I was comparing answering the door to discovering a new continent but considering my present predicament, it was a big step. Besides, nobody ever called on me and certainly never any midnight callers. I had a sudden image of the angry zombie woman from Waterstones having followed me home, ready for another spat. "Well, I'll give you a bloody spat," I shouted and was this time sure my voice carried. "You hear that? I'm coming!"

I loosened the knot, slipped it from my neck and lowered myself to the floor, almost stumbling due to my alcohol and attempted suicide induced shaky legs.

After taking a deep breath, I grabbed the poker that was propped against the wood-burning stove, entered the hallway, peered down the flight of steps and began my descent whilst ensuring I kept a tight grip on the bannister as I went. The boards groaned against my weight and then the usual step crunched as my shoulders pinched against my ears. I reached the floor, squeezed the butt of the heavy iron jabber, which could surely do some damage if the need arose, slid off the latch, grasped the doorknob, took a breath, allowing the oxygen to enrich my brain and improve my reactions, just in case, then...

I yanked open the door.

A single street light shone on the slender feminine figure like a spotlight from a movie, the immediate area behind her was darkened and beyond that the mist that had seeped in through my window also filled the courtyard, blotting out everything else. The minster, usually so large and dominant couldn't be seen and nor could the usual Friday night drunks be heard. Indeed, it was the silence that struck me, apart from the woman who now stood at my door. Her most obvious detail was the sweet yellow bonnet she wore, the string tied into a neat bow beneath her chin, its brim framing her face and the top edge projecting forward, and because her head was tilted down, prevented me from seeing her eyes. Long golden hair tumbled out in curls and I felt my grip slacken around the poker.

She stood leaning back slightly, both hands holding a clutchful of dress to save it from traipsing across the floor. The dress itself was long and dark green, which gave way to its white inner garment that covered the lower portion all the way to the paving stones. The beautiful fabric covered even her arms, leaving everything to the imagination and revealing a V-shape from a long slender neck only as far down as her delicate collar bones. A thick dark green cord was pulled tight around her waist. It was pretty much what you'd expect to find on any stylish Victorian lady at the ball, or on someone who'd stumbled out from a fancy dress party.

"Yes?" I asked almost in a whisper as I propped the poker against the small section of brickwork between the door frame and inside wall.

She slowly tilted up her head to reveal large green eyes. "I'm here."

"What?"

"Miss Buckingham?"

"Yes?"

"I'm here."

The mist was thick, obscuring everything beyond the strange girl but still, I looked out beyond her, expecting to see what, I wasn't sure. Cameras? The local dance troop?

"I can't stay long, Miss Buckingham." Her voice was quiet and refined with a local accent, almost. One of the nearby privately educated girls who went to St Wilfrid's perhaps, who'd managed not to mix with the local riff-raff and had thus avoided acquiring that broad Yorkshire drawl that frightened so many people.

I thrust my head out beyond the door frame, as far as I dared, and glanced both ways, but there was nobody else around. She didn't shrink or draw away despite the proximity. It was cold outside, but she didn't shiver, probably due to the expert tailoring of her dress.

"I was just in the middle of…never mind." What harm could it do anyway? Inviting some strange midnight lunatic into the house, dressed in Victorian garb. It wasn't as though I was suddenly concerned for my wellbeing and longevity, or what the neighbours, whoever they were anyway, thought about my admitting a young girl inside at this late hour. None of it mattered right now and so I beckoned her inside with a hand. "Come on up, if you must, but watch the second step. It's a little wobbly."

The sides of her mouth curled into an elegant smile and she lifted her dress a little higher, stepping inside. I manoeuvred around her within the tight confines of my entranceway so I could close the door and she took an extra step backwards. "The second step, you say?"

I nodded, "I'm sure you'll manage it."

She glided upwards with barely a sound, leaving in her wake a wash of perfume not unlike something I remembered from my grandmother as a child.

I scratched my head, applied the latch and ran after her, having remembered something. "Wait, wait, wait, don't go anywhere just yet."

But it was too late, she'd already wandered into the living room and I braced myself for the inevitable scream that could only follow sight of what waited. Astonishingly, there was only silence and so I followed cautiously after her.

She was standing by the window, gazing outside into the gloom, with her back to the sinister spectre that still dangled menacingly from the crossbeam and I could not envision how she might have missed it. Though rather than emitting any sign of horror, she instead clasped her hands at her front, most unflustered, and hummed something vaguely familiar as a nursery rhyme. The girl appeared to be in her early twenties and so I wanted to spare her the grisly sight of my method of intended suicide, whoever she was.

"If you could just stay where you are for a moment…keep looking away." I blathered, jumping and lamely trying to uncoil the damned rope from the beam and with each landing causing a crash of boot against floorboard.

27

"I do so admire your abode," bless her, she pretended not to notice.

"Excuse me?" Dropping my futile method, I dragged the stool into position and pulled up and over the long length of the rope in an effort to uncoil it from around the beam, which meant the task would take a little longer. Stupidly, I'd set the thing so that the rope was wound far across the joist, the other end of which was two metres away. It wasn't like I'd intended on taking the thing down myself; that task would have been left to some other poor soul probably months from now. "Could you repeat what you just said?" I asked, preoccupied as Oscar Wilde's stool wobbled beneath my feet.

"I never visited York until now, but I'm so very pleased I made the trip." She still had her back to me but was now glancing over the bookcase that had once belonged to Bram Stoker. "My mother possessed one similar to this, though not quite as well polished."

It was a beautiful bookcase, alright, containing five shelves and all encased within a glass cabinet. The oakwood design had wonderful ornate carvings and I loved the thought that the great man had once kept his own books in it. Now, however, it contained books I regretted ever reading and would never touch again, books that had at one time inspired me to try make a difference but had only contributed to the heartache I'd caused with my loved ones. Karl Marx, Betty Frieden; those sorts, and I only kept them to serve as a reminder. My own book was also there but on a different shelf; sandwiched between *Wuthering Heights* and *Jane Eyre*. Call me full of it, but I was only acting on the praise of the critics, and it wasn't like I'd ever reproduced the success and acclaim of *A Petal And A Thorn* anyway.

"You've never been to York?" I was distracted from the task at hand because my speculation she'd grown up in the area was evidently false. I finally pulled the rope free, quickly coiled it up and tossed it inside a set of drawers. "Oh, you may sit yourself." I found my manners whilst using my feet to shift the broken glass into the nearest darkened corner along with the bent and twisted metal of my former chandelier.

She turned around, smiled briefly then glided across to the divan in such a way that eliminated any bobbing of the head. People always bob their heads when they walk. It was the biomechanics of the human being. In fact, there was only one group of people who did not bob their heads and that was only because…

"I do hope my calling on you unannounced at this late hour has not inconvenienced you in any way." She didn't say it as in a question, but rather as a statement.

Inconvenienced me? Well, chewing on it for a second, she did rather alter my plans, yes. Though I wouldn't tell her she'd saved my life. For one thing, it just wasn't polite conversation, nor believable.

"Well, you're here now so I hope my couch is to your liking. Can I get you anything? Cup of tea? Biscuit? Tot of Scotch? An endorsement for whatever play you're auditioning? My name may still carry *some* weight, but I've made a lot of enemies in this town, and others too come to think of it, especially within the so-called artistic community."

She sat with the most perfect upright posture and now placed both hands into her lap, turning to face me where I stood by the window, unsure of what to do with myself. She did not humour my damned impertinent questions and so a short silence ensued. Unlike nearly all people, this one wasn't intimidated, at least not by me, and I wondered how much she'd drank tonight, before deciding to make a nuisance of herself at one of York's most sought after addresses.

I squinted in her direction and scratched my head. "Seriously, which troop did you say you were with?"

"I am not preoccupied with any troop, acting or otherwise. I am here merely for you." She brought her hands up to the two loose cords either side of her bonnet's bow, pulled them outwards, unthreaded them and I held my breath as she removed her headwear. A single long clump of golden curls rolled down her face to join the others and with the backs of two fingers, she delicately moved it away from her eye and tucked it behind her ear.

I was still holding my breath and of their own accord, my eyes flicked across to the nearby table toward the sketch but unfortunately, it was buried beneath a tonne of crap and a whisky bottle. In truth, she didn't look a thing like my useless sketch, well, not really, but in other ways…

I'm no sketch artist, as I know full well, but although the childlike attempt I'd made was still somehow reasonably attractive, it still barely looked human. But this, this girl - She was human, alright.

Oh my, but she was the very image of perfection. Her golden hair seemed endless, much of which was tied into a bun that rested on the crown of her head. Large clusters were left running untamed and rampant down her cheeks and shoulders. Now the bonnet was removed, her finer features were visible with no distractions. Deep green eyes that lay perfectly above a slender nose and lips wide and thin. Of course, her features were perfectly symmetrical, her skin as clear as the purest stream - Flawless in her beauty. At least facially she certainly was and I silently cursed that she'd called around in such a dress, beautiful as it looked on her, but it did nothing to showcase her figure, however she looked beneath it. Considering how attracted I was merely to her face, that I couldn't be seen to drool over her curves was probably for the best.

I recalled her answer to my question and, sensing bullshit, stamped my foot. "No, no, no, don't play games. What the fuck are you doing in my living room on a Friday night if not for an endorsement? And what's your name anyway?"

"My name? You mean, you don't know?" She stood and again did that gliding thing in the direction of the framed photos on the wall. She tilted forward, apparently admiring them. "Why do you attire your abode in the traditional manner, yet conversely opt for strange colour photographs to adorn your walls and mantelpiece," the beautiful idiot considered for a moment, "do they not lack the demure and charm of the real thing? And why must you act so familiar with men of whom you are unwed?" She still leaned forward, taking small sidesteps as she moved along the wall and pointed a dainty finger at one particular frame. "Is your arm not held firmly around the posterior of this gentleman?"

I didn't know what to make of this and rubbed the back of my neck. "That is no *gentleman*. That is Tony fucking Blair, for what good that creature did anybody." Beautiful idiot indeed. I took a single step toward her. "I don't know how much you've been drinking tonight, but I'm in need of a dram myself."

The Talisker bottle still sat on the table, which I grabbed and selected two glasses from the cabinet. When I turned back, she was watching me from her position by the wall.

I held up the glasses. "I like you. You amuse me and you're probably a little better…just…than the alternative I had planned for tonight. Whatever your name is, please say you'll join me for a tot?"

She looked amused but did not laugh. "A *tot* may not be

31

very ladylike, indeed, such things are best left for the gentleman within our company."

"What?" Was she for real? I gestured about the entirety of the room with my arms. "What gentlemen are you talking about? And feel free to break character at any minute." I poured a token measure into the glass, giving myself the same since I was already delirious, evidently, and held it toward her.

After a small hesitation, she reached forward to claim the dram. "Well, since we are to be acquainted, perhaps I can make an exception on this occasion, Erica."

I nodded and held up the glass in a sign of cheers, which she mirrored. "Hmm, quite, yes," I said, mocking her dialect and damned proper way of speaking. "That is rather presumptuous of you to assume we are 'to be acquainted,' as you so elegantly put, but…" I paused for effect and bit my lip, "more to the bloody point, love, how the bloody hell do you know my name?" I might have kept my composure when she dropped the E-bomb, but inside my head alarm bells were ringing.

Her eyebrows dipped and she paused halfway toward taking her first feminine sip, holding the glass between thumb and forefinger. "Why, Erica is your name, am I not correct?"

My grip tightened around the whisky glass. "I just told you it was, but how do *you* know that? Everybody knows me as *Clara Buckingham* and not even the post office or Wikipedia know any different."

"Wikipedia?" She shook her head in the most delightful way. "Besides, I hardly see it as such an issue of inconvenience for you. Why, where I'm from everybody knows everybody and only those who routinely engage in mischief or other such miscreant behaviours are offended by such intimate terms." She sipped her dram and gave a mischievous grin, the little minx, and I knew she was playing with me. "Do you routinely engage in mischief, Erica?"

The damned familiarity of the girl was like nothing I'd ever experienced, at least not with someone I'd only just met. I cut rather an intimidating figure and that was before taking my fame, riches and oftentimes sheer nastiness into prior consideration. The truth was I wasn't even sure how to react to being spoken to in this way, so I just took a step forward and stomped my feet against the floorboards. She didn't flinch, the minx. "Mischief? Now, I hardly think that's any of your business, Miss…"

"Excuse my rudeness. I made incorrect presumptions," she half-turned away, almost abashed.

As I stood before her, all I could do was smile as she continued taking pitiful sized non-sips of my premium Scotch, glancing around at the furniture and making small expressions of approval with her sumptuous lips, one time even scanning the sketch that lay partially uncovered now I'd removed the whisky, but betraying no opinion as to my skills with a pencil. She'd taken huge liberties, not only by calling around, the imbecile, but also in how she spoke to me, but for whatever reason, it was hard to remain peeved at such a beautiful woman - Bat shit fucking crazy, yes, but beautiful all the same. I held a fist to my mouth and coughed in an attempt to reclaim my composure and serious tone, which I seemed to have all but lost.

"Well anyway, where I'm from, calling on a stranger at midnight, under the guise of…of some Victorian maiden and concealing the fact you knew my name all along, well, we call that kind of behaviour stalking and because of my position," and the fact more than a few people would love to see me dead or at the very least suffering in extreme agony, "I have to be careful about who knows my real name," as well as which feminine creatures I admit to my six hundred-year-old genuine Tudor house.

My God, she was beautiful, but just so weird, and without knowing my eyes began roaming over her dress, trying to forge some sort of clue as to how she bared beneath. But the dress resembled a tent if anything, bloody Victorian decency, and I could gage little as to the curve of her hips or the size, shape and fullness of her breasts. There was no cleavage on display for me to ogle, which was frustrating but probably for the best considering she was far too young for me, way out of my league and I was suicidal as it was. Why tip the thing over the edge by seeing what I couldn't have? I laughed to myself, "and you don't give a shit either, do you? Where are you from anyway?"

She surprised me by downing the remainder of the dram in one. "After going through what I have, women like you no longer trouble me, Erica." Taking pleasure in repeating my name, she snatched the whisky bottle from my hand, glass from the other, and refilled both together before handing one back to me. Well, I'll be damned. "And if you have the desire to know, well then, I grew up in Whitby, where I remained until I absconded, under duress, I might add." She thumped the bottle down atop my sketch.

My weary eyes had been leering at her collar bones, about the only skin on display, but now they lost all focus at the mention of the word, and it wasn't due to my inebriation. "Whitby? That town's very dear to me."

"Then you will know why I may never return." Her previous good humour had dissolved with my question and my hand twitched around the glass.

"What…what happened?"

She straightened, raising her chin, and in so doing assumed an aura of conviction, of deliberation, quite unlike what you see in the young these days, like she knew of her purpose and would not deviate. It made her look older, but only for a flash. "What happened to me is no concern of this night. As I already divulged, I am here for *you*."

"Me?" I scoffed and tasted whisky in my sinuses. "Nobody cares about *me*." And least of all some eccentric Goddess who got drunk and parted from her friends before accidentally stumbling across my home. Which tour guide was giving out my address? Shackleton probably. I'd have words with him, which would probably include the threat of another litigation. My expression softened again. "Look, I can maybe call in a favour and get you an audition with the director at York Theatre Royal. You're too late for Puss in Boots but there'll be other plays for sure." An obvious thought struck me and the pitch of my voice heightened with excitement, "or how about the York Dungeon when it all goes tits up?" Which it probably would and not because this girl couldn't charm or sleep her way to any part she wanted, but out of sheer spite that it was *I* who'd recommended her. Oh, how I'd burned all my bridges. "Honestly, they'll take on anyone at the dungeon. Can you lie still in a bed, pretend to be a sleeping vampire and then jump out to scare the shit out of people?"

She swirled her whisky around in the glass as one perfectly trimmed eyebrow dipped. "I don't understand. You would help me?"

I waved a hand dismissing her question. "I know, I know, it's a one-off, so don't get used to it, ok."

"But how many times must I tell you? As I've already divulged, I'm not after anything from you. I'm here for *you*." It didn't matter how many times she said it, I wouldn't believe her.

"Oh, come on. Everybody wants something. It's human

nature. And from my experience, young pretty women usually want the most and when you give them everything and it's still not enough, that's when they run off with…" I stopped, not wanting to go there, and swallowed, trying to fight back the tears I could feel building behind my eyes. "Now, it just so happens that…excuse me," I clenched a fist and held it over my mouth before regaining my composure. "It just so happens that you *may* have done me a good turn tonight, by the grace of God you may have. So I'm in your debt, whoever you are, so let's hear it. No more messing around. What do you want?"

I saw her expression. It was nothing but love and warmth for another human being, which I didn't deserve and I gritted my teeth as I turned away.

Almost immediately I felt the warm hand upon my shoulder. "You've suffered much and you have reason to be bitter." She spoke as though she knew; the understanding and kindness in her voice and of its own accord my head sank against her hand.

I whipped back on her, pointing a finger. "There's something about you. I can't pinpoint it exactly, but there's something about you, love. It's rare to meet a person who gives such a fuck."

Her face changed in a flash, quite unexpected, and my heart thudded. "There is no need for such continuous profanities. The first and only time I spoke in such a way, my mother rinsed out my mouth with soap." The girl turned away and stomped, for the first time she didn't glide, toward the TV. "And what a strange contraption. It doesn't quite go with the rest of your fittings and fixtures. What is it? Some kind of an elaborate table?" Either she genuinely didn't know or she really was a great actor. How could she not recognise a TV set, dated as it was.

My mind went into a temporary limbo as I tasted the soap and felt my mother's hand pressed over my mouth. Apart from myself, I'd known only one other who'd experienced the same. I took a single step toward the girl. "Who are you? I once knew a girl whose mother rinsed out her mouth with soap."

For the first time, I noticed a discoloured piece of string around her neck, which must have shifted position as she stomped across the floor. But what, if anything was attached to it, I couldn't tell.

She glanced at the grandfather clock, its constant strumming evidently having been hard at work, although I'd barely noticed - It was late. She smiled at me, "I must go. If you would be so kind as to see me out?"

My heart sank; the feeling of a saviour come and a saviour lost - Emptiness. I made a large drunken step toward her. "But will I see you again?"

She straightened and for the second time appeared older than I had her marked at. "I will return tomorrow night," she said with a conviction I actually believed, which was obviously foolish of me, at my age, "if you would desire it?"

"I would," I said without hesitation, my foolish side winning out. And then she was heading out the living room toward the stairs to where Percy was now busy biting chunks of wood out from the uprights. I'd deal with him later, I thought, as I rushed to catch up. "Wait, you wanted me to see you out."

She watched my destructive parrot with interest before again descending the stairs without a sound as an odd, indescribable feeling washed over me. I hadn't experienced this kind of interaction in as long as I could remember and it had all happened so quick, in my state of mental anguish. There was something quite ethereal yet mystifying about her and not knowing distracted me intensely, and then I realised something extremely important.

"Who are you?" This time it was more a demand than a polite ask.

From the living room, the clock chimed six in the morning. How was it that time already? And then we were cramped together in the small space by the door, inches apart.

"You know who I am, Erica. You're just too afraid to say it." She leaned forward, I didn't see her bring up her hands as they gently cupped my jaw. The clock silenced and the world stopped as her lips touched mine; gentle, closed-mouthed, too quick but heaven. She pulled away and I needed a few seconds for the fuzziness to recede.

She grasped the doorknob, opened the door and stepped outside giving me one final smile. "My name is Tilly."

She disappeared into the mist.

3

MISSION

In the foyer of the York Theatre Royal, the cleaner mopped the floor as I sat hunched forward, playing with my hands, twiddling my thumbs, tapping my feet. Piano music chimed a happy song from several rooms away and I pictured the cast of whatever play they were performing rehearsing and dancing in flamboyant costumes.

The foyer was empty, save for myself and the cleaner, who ignored me for the most part, other than for the occasional glance when I had to stand and move my chair elsewhere for her to mop. I'd been here forty-five minutes already and I knew David Maher, the director, was intentionally making me wait. For one, the same song had been run through at least seven times, the vindictive swine.

Years ago, he'd withheld box seat tickets he'd promised for a former partner and myself, so I'd repaid him by repeatedly delaying endorsing his performance in Joseph and his Technicolour Dreamcoat and as a consequence, the marketing had been so late they had to postpone the start of the show. For payback, he spread rumours about me and when he saw how little I cared, began a blog criticising my work, the crap I'd released since *A Petal And A Thorn*, which he was right about, but I could hardly let that rest, so I'd gone out of my way to find a boyfriend for his longterm crush. They married last summer and moved to Portugal.

Not without reason, I've known for a while I've had it coming and that it was only a matter of time before the man made his move, though why he'd think sending over a beautiful woman to be suitable revenge was the big question, kind of the opposite effect, in fact, but then, there was no getting inside the head of David Maher and to try understanding the motives of a fellow eccentric was an exercise in futility. Now that I was winning this feud, he was hardly likely to drop it there and was honour bound to find some new and elaborate method of making my life miserable, after all, I'd done it to him and had thoroughly enjoyed it. The joke was on him, though, because he'd unwittingly saved my life. If only he knew.

"I'm not angry, just bloody curious," I muttered and who could blame me for that?

I checked my watch, fifty minutes and counting, and there was nothing to do but attempt to make sense of the night I'd just had. Indeed, I'd thought of nothing else since and likely would think of little else again until the bloody thing was resolved.

Trying to get inside the man's head, the best I'd managed to come up with was that Maher had sent 'Tilly' around to my house in some new and sick revenge plot. "Have me fall in love and then pull out the rug, right, David? What a bastard!"

After *Tilly* had left, I'd laid on my bed until ten in the morning, unable to sleep. How could I have? One moment there was a noose around my neck, the next my vision had disappeared inside the perfect kiss, which I'd replayed in my head countless times since and not without reason. It was driving me crazy.

Why the fuck had I allowed her to leave?

And who was she?

Some crazy fan who possessed an uncanny physical resemblance to my own perfect image of Tilly, who'd tracked me down for a laugh? She'd be far from the only *Clara Buckingham* zealot I'd encountered but that line seemed to have dried long ago, twenty years after the book was released, five since the movie, people no longer gave a shit.

Had she been a struggling actor who'd thought I'd somehow be able to advance her career? I'd offered and she'd turned me down. Twice, in fact.

It was small wonder I couldn't sleep.

No, it *had* to be Maher, it *had* to be. It was the only logical answer. That he'd finally come up with something elaborate and spiteful enough to satiate his sick mind and I could almost see him now, laughing behind those closed doors, in a room where a piano played the same song over and over, while I waited and wasted my day with only the cleaning lady for company. Not that I had anything better to do anyway, mind.

But after *that* girl, and *that* kiss, I had no choice other than to get to the bottom of the mystery. I didn't know what I'd do once I had the information but that was beside the point.

"Erica, darling," Maher swaggered toward me, one hand on hip in his usual over the top flamboyant way and opened out his arms, "hugs and kisses." His cheek barely touched mine, then the other, before he pulled away with one hand clasped to his face from where he performed a little on the spot jig thing I couldn't even begin to fathom. It was all for show and far too excessive but it was his style and so I'd humour it, irritating as it was. Heck, I'd watch him all day and pretend I was at the Vienna State Opera if he gave me what I wanted.

"David, how nice to see you, darling, I must come by and see your new play." Of course, I had no intention of the sort, and he knew it, but one has to play the game.

He settled down after what was probably about fifteen seconds. "Of course, you must and I should get you balcony tickets," he said in such a way that left me guessing whether or not he was joking. Though considering everything, he was being just a tad too friendly. Beware the false friend, and they did not come much more false than David Maher. "I trust Edith kept you company during rehearsals?" He glanced over my shoulder toward who I assumed was the cleaning lady.

I was not about to give him any satisfaction here. "Of course, turns out we both have an interest in local history. She's an old hand at the Viking invasion."

He grimaced and then quickly masked it with more arm flamboyance. "Erica, what can I do for you?" He said, all seriousness now.

I gave him a knowing expression, clenching my lips whilst tilting down with my eyes pointed up as I awaited his imminent confession.

"My dear, are you quite alright?" Clearly, he was determined to continue with this silly charade.

I came to arms akimbo. "Don't play the bloody innocent with me. We both know what you've done."

He took a large step back to over-exaggerate his taking offence, which looked ridiculous. "My dear, whatever are you talking about?"

I shook my head. "This is payback for Julian, isn't it. Well, if you were ever a true friend to him, you should be ecstatic I made him happy."

He smirked at the ground. "Erica, I was never able to thank you for what you did, not just for him but for me as well. We were never going to happen, and I couldn't see it, but you made me see it," he reached out and squeezed my arm, "who knows how many years of heartache you saved me. Sure, it hurt at the time, and I wanted to do some incredibly cruel things to you and cause some extreme physical as well as emotional pain, but," and now he beamed in a way I'd never seen him do before, "if it weren't for you forcing me from my life of denial, I'd never have met Brett."

"Brett?" I yelped, unsure what to make of this. And the thought did pass, for the briefest of moments, that maybe I ought to repay Maher in some other way, perhaps by setting up *Brett* with the gay catalogue model I knew, but no, I remembered the reason I was here and pulled away from his hand that still clutched at my arm.

"You mean, you've not been plotting revenge on me? In any way whatsoever?"

"My dear, you regard yourself much too highly." No, that wasn't true. I knew precisely what I was. "And like I said, I owe my present happiness, in large part to you…unwitting as I know it was, but still."

"Hang on one minute…" I scratched my head as I tried to reconcile this news, "you've not done a single thing as far as vengeance goes?"

"Well," he trailed with the word, "we'll have to see won't we," and then he absolutely winked, the fiend. "Could you possibly be a little more specific?"

I'd wanted him to admit to what he'd done, rather than say it myself and have him take credit for it. He was like that, you see, completely incapable of invention, and he a stage director, of all things. But we were getting nowhere with this conversation, so I sighed and gave him it. "David, did you send a girl to my flat last night?"

He made a pained expression, "my dear, Erica, if I'd wanted to pay you back for what you did to me, I would not do it by sending a girl around." He laughed and glanced back toward the door from whence he came, "I must return to my work, so…"

"…Wait, David," I reached out, grabbing his arm and he looked at me with alarm. He wasn't escaping until I was absolutely sure. "The thing is," how could I put this without sounding even more insane than he already knew me to be, "she was a bloody good actor, and I thought there could be only one person's tutelage she must have been under." Like I said, I could play the game, and knew when and how to lay it on and Mr False here enjoyed nothing more than being complimented on his work, which was why my withholding an endorsement had sent him into such a prolonged period of concentrated revenge in the first place.

He shook his head but was sympathetic, "Erica, I don't understand. Why would I send an actress around to your flat? It beggars belief, my dear. It's simply not something I would ever even think to do. To what end exactly?"

Well, I'd assumed for revenge, although even that had been a long shot, and deep down I'd known it, but I needed to find the girl and this was the obvious place to begin. But I still knew she was here. Oh yes, somewhere in this building, she was here, probably giggling in a corner after all the trouble she'd caused, the little minx. And I'd find her. "What play are you rehearsing for?"

The change in subject prompted him to check his watch, bloody rude. "It's a very famous historical play, though I highly doubt you care one jot for my work." Historical play? He half turned and I grabbed his hand.

"Please, David, I have to see your actresses." I sounded pathetic, but so be it. "And I'm sorry about the Joseph and his Technicolour Dreamcoat debacle." I wasn't, in fact, but I now had to act like I was and pray that I could convince this director of my sincerity. Time to see how good he really was, a hard task, considering I was a supposed author, not an actress. I inhaled deeply, the air in his proximity tasting of vanilla, and paused for effect. "Oh, David, the truth is I was in a bad place back then and was so sorry to lose your friendship, which I valued so highly." Don't overdo it, Erica. "You see, I was truly hurt when you withdrew my tickets, and I never understood why…"

"…you slept with the director's girlfriend." He folded his arms across his chest. "It was *he* who withdrew them, not me. If you'd have taken the time to ask, this whole sorry business might have been avoided."

My head dipped, part involuntarily, part for effect, although I did feel pretty small right about now. "Is that a fact? Now I feel so much worse. We could have been truly great friends, you and I. I was on the rebound, you see. Like I said, I was in a bad place back then." I sniffed and peeked up from my hunched over position, only to see his arms still folded over his pigeon chest.

His jaw clenched, "Erica, do you know how many substandard acting performances I've had to sit through in my life?" He didn't give me chance to reply, which was just as well, "most of them, is the answer. But what I've just witnessed is easily one of the worst." He sighed and threw down his arms. "Oh, I don't know, if it'll shut you up and put an end to this silly grudge, I'll bring them out. Just promise me you won't ever audition for any of my plays."

I straightened and tried to subdue my grin. "Of course, I wouldn't dream of it." And that was the truth.

He began walking to the door, stopped mid-stride in seeming hesitation and shook his head before continuing.

For a few minutes, the foyer was empty and I was left to ponder my actions once 'Tilly' had been exposed. How would she react after waltzing through the doors with her colleagues to be caught and shamed before me? Though truthfully, I wasn't sure I even wanted her caught and shamed. Surprisingly, I'd enjoyed her company and she probably did save my worthless arse from a soggy end. Though it remained that, being an inquisitive woman, and an author at that, the curiosity was far too overpowering. I needed to know just who the bloody hell she was, find out about the *true* her, the girl's real name and, well, everything else. I wasn't so stupid as to think it could go any further between us, but then, she had been the one to kiss me.

David's voice blared from somewhere down the corridor, "this way my children, a surprise guest would like to inspect the cast," and for the first time, my heart rate increased uncontrollably, as sweat beads pricked at my forehead. I held my hands in front and clasped them together then the door swung open and David trotted out three costumed females who each lined up to my fore. "Now, are any of you aware of Miss Clara Buckingham?" He held out an opened hand toward me but only blank expressions were returned.

I quickly scanned all three girls and almost simultaneously, David introduced them.

"This wonderful creature, Clara, is Tabby the Cat."

Tabby, all four and a half feet of her, and in full feline costume could be discounted immediately. Even through the heavy makeup, it was obvious that she could not be the girl who visited me. She made a clawing gesture with her mitt followed by a shallow curtsey, which I rolled my eyes at.

"And then we have Miss Ciceley, the Chef." The

characters were beginning to sound familiar. This woman, although of similar height, possessed dark hair that was easy to spot beneath the misplaced straggly wig. She was much older too and fit very well the description of an overworked chef.

I almost dared not look at the final girl.

"And last but not least, may I introduce Alice Fitzwarren." This girl was very beautiful, with long blonde hair, well groomed, tall and slim. But she wasn't the girl from last night. More than anything else, it was her facial expression that gave it away. The girl last night had happiness flowing through her. This girl, I sensed, had no real wish to be here; not only to meet me, but I had the impression she thought she was far above the art of theatre and was either an out of work TV actress or had ambitions far above her present station. Her costume, although middle class like the girl from last night, was from an altogether different period of time.

I coughed and smiled at the girls. "Say, David, what play is this exactly?"

He gave me a look as though to wonder if I was stupid. "Why, it's Dick Whittington, of course."

"Dick Whittington?" I gathered my bag from the seat. "You moron. That's 14th Century. I need Victorian."

I stomped out the building with their curses hissing in my ears.

❄

ALONG THE RIVER OUSE, outside the famous King's Arms, the 'Pub that floods,' the queue stretched beyond the neighbouring alehouse where tourists, and myself, awaited the arrival of the tour guide.

There was never much risk of being recognised because I

wasn't exactly J.K. Rowling or E.L. James. The days of my being stopped in the street and asked for a photo or signature were long gone, but since leaving the theatre, I'd donned my scarf and a beanie hat, which pulled down over my ears, for concealment regardless. It was for the benefit of a certain tour guide I knew, 'Hector Shackleton,' and I'd decided it might be fun, as well as necessary, to blend in with the tourists.

"Is this the line for the Ghost Tour Walk?" A large man asked with an American twang. It was then I realised I was leaning against the sign and when I pulled away, he read aloud from the plaque for everybody's benefit. "This is the meeting point for the Ghost Tour Walk, which begins at 8:00 pm every evening. If ye are late, ye can join the tour at Clifford's Tower, the halfway point, at 8:30 pm." He sniffed and perhaps sensing aloofness from myself, asked nobody in particular. "Well, where do you pay? Does anybody have a ticket?"

"You pay the guy when he arrives," I told him, wondering if I had the patience for all this whilst glancing toward the back of the line where the stragglers had more space to avoid the small talk. The Ouse looked equally appealing.

It was as though he phased out from one of the walls; Hector Shackleton appeared like a character from some Victorian horror scene. Black cloak that trailed down to his boots, slicked back grey hair beneath black top hat, cane in hand, long thick stuck on mutton chop sideburns; a kind of Ebenezer Scrooge from your nightmares - Attractive, not at all, but perfect for this gig. "Follow me." He motioned with the cane toward a clearing away from the camera flashes and rowdy tourists and locals who drank together at the tables along the river bank.

There were at least three dozen on the tour, a mixture of children and adults doubtless from all over the world. I hung back at the rear and made sure to keep a distance from one particular large female who I guessed would have difficulty tonight, as well as draw attention to herself and therefore anyone around her. The poor soul. The river was high with the usual ducks and geese splashing about to everybody's enjoyment. It might only be a few more days before the tourists were treated to the near annual spectacle of this part of the city flooding, along with the entirety of the King's Arms pub.

Shackleton stopped beneath a tree and made a gesture to gather in. "You see that bridge over there?" Everybody turned around to look. "That's the Ouse Bridge where for hundreds of years, traitors' heads were placed on pikes and displayed for all, as a warning. To get to the brain, crows would often peck out the eyes, which would then roll along the bridge to the adjacent streets on the wind." That the present Ouse Bridge dated only to 1818 and was not the original wasn't mentioned, but why spoil a good story, the crowd were enjoying it and getting a taste of what was to follow. Shackleton grinned, "and now comes the worst part of the entire tour for us Yorkshire folk…parting with our cash." He held out a crooked hand. "That's five pounds each."

Five multiplied by three dozen equals one hundred and eighty pounds. Not bad for an hour of work, cash in hand and untouchable to the taxman should he choose to keep mum regarding the number of paying tourists. Given I knew more about the history of York than this guy, I should probably consider a change in career from failed author to ghost tour guide.

I handed over my fee with a bowed head, not that there was need for me to worry since there were so many other tourists utilising his full capabilities.

He waved his cane and addressed the flock. "I like to

think we get transported back in time for my tour, but present-day health and safety deems I must warn you about the corner as we make our way to the first story point. We pass the York Dungeon, where terrified tourists have the opportunity to bail out at the halfway point through the fire escape, only to find themselves standing on the main road with an oncoming vehicle. Please be careful of the tourists."

Laughter. And there goes the illusion.

He began leading us toward the next story point, wherever that would be, his pockets heavy with our cash. The late evening chill was making itself apparent, the breeze flowing over us as we entered a park and Shackleton made the usual conversation with his tourists, asking where they were from and pretending to be interested.

What was my plan? Good question because I hadn't a clue. All I knew for sure was that I'd drive myself crazy staying home when I could be out at least attempting to discover *something* about the girl. Naturally, I again thought about that heavenly kiss and once more, silently cursed that I'd so stupidly allowed her to simply walk away without so much as demanding documented proof as to her real name. What could I have done though? I'd treated her as such a joke that when she surprised me by pressing her lips so tenderly to mine, I'd been completely knocked sideways and rendered insensible. No, there had been nothing jokey in that and no longer did I find it funny. Would she have anything to do with this stupid tour? It was more unlikely than likely. But what else could I do? I just hoped to learn something by the end of it.

Whatever happened tonight though, I'd have to confront Shackleton at some point and demand to know whether he was sending tourists to my front door, and what the bloody hell was he playing at? And no better time than the present, because to confront him now would spare me the next fifty-five minutes of Hector Shackleton.

I made my move, stepping out from behind a young couple holding hands, only to be cut off by the large woman who plodded plum into my path. "Exactly how much walking is involved in this tour?" She panted and sweat glistened on her arms.

"This is the Ghost *Walk* Tour, madam," Shackleton confirmed to an audible groan.

My fists clenched without any instruction from my brain, I'd most likely have to suffer the tour. There was nothing about York that Shackleton could teach me and I'd have to physically stop myself from making corrections or adding to his anecdotes. I breathed, reduced my pace and decided to try enjoy the thing. The tourists, for the most part, were smiling and I scanned around the group for anybody who might be a plant working for Shackleton, perhaps with the intention of jumping out to scare the shit out of everybody but now I knew I was getting paranoid, and perhaps with good reason, considering an attractive girl claiming to be Tilly had spent last night sharing my Scotch. How crazy could I be, really? The group included nobody who could even remotely be described as last night's enchantress, nor anybody in vintage Victorian clothing, Shackleton apart. But I knew this slimy toad, and that he'd take pleasure in causing mischief.

Outside Clifford's Tower, a knot of people waited at the foot of the motte and Shackleton spoke with them before they began handing over their reduced fees. A middle-aged couple from Japan laden down with bags and heavy photography equipment, a man who spoke to the air above Shackleton's head, oh and one young lady who caught my interest immediately. She wore a plain dark blue gown of percale with a large white apron with frilly shoulder straps. A black ribbon was tied around her neck and on her head she wore a white coronet with lace edged frills pulled tight, its rim concealing her eyes. In all, a neat appearance, if not totally plain, but certainly an attempt at looking like a Victorian maid. But what really put me on edge was the fact she didn't pay her fee. Why was she so special? Was she a plant or part of the tour? Either way, I'd keep an eye on the girl who, when she turned sideways, revealed herself to be a brunette. All this whilst Shackleton told the story from 1190, of when the local mob chased the city's thieves into the tower from where they committed mass suicide. I'd heard the story so often I'd become immune to it, but the strange maid, who'd probably just finished her shift at Betty's cafe and stumbled upon the tour, scrunched up her face and turned a shade paler. That ruled out her being a plant as surely, she'd be used to the gory details by now. I sighed at the thought of turning prematurely paranoid.

I hung back as the tour continued. The large lady had sloped off at some point before Clifford's Tower and now we approached The Shambles from the far end to my flat, to face another famous York attraction.

Shackleton pointed across the road. "This is the oldest and most haunted pub in York, where men are often seen to fall down at the bar."

Almost everybody laughed at that, as I shook my head and turned away, trying to decide if I should slink off myself. I couldn't take much more of it; the lame jokes, tourists, walking around a town I knew like the back of my arse while pretending it was all new, Shackleton himself. But something made me stay, which was lucky because things were about to get interesting.

We continued along The Shambles and emerged in the Minster Courtyard close to the statue of Roman Emperor

Constantine, who'd declared himself emperor in York in 306 AD, which also happened to be around the corner from my flat. It really was a beautiful place to call home, part timber-framed with the roof protruding beyond the outer facade in typical medieval style. Upon seeing my property, people within the group took out their cameras and began taking pictures. It was one of the things that riled me up more than anything else. For one, it drew attention to me and my precious abode. Like owning a Ferrari, one simply could not drive to the shops, park it for ten minutes on the roadside, return and expect to find nobody had spit, scratched or taken a blade to the roof, shredding the vinyl. Few knew it was I who lived there but that had never mattered. The number of times I'd needed to use wood filler to erase people's names carved into the timber frames, scrape chewing gum off the front step or clean eggs off the windows. Was it any wonder I suffered a permanent manifestation of bad karma? It was only after the case of flour and worse deposited through my vintage letterbox that I'd had it removed, a new door fitted and now had to collect my mail from the post office. The worst thing was, without a postman I could go weeks without speaking to a single soul, with the exception of the barista at the coffee shop. But I would not give up my flat, no matter how hard they all tried because I loved it too much and I'd never let the bastards beat me.

I dared inch closer to our guide to concentrate on the next story and given our location, I did not want to miss this one.

But Shackleton left me astonished.

Because instead of stopping, he simply pointed with his cane toward Monkgate and even physically pressed a hand against the back of one man who was taking particular interest in my wooden window shutters. "Let's go, folks, nothing but a cold chill around this place."

Ooh, the little toad, and I found my feet fixed to the spot as I stared a hole through the back of his head.

Not a word about Clara Buckingham?

Really?

The group had diminished in number and now probably resembled about half the original turnout. I hurried to catch up as they headed toward Monkgate, once the area of the city known for its brothels but now a very pleasant set of streets with upmarket housing and weird black cats nailed to the walls as part of an old legend about chasing away the city's rats and pigeons. The tour was nearing its end, at which point I could finally throttle a certain somebody, ironically for *not* sending tourists to my home.

Shackleton assembled the remaining tourists into a semi-circle and pointed to one tidy property, which, according to him, was where he used to live. The story, he continued, was about his neighbour who won millions on the lottery, proceeded to spend it, lost it, then died penniless with no friends or family. "What is money if it doesn't bring happiness?" He spoke with solemnity and everybody nodded.

I checked my watch and waited for everyone to scatter. Shackleton had warned us not to clap, since he'd received complaints from the locals about the noise; I'd thought *I* was a misery, but instead, he asked that we touch the ball on his cane's handle for luck. As the last person present, finally, he held the grubby thing out to me and I pushed it aside.

"Hello, Hector Shackleton, or should I say, Glen Atkinson." He gaped and squinted with confusion at me behind my concealments. I continued, "I hear you've been directing tourists to my property." I stepped into his personal space and folded my arms. "I wonder what the judge will have to say about that."

His neck stretched forward, "what…who…"

Running out of patience, I tugged off the beanie. "Oh it's me, Clara, you remember?"

For a moment he just gawped, then it clicked. "Oh, Clara. Did you enjoy the tour?"

I tapped a foot. "It was tolerable. Well?"

"Clara, you just saw me skip your precious property entirely and I've certainly done no such thing as *direct tourists,* as you accuse me of." He removed his hat and I grimaced. "In fact, it's a shame we need to pass by at all, but you do live on the path between Stonegate and the pub, which is hardly my fault." He scratched his silver head and made a pained expression. "After the court case, I was rather hoping I'd never see you again, but here you are."

It was two years ago when I'd lost a court battle to have him stop bringing tourists to the courtyard, right up to the front of my property and especially for him to stop pitching for business, literally three steps from my front door. The judge found in his favour, since the pavement was not considered private property, but as a gesture of goodwill, he'd removed himself anyway, only for some other ghost walk company to take up position almost immediately after. They were still there and always would be unless I could figure out a way around it, which I never had. But, as it transpired, after winning and still giving me everything I wanted, my privacy, Shackleton was not, as punishment, sending attractive women to my address. And the more I thought about it, that kind of made sense.

Feeling somewhat dazed, I massaged my forehead. "Well, has anybody ever asked where I live?"

His upper body jerked back and he almost dropped his cane. "Yes, that's all I'm ever asked. It was only yesterday when a girl wanted to know, 'where does the author of *A Petal And A Thorn* live?' and I pointed her in your direction for an autograph," if only he knew how close to the truth he was with his sarcastic mocking, "and I see the solitary confinement in your little madhouse has finally eroded your brain whilst simultaneously inflating your ego. I bet it's been so long since you've had a visitor that you're creating them within your own mind."

I tried to think up a witty putdown. "Watch the crows don't pinch your sideburns." It was pretty lame but the best retort I could come up with at such short notice. The annoying this was that within ten minutes I'd think up something worthy of my next book, but by then it'd be too late.

Enough of Shackleton. Clearly, he wasn't giving away my address, or even allowing tourists time enough to photograph my home. I turned away from him…

…and froze.

How had I forgotten?

The vintage girl was standing alone under an arch by the alley.

My chest thudded as we made eye contact.

I whipped back on the rogue and bared my teeth. "That girl, she didn't pay. Who is she? Does she work for you?"

He looked at me like it was *I* who was going mad. "What girl?"

My eyes glassed over as I turned back to the alley in time to see her dark blue gown disappear around the corner. "Huh? Oh, nothing. Come up with some better jokes," I shouted over my shoulder as I strode beneath the arch. Luckily, I'd worn trainers and they struck the cobbles hard as I swerved right and then to the left past two alley lurkers. Around another corner and along a passage, I had to be catching up, and then I emerged through the other end to find myself on Stonegate with its quaint independent shops and so many tourists it was impossible to see much of anything.

And as I looked frantically both ways, again and again, whilst sucking air into my lungs, I knew I'd lost her.

Whoever she was.

4

TRIAL

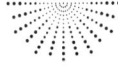

*T*en minutes before midnight, I found myself pacing around the living room, occasionally scrutinising the scene outside the window, looking for signs of a girl who'd have to be as insane as myself to return.

Since arriving home, I'd given it some thought and my conclusion - There was literally no reason for her, whoever she was, to come back - Yet still, I found myself leaning against the glass, my heart filling with hope at every passing pedestrian, only for it to be dashed.

A drunken lout sat, half leaning sideways on the bench on the small strip of grass opposite my front door, faithful dog in his lap, whisky bottle clutched in hand. If the man was asleep then that was some acquired skill. I grasped tighter to the bottle in my own hand and wondered that if not for all my money, that man's situation could well be my own. Replacing the half-empty bottle to the table, I continued pottering about, but did make some use of myself, by bringing out a clean glass for her inevitable no show and when the time came, I'd drink myself into a rare stupor.

The grandfather clock chimed its steady rhythm, each

strumming sound reminding me I was that little bit closer to midnight, and disappointment. There was still some hope in my head, otherwise I'd have gone to bed. Given I hadn't slept last night, I was understandably feeling the effects now, as I enjoyed a deep yawn and peered again outside.

Two minutes to midnight. "Two minutes to nothing happening and then bed with my bottle." I'd wake in the morning and then reconsider my position from the night before, but this time not with a rope. Too grisly. And I didn't fancy the thought of some poor bugger finding me after many months, years even, still swinging. Surely, I had enough whisky to finish the job. A nice bottle of sleeping pills and the whole thing would be over. I could then take my rightful place in the ranks of Bronte and others, assuming they'd have me.

Outside the night turned grey, concealing the lout on the bench, as that bloody mist returned. The windows were closed tight, and so none of it seeped inside, but there was the sensation of the room decreasing in size even though I knew it was all in my head. Then Percy squawked, which was unusual for him at this hour.

Knock, knock, knock.

The same distinct three thuds of brass and my heart jumped into my mouth. Thanking the stars I was sober, I ran down the steps and lunged for the handle. Then stopped.

It was the sight of the poker, still propped against the doorframe that checked me, and just in case, I clutched a clammy hand around the handle. I had to be careful. It was midnight and I still had doubts as to the identity of the caller on the other side of the door and besides, there was a drunken homeless guy lurking out there somewhere, though the truth was that deep down, I expected disappointment because that's all I'd ever really known.

I carefully pulled open the door as small wisps of grey bled inside and I relinquished my grip on the iron as the golden haired lovely smiled at me from the outside.

She had much the same appearance as the other night; same dress, same bonnet, same aura of love and perfection. She didn't need to say anything, the smile did everything for her.

"Do you bring the fog with you?" I asked, not giving a shit about the weather as adrenaline fuelled my tired body, my legs still quivered though, which was only natural and I dared allow the happiness to show on my face. Oh, but I was more than curious about this harmless little imbecile "Well, come on in." I held out an opened palm toward my abode's interior.

"Gladly, Erica," she did a cute little curtsey, raised her dress and glided beyond me and up the stairs.

"Watch out for the second…" how did she do that?

Her scent again poured over me. Yes, it definitely brought memories of what my grandmother used to wear. That wasn't too weird, was it? According to psychologists, the olfactory system stimulated the most vivid memories but why was I thinking this shit now?

My eyes roamed over her rear, and I finally realised that whoever she was, she'd managed to locate a dress identical in description to the one Tilly had worn at the Annual Whitby Ball. "She's just a crazy fan," I conceded as Percy chirped with excitement above. "But it'll be fun catching you out, you little minx." Oh, yes, I'd catch her out.

I followed her upstairs but made a detour toward the kitchen. "Would you care for some tea?"

"Oh, yes please, have you any Taylor's of Harrogate?" Came the dampened response from two rooms away.

Taylor's of Harrogate? Established 1886. A popular

Victorian brand. "No," I shouted back, "I have PG Tips. You know, the brand with the monkeys in the TV ad?"

I strained my ears, waiting for the response, and then, "oh…well then…extra milky, please."

After preparing the tea, I carried the two mugs into the living room to find her standing, politely awaiting my invitation to take a seat. Good manners were always welcome. She narrowed her eyes at my rainbow mugs, then took one and placed it carefully on the table.

"Sit!" I demanded, in a voice that sounded harsh as intended. She backed up toward the divan and was halfway to sitting when I barked, "no, wait," I held out a hand for her to stop, which she did before returning to a straightened position.

She raised a golden eyebrow in a most delightful way, "Erica?"

"Take off your bonnet." I rushed toward the book cabinet, pulled out a leather-bound volume and was facing her again in time to watch the golden curls tumbling out.

She again did that thing where she tucked a cluster of gold behind her ear whilst looking down and then delicately grazing her jawline with the outsides of her fingers.

My hand tightened around the book as my teeth bit into my bottom lip. She was too good a study and had the character down to the most minute of mannerisms and I made a mental note to check if any production companies were in town filming. The girl was far too good an actor to be pissing her life away with Maher down at the local theatre, or wherever she was treading the bloody boards.

"Oh, I do declare, but you look at me with eyes most… curious." She chose the final word carefully and I knew she was either too uncertain, too kind, or too downright scared to have said *lust*, or *with the eyes of a pervert*.

Yes, I wanted to see what lay below that stupid cumbersome tent she'd again togged herself in but for now, I'd have to settle for the removal of her bonnet. I held the book out to her. "Now, wear it."

That startled her, again in a delightful way, and my not totally unreasonable request gave me a small amount of satisfaction, to see the façade chip just slightly. Her hand pulsed toward the book but then hesitated. "You wish for me to wear a book? I know you think I'm dicked in the nob, but come on, Erica."

Ignoring for a moment her hesitation, the repeated use of my name and just how the bloody hell she'd come about it, I instead went with the obvious. "Dicked in the nob?" I bawled out, unable to control the volume.

It wasn't exactly a saying the English had used since, well, Victorian times, and what's more, the term had not once been used in *A Petal And A Thorn* anyway. All I could do was question where in the bloody hell she'd heard it and how far into studying Tilly, as well as her era, it would now appear, this girl had gone?

Because now she was beginning to take on a life of her own.

People simply did not speak like that anymore, which was a damned shame. I'd come across the term only when visiting the British Library in London whilst carrying out my research, where I'd read transcripts of actual conversations between Yorkshire tradesmen from the 1880s, but I'd decided against using that particular phrase on account of it being not just obsolete, and not just that nobody would have had a clue what I was talking about, but also that it would most likely be misinterpreted. I gaped, awestruck at the fascinating girl before me and had to warn her.

"Dicked in the nob?" I said again. "Please, just promise

me you'll never repeat that outside these walls. I think you'll find it means something completely different these days, and you'll find no lack of volunteers, I might add." The very thought of some naked sweaty barbarian clambering atop this delicate piece of perfection brought up the bile in the back of my throat.

Ignoring my discomfort, she reached forward and took the book from my hand before holding it up to read the cover. "*A Petal And A Thorn*." Her face became suddenly animated, totally endearing. "Oh, oh, Erica, really? This is the first time I've ever seen it. Oh, please say you'll read to me, do? You truly must, Erica."

I'd been engaged in the process of swallowing tea and a small quantity went down the wrong pipe. "Like hell…" I coughed, making all kinds of attractive noises and I could swear she was almost concerned for my wellbeing. Once I was settled, my finger found itself wagging at her. "Like hell it's the first time you've ever seen it, you little minx." I gave my chest a few thumps with the inside of a closed fist. If anything, with her last remark she was now overcompensating, going out of the way to make it look like she'd never read it. And now I smelled bullshit. No, she'd pushed the envelope too far and for that, I'd make her pay for it. "Would you just wear the bloody book before you make me make you wear it." I took half a step toward her and stood arms akimbo, all business and not to be misinterpreted.

Unable to meet my eye, she clasped her hands at her belly, book dangling between them.

Gotcha, you little fraud. And I'd barely even tried. She'd caved at the first challenge. After all, how hard was it to wear a book?

I was about to demand, possibly backed up with the threat of violence, that she divulge her true identity at once, when she swallowed, slowly raised the book and placed it atop her head. She took a few seconds, steadying my precious work before removing her hands and opening them out in front as she looked me in the eye.

"Tah-dah."

And I swear she even winked.

But I wasn't having this. Not quite. I moved out of her path and gestured to the far wall. "Walk."

"You wish for me to walk now? But my dress. Oh, never mind." It made it harder, not being able to use her hands for balance, but instead to prevent her tripping over the unnecessarily long frilled edges of her teepee, which she now held up in her hands. "Oh, I dare say, I'm intrigued but this is so much fun," she stepped toward the cabinet, eyes forward and stepped again. Then she shocked me by taking four large steps in quick succession and was now at the room's limit. She turned around and voluntarily started toward the other side, increasing her speed before stopping in the centre of the room.

As she began kicking her legs out in some bizarre skipping movement, I became vaguely aware of tea spilling over my mug. She let go of her dress and now waved her arms about, dancing, totally playing the goat and all the while, as I felt burning tea scolding my leg, the bloody book stayed put on her head.

"My mother used to make me do this. *It will make you walk like a lady*, she'd say. Oh, you do so remind me of her." It wasn't exactly what I wanted to hear. "Look at me, oh I do declare…Am I ladylike enough for you now, Erica?"

God only knew how my face must have looked, though probably a contortion of amazement mixed with searing pain from spilt tea.

But she was a sight to behold. The very image of

perfection, dancing around in my own living room, with a book on her head, no less. And try as Newton's laws might, that book would not move, shift nor fall; no easy task as I recalled from my research of twenty years before. Correct, I'd not attempted the former popular pastime of our nation since. Book balancing to instil a girl with a lady's grace and poise. Much like stonemasonry, a lost art.

I shook myself out of the trance she'd put me under. "Ok, remove the book." I didn't wait for her to remove it but grabbed it myself and chucked it to the divan. It landed with a thump and the smirk left her face.

"Erica! How dare you treat a book in such a way." Great, I was getting reprimanded by a twenty…actually, I had no idea how old she was.

The flowery green dress I'd worn was now stained, even if the pain had subsided, and I rubbed the sore spot while I tried to gather my thoughts, the next part of the plan to expose this beautiful little fraudster. "Your bag, hand it over."

She straightened but did not object in any major way, at least not enough to make me rethink my perfectly reasonable request. "My bag? You mean my purse?"

I exhaled and motioned for her to come closer. "Yes, your bloody purse, give."

She stepped back. "Erica, a lady has her secrets. Surely you don't wish to see my private possessions?"

I moved into her old space, examining her eyes for contact lenses. Nope, she was clean. "You mean, you don't want me to see your car keys, mobile phone, Tampax and whatever other crap you youngsters carry around these days?" My foot tapped a deliberate rhythm of impatience.

Her eyes widened and she clutched her hands in tight. Gotcha, you little fraud. And now she would be forced to admit everything, not least of all just what the bloody hell her game was.

I was about to demand answers when she delved inside some fold from deep within her inconvenient enclosure. And then what happened, but she only proceeded to produce a small reticule type thing tied on a piece of pink ribbon. It resembled a single piece of cut leather, shaped into a pouch with the ribbon drawstring holding it all together. If she was being a true, albeit lunatic, follower of my book, then the other end of that ribbon would be tied around her waist. Oh, to see such marvels.

But wait - It was another of those things that was never fully divulged to the reader because it was such a minor detail that it hadn't even worth mentioning. If *Tilly* here had indeed tied the other end to her waist, then it meant she'd carried out even more research on her own. It was just a damned shame she'd not thought to visit in something a little more revealing, though so far she was humouring my, let's admit it, demands that were now bordering on becoming hostile but I guessed that might soon end if I demanded she strip. Pity.

Finally obeying, she held the purse out to me. "One must be careful when one ventures into the big city."

"Quite." I took it, untied the string and rooted about inside, removing items one by one and placing them on the table. "Handkerchief. Door key. Small bottle of grandma's perfume. Needle and some thread." The coins were at the bottom and I jingled them in my hand. "Shillings, florins and even a half-crown." I looked at her with a jaw most gaping. "Where the bloody hell did you get these?"

She grinned, showcasing immaculate teeth; straight, white and symmetrical, perhaps too perfect for the 1880s but then, I'd created Tilly that way - Perfect. "Why, I have an allowance, silly. A lady has business in which to attend. Suppose I was meeting an acquaintance for tea?"

My eyebrow raised of its own accord. "An acquaintance? Do please enlighten me." I sounded full of doubt at this, which masked my interest.

She counted on her fingers. "Well, let's see, there's Emily, nurse Bennet, aunt Dorothy, Frances and Lindsay, although she hasn't spoken to me in a while, at least not since her mother stopped her calling around on account of the rumours."

"Uh-huh." All periphery characters, which didn't prove anything either way. So she knew the book, that was kind of why we were doing this in the first place. Although come to think of it, Lindsay was a new one to me. I threw down the purse so that it came to land beside the book. "Nice prop."

"Prop?" She gave me a slight reprimanding look, totally delicious, before retrieving the purse from the divan, ravelling up the ribbon and concealing it again in some invisible fold. "Why, whatever do you mean, prop?"

As much as I enjoyed her company and admired her perseverance, this pantomime needed to come to an end. If I didn't learn, and quick, just why this stunner was visiting *me*, her true identity and what her real motive was, I'd go even crazier than I knew myself already to be. Thankfully, I still had my ace card tucked away, and it was now time to play it - Literally.

"Look here, *Tilly*, you may be able to fake your looks, your dress, even your bloody purse. You may, with a few days practice, learn to walk and prance and dance with a book sitting on your smug little head, but what you can't do is fake the ability to play the piano better than any girl in Whitby." I pointed into the corner and at the 8ft rosewood cased grand piano, polished to a perfect shine by my own hand, never played because I'd never bothered to learn, built at Broadwood in 1865, with an expression of victory. Gotcha, you little fraud. Now fold like a good girl and spare us this charade any longer.

Her face came alive as she clutched her hands below her chin and hopped up and down on the spot. "You have a pianoforte?" She ran toward it like an excited teenager and without my permission lifted up the cover. "Oh, I thought you were going to make me knit, embroider or something else horrifically boring, but this will certainly do. Erica, please permit me to play for you?"

"Say what now?" It occurred to me to ask just why, since she was so excited, she hadn't noticed it before this moment. It wasn't like the expensive piece of furniture, since it was nothing more, failed take up a stupid proportion of my living space and forced me to squeeze past every time I required access to the cast iron weighing scales with set of kitchen weights or the spare paraffin lamps I kept in the cupboard behind it. Sometimes, I thought my obsession with Victorian England, and certain people from it, went a little too far.

"Oh, I spent many an hour as a child playing the pianoforte. Why, my mother would rap my knuckles raw with a cane should I ever miss a note. Oh, Erica, please allow me to play Edvard Grieg, do?"

Since she'd already pulled out the stool and plonked what I imagined to be one heck of a shapely arse down on it, if she was indeed bluffing being able to play the confounded thing, then I would damn well call her bloody bluff. The thing hadn't even been tuned since it took a nick out of the wood timbers when they hoisted it up through the window six years ago and I very much doubted even Grigory Sokolov could get much pleasantness from it, so what could this unsuspecting fraud possibly do, other than finally expose herself? I had to hand it to the girl though, she played a good game, for what reasons, I couldn't even begin to fathom, but it was all about to come to an end.

I gestured for her to begin as I quietly anticipated what might come next. What would I do? Kick her out? Call the police? Or politely push and prod her toward the bedroom before applying the locks?

She made a feminine coughing sound, which was only delaying it.

"You don't need to sing, dear, you just have to play. Good luck with that." I muttered the last part under my breath.

"It's an old habit and helps me concentrate." She pulled the seat further in, like a pointless fraction of an inch.

I folded my arms. "Take your time. Carry out any and all rituals you have. It's your own grave you're digging."

She'd been placing her fingers to the keys but brought them back into her solar plexus. "Well, now you're being awfully unfair and placing me under such undue pressure. I'm used to my mother standing over me, most often with a cane bearing down, but not *you* Erica. It's almost too much." She'd spoken in a reprimanding tone, which was strange because her words contained admiration. It was all in the way she'd said *you*, which almost had me thinking I was something special to her.

But I wasn't special to anyone and arguably never had been, and I saw a sudden flash of red. "Will you just play!" I shouted, immediately regretting my loss of temper.

She didn't flinch but swivelled bodily toward me on the stool. "Oh, Erica, have you never wondered whether it's your eagerness to berate people that is the reason you spend your weekends alone in your wonderful home? Why, both Friday and Saturday we meet and I've seen nobody else. Is not a life shared a life tripled?" Despite the uncalled for cheek from the

69

girl, she'd spoken in such a playful tone that it was impossible to rebuke her for poking her nose, yet further, into my business. All this despite my earlier anger, and still nothing but warmth cast from her. She'd finished her words with, what was in her way, a philosophical question, which, should I choose to humour it, could only have been intended as a further distraction from the piano. I'd return to that later but for now, there was another matter, because something else she'd said jabbed at my heart and it was almost as if she'd looked through a window into it.

"How do you know I've been alone in here both nights?" I asked with genuine hurt. For all my faults I was still a woman, and we women like to think that any potential partner, not that I had a chance with this one, mind, was at least popular amongst others, that they had options, that we could possibly lose them at any moment, because it spoke more about ourselves if we were able to attract partners who attracted others. If nobody else wanted those we were with, then what did it say about us? The psychology of the female mind, something as an author I was required to understand, even if it had never helped me in life. "You only ever arrive at the stroke of midnight, you big freak, so who are *you* to say I didn't have a house full of people, most of them extremely hot women, before your arrival, huh?"

She remained expressionless, save for the quirking of one perfectly trimmed golden brow. "Did you?"

I scoffed, "no, of course not," but still, it was the assumption that bothered me. I mean, did she take one look at me and think, hmm, Erica's the kind of woman who spends the weekends all alone. It hurt dammit, but only because it was *her* thinking it. Let's face it, usually, I couldn't give three flying figs for what people thought about me or anything else. "Maybe I had guests here Thursday night, or maybe I'm hosting a party tomorrow. How would you know any different, you haven't ask…" I slapped my forehead and laughed. "Oh, you're a sly one, I'll grant you that." I shook my head and now regarded her with even more admiration than previously, what with the book thing.

"What?" She asked, again bringing both hands into her belly.

"I bet you must get away with all sorts." An image flashed through my mind of her distracting lovestruck young men as her accomplice carried out the pickpocketing. "And I'll give you credit because you very nearly succeeded. You'd have me ramble on for an hour, about all kinds of subjects, before you played even a single note, because, let's admit it, whoever you are, you can *not* play the piano." I turned away and gathered up the mugs…

…The music froze me to the spot…

…And then the wall before me disappeared to reveal a large open meadow as bright green grass sprung from between the cracks in the floorboards. Wind rustled leaves high in the trees, dandelions swayed likewise, the crisp smell of cold autumn air flooded my lungs. Beautiful swans played in a crystal clear pond, ducking their heads before pulling them out and swishing the beads from their necks. I stood surrounded by nature, alone but for this girl's music. Grieg's unmistakable Morning Mood riveting from her magical fingers as the scene evaporated before me to reveal her again in my living room.

I wiped away a tear, the teacups having returned in my trance to the table, and I collapsed into the divan.

The floorboards morphed again into grass as I sat and watched the wild hares dare approach my bare feet as I sat upon a tree stump. Birds sang from a hundred nearby trees, while below, horses licked up water from the trickling stream.

It all unfolded in front, next to and all around me. I was enveloped by it and always, the girl's music came to the fore.

I wiped again at my eyes and concentrated on her image, trying to ignore the silly sheep, in much need of a shearing, that rubbed against my leg. She, the girl, her perfectly slender frame swayed back and forth on the stool, living every magical note with her body. She played with closed eyes and an ease that could come only from years of practice.

My tears were flowing now, not so much for the music, but for the proof, the truth that refused to be silent. This strange, mysterious girl, she could be no other.

Tilly!

I'd known it was her all along, you see, never doubted it for a moment, but with such things, one has to be absolutely sure.

I grabbed the bottle of Scotch from the table and held it up for inspection. *Talisker - The only single malt Scotch whisky from the Isle of Skye. Specially vatted from selected casks to celebrate the 175th anniversary of the Talisker distillery.* "How much of this stuff have I taken?" Over the years, there was no way of knowing for sure but I squinted hard at the smaller text on the bottle, unsure I was seeing what was actually written. "*From the magical shores of the Isle of Skye, in the tall shadows of the Cuillin Hills, comes a single malt,*" the handwritten font decreased in size, "*so fun,* or is it *fine?* something…something…something, *full-bodied spirit…oak casks in orphanages…long-standing tradition…Scottish Highlands…makes fantasy* or is that *fantastic?…spirit…limited edition,*" I swished around the remaining Scotch inside. "Is that '*fantasy spirit*' or '*fantastic spirit?*'" Either way, it was certainly full-bodied. I gave up. What did it matter anyway?

I gazed at Tilly. Just thinking her name in my own head,

while she sat at my piano, playing Morning Mood, was enough to fill me with the kinds of anxiety not even Talisker could mitigate.

She had come to me.

At some point over the last few days, I really must have gone *dicked in the nob* myself.

Tilly!

The one character I'd created out of my own image of perfection. The way the ideal woman *should* be. *My* perfect woman. And she was here. In my own front room, no less. Right now. Playing Edvard Grieg on my own piano…forte.

I'd often considered that I was teetering on that thin line between genius and madness, between sanity and being carted off to the Bedlam lunatic asylum, or whatever the none Victorian equivalent was. They'd called me mad, amongst other things, but none of that mattered now. Not now that she'd come to me. Everything before this point in my life, all the misery and loneliness, the names and the isolation, the lawsuits and the public boycott campaigns, my upbringing and everything else, it was all worth it now.

I only now realised I'd been swaying along with Tilly to the music, parallel with her, my shaking hands clasped together in front of me. "I can't believe it." My whole body trembled. Could I only now, aged thirty-six, finally allow myself to become truly happy for the first time in my life? The things I could show her about the modern world; travel, technology, cuisine. The things she could teach me about the past; how they lived, how they spent their time, their ways. The life we could have, the love we could share. I did not wish to throw my heart in too far too fast as I knew that to be foolish, but I did always love Tilly. Nobody else ever came close to her, in life or in fiction and it was not only a contributing factor in all my failed relationships since I conceived of her, but also in my failed stories. Not one person, real or imagined, had ever compared to my beloved creation.

And for Tilly's part? Well, she did return for the second time.

She played out the last few notes, Grieg himself could not have bettered, and twisted on the stool to face me. "I do hope I didn't disappoint. Mother says I have a propensity to play such modern dross, rather than the classics of Mozart, Lully, Bach and others. I just find them all so boring. Is it any wonder my knuckles reddened so?" She leaned forward and waited patiently for my answer, which seemed to mean a lot to her.

I dabbed at my eye with a still quivering hand. "You were perfect, as always, and so are your knuckles."

"You really think?" She stood and ran toward me, pleasantly surprising me by leaning down and throwing her arms about my shoulders where I sat. I inhaled her intoxicating scent, which almost sent me giddy and, with my eyes at the level of her beautiful collar bones, that was when again, I noticed the string about her neck, frayed and brown stained, the edges of what looked like, and what I knew to be a shell just barely visible down the hem of her dress. When she retracted her arms my book was in her hands. How did she do that? "You promised you'd read to me."

"Did I now?"

She bounced on the spot. "Oh please do. It is about *me* after all, is it not? And I'm dying of curiosity."

I hadn't promised, but I'd rather die than disappoint her? I took the book and ran a hand down the leather-bound cover. "I'd dearly like to hear your darling voice, Tilly. Maybe you'd like to read?"

"Oh, but to hear it from *your* lips, the genius who created it would be a rare treat indeed." She looked down upon me with a pretty please expression and I could have melted into the divan.

I patted the space beside me and she plonked herself down. I slid even nearer, closing the small gap between us. "You know, I had my initial draft and notes bound into this cover. It's sort of the master copy, so to speak, and is truly very special. It's worth a lot of money. Not that I could ever sell it, you understand." I flipped through the pages and showed her my scrawl. "See? All handwritten, including detailed descriptions and pretty damned poor sketches of you, I'm sure you'd agree."

Bless her, but she didn't criticise my drawings and instead seemed to be analysing my style. Naturally, Tilly was a gifted artist herself.

I decided to be bold. "I see that you're even more beautiful in real life…Tilly."

She turned a delicious shade of red around the nose before looking down and away. Finally, I'd rendered her mute.

To spare her further embarrassment, I opened the book to one of my favourite parts, and since she was already wearing the dress that came from it, the scene at the Annual Whitby Ball seemed like the ideal chapter to read.

5

THE ANNUAL WHITBY BALL

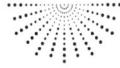

hrough the occasional gap between the dancers in their pomp and finery, none other than that rogue, that creature, the mill owner's son, Master Daversham was dragging Elspeth, terrified and unwilling to show it, yet still handsome, through the study doors from whence they closed, trapping the innocent within and all at the brute's mercy.

What could the confined beauty do? For her father owed his occupation to the mill owner who doted on his rotten son, who even now was undoubtedly taking liberties by occupying his hands as he saw fit.

Tilly barged through the disgruntled pack who frisked and frolicked without a care at the Annual Whitby Ball within the Bagdale Hall Hotel, owned by none other than the mill owner, Sir Daversham, himself. It was of a matter most delicate indeed and Tilly had to act with the utmost care and consideration lest the groper have his defiling way with a very special innocent, who'd merely been fulfilling her duty as maid by offering wine to the guests. The reprobate had taken more than the full tray for himself and something had to be done with haste.

Salvation came in the form of the utterly rotund yet thoroughly decent Lady Carrington, who'd tired beyond all hope of recovery, no fewer than three purebred Irish horses on the short journey over from Scarborough. Even now, the floorboards creaked beneath her ample tonnage as she waltzed to the violins' trills, second champagne glass, à la Elspeth, in hand.

"Pardon me for the interruption ma'am, but I do believe that Miss Wakefield has finally arrived with her entourage and even now waits patiently in the foyer for an introduction." Endeavouring to remain forthright and unrumpled whilst under the most pressing of circumstances proved most challenging for Tilly, who carried off the feat with her usual charm, but only just. As it turned out, being privy to the town's gossip did indeed, every once in a while, have its advantages.

The stout lady threw up her arms, causing something of a ripple effect and upsetting her partner, a poor rake of a man whom Tilly had often seen at the library. "It is about time," declared Lady Carrington, perspiring somewhat from her meagre exertion. "Now I may finally make a match between her and my nephew and there is but no time to waste," she leaned closer to Tilly afore confiding, "for I hear the local jezebel has her hooks set on Master Daversham, and his fortune too, I might add." She peeked to and fro through the oblivious masses for the errant master come polluter of purity and Tilly, nearing the point of combustion, almost shouted with impatience.

"I do believe Master Daversham took leave to the study, your ladyship," pointed Tilly to the oak door that may as well have been death by suffocation itself.

"Ah, that'd be Billy, my beloved nephew. Always with his nose in a book, that one. Lead on my dear, do."

Tilly was already moving, dragging the dear lady, who might easily have been a broken down barge on the Leeds to Liverpool canal, through the irritated and heavily put upon prancers, whilst the violins, cellos and pianoforte played on obliviously.

Finally, and with an agonising heart, Tilly threw open the door.

"What the devil is the meaning of this?" Master Daversham, with a hand clasped firmly around ample bosom, glared at Tilly afore noticing the looming and imposing form of the canal barge occupying near the entirety of the threshold. How he'd seen the former afore the latter, only the Lord God must have known, for his mind must truly have been fizzed. One's first touch of bosom can often have that effect and indeed, the lustful master was almost salivating. "Aunt Agnes," acknowledged the young deviant afore straightening and forlornly shielding a terrified, yet still handsome Elspeth from the unwelcome glares of Whitby society.

Tilly coughed and nodded to her ankle, which was partially uncovered due to the frolicking, and Elspeth hastily covered the naughty appendage afore scandal and ruin became her, and disoccupation her beloved father.

If the ever-hungry lady saw any wrongdoing, then she displayed no outward sign nor signal. "Master Daversham, I do believe there is a Miss Wakefield awaiting an introduction and subsequent offer of marriage. You will join me presently in the foyer so that I may complete my life's work of interfering in other people's affairs."

Master Daversham straightened his collar, adjusted a cuff and replaced an errant cluster of matted black hair. "Oh, please lead the way, my prying aunt, do."

Tilly stepped aside for the miscreant who remained

completely unperturbed after his wrongdoing and she silently vowed never again to allow such a man to be alone in the company of her childhood friend. She slammed the door behind them, shutting out the trills and taps from without, afore rolling an old perambulator, sans child, in front of the door and applying the brakes.

"Oh, thank heavens you came, Tilly," approached the heavily put upon maiden to within an arm's length, "another moment and it's a wonder I shan't have screamed."

A trickle of unladylike perspiration ran down Tilly's back within the confines of her specially chosen ball dress. "The brute. Please tell me he made you no harm," Tilly dared ask whilst closing half the gap.

"Oh, but it's all thanks to you. You always had my best interests at heart and if not for your timely intervention, who's to say what harm he'd have caused," panted Elspeth an unfamiliar shade of red that contrasted most handsomely against her brown hair tied up into an elaborate bun for the ball.

"Come here, my sweet," Tilly opened out her arms and clasped Elspeth within their grasp, "we have Lady Carrington to be most thankful for."

"No, I have *you* to be most thankful for," gasped Elspeth in a muffled voice, her breathing apparatus pressed most inappropriately against Tilly's bosom.

She pushed Elspeth back to arm's length. "You're so brave, but upon my soul, I shall never again allow such unwarranted attention to come your way." Tilly rubbed upon her friend's arm, straightening her dress, getting that damned crease out, removing a piece of fluff and touching once more for luck. "Unless, of course, you'd welcome the attention?" Enquired the golden-haired lady with a raised brow.

"Tilly, I could quite happily never again look at another

man," replied the girl who was in no way a jezebel, no matter what the town thought, as she straightened Tilly's sleeve, tugged it down over her wrist, readjusted her friend's bracelet to face the correct way and then touched her hand again for luck. "It's true what they say. Men are all such pigs. I'm so eternally lucky I have you for…a friend."

"Yes and I will always be here for you," panted Tilly as she stepped back and then forward again as another drop of unladylike perspiration trickled down her back.

Elspeth wiped a clammy mitt over her maid's dress and swallowed. "But what happens next?" Whispered she, glancing between Tilly and her hands. "Help me. I don't know what to do."

Jezebel indeed, thought Tilly, almost certain in the knowledge that Elspeth was in no way referring to reentering the ball with the tray of champagne, but what else could she have meant? Tilly grabbed two handfuls of ball gown afore drying her own perspiring mitts. "Oh, Elly, if only I knew."

❄

"I'M SORRY, JUST ONE MOMENT," Tilly interrupted, stood from the divan and stepped toward the window before staring out into the gloom.

I closed my eyes and pinched the loose skin at the top of my nose. "Are you ok?" I asked after a few minutes, gazing across at her forlorn figure.

"Whether *I'm* ok is beside the point. It's *you* I'm here for." She spoke with a defiance that almost cracked, like an anxious soldier addressing his comrades and trying to sound brave, before giving the orders to advance. It was the first time I'd seen her, at least in the flesh, as anything other than playful.

I knew what had happened and cursed my stupidity for choosing the wrong bloody scene. Hurting her was the last thing I ever wanted. Well, other than to remind her of a certain somebody else and I knew I had to occupy her mind, and quick, on something else.

I approached her at the window and ran a soft comforting hand down her arm. She slowly turned to meet my eyes and with my hand now stroking her, she could not be mistaken of my intentions. But just in case - A cluster of golden curls flowed down her face and I gently tucked them behind her ear in a way that made her shiver as she sighed sharply. She wasn't flinching or showing any signs of objection and my heart soared. I stepped closer and grazed her jaw with delicate fingers until she closed her eyes in preparation for what I desired more than anything else in this world. Her breathing increased and I sensed the slightest tremble from her body, or was it mine? Her lips parted slightly as I leaned closer toward her perfect features. It was so hard to believe, it couldn't be real, yet here she was and our lips touched, so softly as I inhaled her scent and ran a hand through her hair. I pulled her closer and deepened the kiss, opening my mouth as did she, inviting my tongue to caress hers and I grazed her bottom lip, exploring, experiencing her taste. Her tongue connected with mine as I felt her hands reach around my back, clasping me tight. My knee shook as our breasts crushed together and I released my hand from her hair to stroke her cheek with the outsides of my fingers. Her skin was so smooth and perfect, her kiss so soft yet passionate and I floated away as my body felt so light, my head spinning from some unknown entity. Finally, we pulled away as the need for oxygen overcame us. We breathed deeply in time with each other and smiled as we brought our foreheads gently together.

I was overcome by feelings more intense than I'd ever

experienced, or perhaps it was just because it had been so long, but I could have wept despite feeling so overjoyed.

"Are you ok?" Typical Tilly, so caring, when it was her I was concerned for, given the circumstances.

I clasped my eyes closed in an effort to regain some self-control then asked her in all seriousness. "Why are you *here for me* as you keep saying?" I feared I already knew the answer but wanted to hear it from her.

The truth was that Tilly was one of the most caring women in life, fiction or otherwise, and I knew I was a deeply disturbed soul. Like I said, she was perfect in every way.

She took a moment, then spoke monotone. "I don't quite know. Something made me come, but I'm not sure what exactly." She glanced outside into the mist and then turned back to me. "Anyway, it's of no importance. I'm here and we can enjoy each others' company. At least, until…"

My heart jumped, "…until what?"

She straightened and in a flash her expression changed. "It's time for me to go."

I sighed and studied her face, trying to burn her image into my memory. "Must you always be so mysterious?"

"I know what you're thinking but don't worry. I will return tomorrow night."

It was all in how she said it that made me believe her.

6

CROWS

I awoke at nine in the morning feeling energised despite the mere three hours sleep I'd managed, though I would not be able to continue like this indefinitely. For two nights running I'd entertained Tilly and it was sure to take its toll on my body eventually, probably by as soon as midday today, despite how excited I felt. Maybe I could get Tilly to call around earlier in future, like most normal people, because the other option, to sleep during the day, I'd always found difficulty with, although if this were to continue I'd have no choice. In truth, I felt like a child on Christmas Eve and I recalled those few innocent years, before I grew up, when the excitement of what was coming the day after prevented me from sleeping. It was the exact same feeling now, Tilly would return tonight. How could I possibly sleep?

I rolled onto my back and felt the slickness between my legs. "Hello, and what were you dreaming of, you little pervert." There was only one thing for it.

I closed my eyes as her vivid image filled my thoughts. Her smile, hair, skin, body, smell, the way she moved, her kiss, her touch. I ran my hand down beyond my belly and began massaging my moist folds until my breathing increased in pace as I shuddered against the bed and I imagined her mouth closed tight around me, the hot damp sensations sending tremors through my body and then, almost as soon as I'd begun, I sent myself over the edge.

I moaned, "will I get to experience the real thing?" And if I did, would it last longer than two minutes?

I stared up at the ceiling pattern as my post-climax cloudy vision returned to full clarity.

Seriously, what was happening to me?

I always knew I was nuttier than a squirrels droppings, but still, I dared not think about it rationally, just in case reason put an end to her visits. What was happening was happening and that was all that mattered.

Although, thinking with *some* rationality, if there was one city in England and possibly beyond where this kind of strange thing could happen, it was York. The city's history was beyond comparison.

York - Founded by the Romans, or more specifically, the Ninth Roman Legion in AD 71. This was the famous legion, the same that marched north into Scotland forty-nine years later and were never heard from again. Nobody ever knew what became of them and Emperor Hadrian had been forced to build his wall to shut out the Scots from the rest of Britannia. Did the spirits of York's founders find their way home to haunt me two thousand years later? It was unlikely, but it'd be foolish to rule it out.

York was later to suffer from numerous Viking sackings, lootings, invasions and underwent everything that involved being occupied by those axe wielding Danes. Their final action on the British Isles in 1066 resulted in them losing to the Saxons at the Battle of Stamford Bridge just outside of York.

During the middle-ages, at least six bouts of the Black Death wiped out up to half the population. And let's see, other than all that we've had civil war twice, the hanging of Dick Turpin and a Luftwaffe bombing.

Put simply, there were too many ghosts and ghouls around these parts and I recalled a documentary that claimed there were 600,000 bodies buried within the city walls alone. Given the present population amounted to a mere six thousand, that was making one heck of a bold statement. One hundred ghosts for every living human.

In a strange way, this knowledge brought comfort because, no matter how unlikely it seemed to the rational mind, York was spooked and the city survived on that. Even my own abode was long rumoured to have a ghost, although she'd not bothered introducing herself to me, yet.

Considering everything, all I could do was embrace Tilly's presence. I'd always loved her, you see, and love meant accepting that person in whichever form she chose to take shape.

I arose from bed, showered and for a change ate a healthy breakfast of porridge oats before cleaning the kitchen and living room. It occurred to me I'd need to make more of an effort with these important details now Tilly was making regular calls. I could no longer eat sausage and eggs every morning, shower only when it suited and leave the place in a questionable state. Being filthy was not in my nature, I did not leave rubbish lying around to fester, however, neither did I carry out regular dusting and because Tilly, on account of having a multitude of household staff in her family's employment, was used to cleanliness, I'd have to start making more of an effort.

I sprayed some Mr Sheen across the mantelpiece, lifting the framed photos as I went, including the one of me with my mother that faced the wall. The small scrap of paper with her number fell to the floor and I bent down to retrieve it. I ran a finger over the handwritten digits and even half glanced at my mobile but quickly snapped out of the silly thought before returning the frame to the mantelpiece, faced it away and ensured the paper was properly concealed.

The phone rang and it scared the complete shit out of me. As it transpired, the damned contraption worked. When I recovered, I dashed over and lifted the receiver.

"Hello?"

"Um, hello, is that Clara Buckingham?" The voice was familiar.

"Hello, Dan." It wasn't that I was such a great person that I could remember people from the sound of their voice, it was more that there was such a limited pool of potential callers that the odds of the male caller being Dan from Waterstones, who I'd dealt with once, was almost a dead cert. How had my life come to this?

"Oh, hello Clara." To be fair to him, he didn't sound as weirded out as he might have but doing it gave me a chuckle, which was reason enough, though he'd probably assumed wrongly I was in high demand. We exchanged pleasantries and then he got to business. "I'm truly sorry for the double booking and hope you've reconsidered returning for another signing?"

The grandfather clock made its continuous rhythmical sounds from nearby and I checked its face, eleven in the morning, a long time to go until...

Dan continued, "we've ordered a large batch of *A Petal And A Thorn* and they'll be waiting for whenever you wish to arrive. Just give a day or two of notice and we'll arrange the promotional stand and place the book on half price, as a goodwill gesture. Authors are usually ecstatic when we promote your books and take the hit from our end. Now…"

"How's the family, Dan?"

"Excuse me?"

"I was just wondering if you had a family, a girlfriend, boyfriend? Or perhaps you found a permanent use for Kiera?" I was grinning but was unsure how he'd take my humour.

"I…" he croaked an odd sound, "I have a fiancée. A woman, Clara."

"Umm-hmm, and did you grow up in the area?"

He made that funny stammering sound again, like his mind was in spasm because I'd changed subject mid-flow and he was having difficulty adjusting to small talk. "I'm York born and bred, yes. You?"

"Aye, the same. And tell me, did you go to university?"

"Yes, I um, studied media at Lincoln."

"Really, media huh? I've heard it's oversubscribed and leads to a life in the fast food industry." Now it was me who made a strange croaking noise while I searched for something else to say, and when I couldn't, "I think next Friday ought to be good for me. That's not when Michael Crichton's due, is it?"

"No. Well, we'll look forward to seeing you."

I ended the call and spent the next thirty minutes either staring out the window as tourists took photos of the minster and my property, or pottering about looking for something to do.

In the bedroom, the underlay behind the set of drawers was protruding out from below the carpet. Something would need doing about that. And maybe I could make enquiries about having the pianoforte tuned?

Finally, I decided on something better. I'd walk to Waterstones and make conversation with Dan and so I dressed and grabbed the brolly, which was always the safe option in York, before heading down the stairs. The usual step creaked as I tramped over it, then I was out the door and swerving away from tourists photographing my house.

Around the side of the minster, through the minster yard, down Stonegate and along the busy shopping streets towards the river. It was while crossing the Ouse Bridge when I made a double-take at the same time as she did, so it wasn't my dicked nob playing tricks. We both stopped and glared at each other before she finally spoke.

"Clara?" She seemed unsure of what to do next and probably, like myself, regretted stopping, but by then it was too late.

A surge of lunchtime pedestrians past us by and I considered following them over the bridge, but something stopped me. "The woman from the book signing."

"Gemma, my name's Gemma." She wasn't peeved at my not remembering but neither did she offer her hand, which was hardly surprising. She wore a nice pair of tight-fitting light blue denim jeans with the odd tear down the front and brown boots that ended just below the knee. She also wore a brown leather jacket to match the boots, not altogether unstylish and I noticed how cute she looked with her brown hair running down the shoulders. It almost made me regret our, should I say, negative first encounter. Not that I'd be in with a shot anyway, mind.

I nodded in recollection, "Gemma."

She continued to stare for a period bordering on becoming uncomfortable whilst her mouth tried to decide what to say or whether to speak at all, kind of like how a goldfish looks at you through its bowl. Finally, she found her voice, "I guess I should apologise for being a bitch before."

Quite an unexpected revelation and I nodded in gratitude.

"It was one of those things, Gemma. The store, you know… what can you do?"

She smiled, probably in relief that I wasn't in the mood for making the conversation any more awkward than it needed to be. "All the same, I should never have lost my cool like I did. It's really not like me, I'm usually the most chilled out person you'd ever meet," and she touched my arm for emphasis, "but I was just so incensed by what you did. I…I lost my good sense. And for that, I'm sorry."

I looked down at her hand as my mind concentrated on *that*, rather than on how to continue the conversation. "I see. Well, there you go then." I nodded, distracted by people filing by either side with sandwiches, pasties and even one man with a large pizza box, at lunchtime? They were stuffing their mouths, bits of pastry dropping to the ground or down their fronts, chewing. I shuddered but hid it pretty well.

She removed her hand and leaned closer. It was kind of awkward.

More seconds past as I wondered what she was thinking then I remembered the obvious subject. "Funny I should bump into you now, I was just on the way to Waterstones to discuss returning for a book signing."

"What?" She stepped back and spoke in a heightened tone I recognised from before. "You mean they invited you back?"

"Of course," I was Clara Buckingham, after all, "and after they apologised and begged me to return, I thought, well, where's the harm." It wasn't like I had anything else to do anyway, other than purchasing some sort of tool to fix the carpet. "They're promoting the book, so…"

"Hang on, let me get this straight," she stepped forward to reoccupy her old spot, "Waterstones apologised to you?" Where was she going with this?

"That's correct," I confirmed with scepticism.

"I see, so, Waterstones apologised. Did you apologise to them for causing a scene?"

I didn't allow her sudden raising of hostilities, albeit in the minute and almost unnoticeable way I'd come to expect from this person, to affect me. "I did not and I will not."

A flicker of anger, most amusing, flashed across her face and she seemed to be reconsidering saying the first thing that came to her mind as she visibly bit down on her bottom lip. "I see, and is there anything you'd like to say to me?"

I'd like to see you bite your bottom lip whilst lying on your back. "No, nothing."

Her chest made a small jerking motion. "Nothing at all, Clara?"

I thought I knew where she was going with this, and couldn't resist the temptation to cause a little more trouble. "Well, there is one thing…"

She bounced on her feet and smiled. "Oh, good, what is it?"

I spoke with as solemn a face as I could pull. "I accept your apology." It was all too much fun and she was so easy she had it coming.

Her eyes widened in shock. "You accept my apology?" Clearly, here was a girl who avoided all conflict and in a way I was doing her a favour by welcoming her to the real world, and neither did I think it could harm her literary career to experience a genuine head case for the first time in her life. Not everybody is nice. Every once in a while, people will encounter one such as me. I was helping her. "And? Is there anything else?" She stammered.

I glanced around as though searching for the answer. "No, I don't think so."

She took another comical step back and thrust her arms out akimbo style. "It is polite, Ms Buckingham," she spoke through totally delicious gritted teeth, "that when you share blame with somebody and that other person apologises, that you should apologise also."

I laughed, not because she'd finally spat out the words and not because she expected me to apologise either, but because this girl could not pull off anger to save her life. She was far too cute to be effective, with a voice several pitches too high to take seriously. A part of me thought to apologise just to see how she'd react to the unexpected but given it was *I* who'd been wronged, sort of, I just couldn't bring myself to do it. "Gemma, if you think you're getting an apology out of me, then you must be seriously dicked in the nob."

Her mouth sagged open and she did that fish thing again. "And what is that supposed to mean?" She continued ranting while another surge rushed past, forcing me to sidestep closer to the bridge railing. "It sounds very vulgar, and coming from you, of all people." She mentioned something about body parts but my mind was connecting strange dots inside my head and her words, although I could hear them, were not being properly processed.

I glanced to my left, across the bridge's road surface, through the vehicles and over the railing on the opposite side to where the King's Arms pub was situated. It was too early for the ghost walk tour but I recalled Shackleton and his stupid story and realised I was standing on the bridge with the supposed hangings and heads on pikes. Without warning, I laughed.

"Excuse me?" She demanded, now almost at the point of bursting.

Two men in suits stepped between us. "Huh?" I asked as one particular pedestrian stole my attention and then I spoke in monotone as my eyes followed the figure down the steps that led below the bridge toward the pub. "Oh, I was just thinking about crows pecking out your eyes." I missed her response as the strange dark-haired woman dressed in vintage maid's clothing bobbed further down with each step and then the back of her head, in white bonnet, disappeared from view. "You are not part of the ghost tour," spittle may have left my mouth but I couldn't be sure.

I held my eyes shut, gave them a rub and stared over the railing to the near embankment. She hadn't passed under the bridge so unless the odd woman was intending on remaining at the foot of the steps on the other side, then she should emerge any second walking toward the York Dungeons.

Gemma placed a comforting hand on my shoulder. "Clara? Are you alright?"

When I looked back from her to the embankment, there was no mistaking the maid and what's more, she was standing inches from the river's edge staring right back at me. "You'll fall in if you're not careful."

"Excuse me?"

The pedestrians were blurs who intermittently obscured my view of the girl but there she was and from this distance, the eye contact we were making could not be misinterpreted, just like the other day at the end of the ghost tour.

She wasn't getting away this time.

"Gemma, keep an eye on that maid," I pointed in the general direction before setting off at a pace. Looking right toward the oncoming traffic before attempting to cross the road, I briefly glimpsed Gemma throwing up her arms before she began stomping off in the other direction. "Hurry up, stupid cars." There was a long line of slow moving traffic, so I abandoned that idea and instead ran toward the steps leading down on the near side, barging through tourists and ultimately being held up behind a teenager on crutches, who selfishly occupied the entirety of the narrow passageway.

"Ugh, there's far too many people in this city." I almost screamed while thinking about adding to the number of corpses buried below.

Why did I care so much about discovering the identity of the woman?

The answer was that I was beginning to fear I already knew who she might be.

Finally, jumping the last two steps, I struck the ground, rounded the corner and ran below the bridge to the footpath on the other side.

But when I arrived at the King's Arms pub, she was gone.

7

BOUDOIR

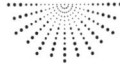

*T*hree knocks jolted me off my arse where I was sitting by the window and I bounded down the steps, two at a time, the sight of the poker leaning against the doorframe checking my step as I landed at the bottom. I wrapped my hand around the handle, feeling the cold iron in my grasp, breathed and then placed the tool back.

I inched the door open and bloomed inwardly at the sight of Tilly.

"Don't think I'm not aware of your delaying while you keep me out here waiting in the cold. Why, I can hear you shuffling around on the other side and can only imagine what you're doing." She pushed the door further open as I lost a great many of my faculties including the ability to think clearly. It had been so much easier when I'd thought she was an out of work actress looking to cause mischief. "I assume you have no objections to my being here, so I'll just take the liberty and enter, shall I?"

"Um, yes, of course," I shook my head clear and beamed, giving her the welcome she deserved. "Come here," I opened out my arms and embraced her, compressing the wigwam in my hold and inhaling her scent. "It's so good to see you again."

"The pleasure, Erica, is all mine."

"Shhh," I placed a finger to her lips, took her hand and lead her up the stairs.

"Ooh, you have oil lamps." Obviously, my plan to take her in silence may come undone here. "I do declare, but you're being very…intense."

Percy squawked as I led her along the corridor and I felt her apply the brakes so we stopped and I watched with intrigue, the fascination in her eyes as she tapped the birdcage. "Such strange paper you use to catch his droppings, Erica, I see glossy smiling faces staring back at me."

Explaining the novel use I'd found for old photos of my ex would probably kill the mood so instead, I tugged on her arm and she obediently followed.

"I sense you're not in the mood for conversation this evening and have other plans for us, perhaps?"

I rolled my eyes, pushed open the bedroom door and tugged her inside, relieved to feel no resistance from her.

"Oh, you have the most beautiful…"

I whipped around on her, kicked shut the door and breathed in her expressions as she contemplated the room and as hoped, my vision of the ideal Victorian boudoir had rendered her voiceless, albeit temporarily.

Above all, it was the exposed oak beams that truly gave the room its character. The four-poster bed, so I believed, had once belonged to Charles Dickens and had cost more than a small sum at auction. Apart from that, I had wood panelling with beautiful carvings, chandelier, cabinets, mirrors, rug, stools, curtains and drapes all either genuinely from the period or else styled in that way and I hoped Tilly would feel at home here.

Apart from my extremely tasteful arrangement, for the evening, I'd made a few additions, not least the dozen candles laid out in contravention of fire regulations.

Tilly picked up a handful of rose petals from the bed, brought them to her nose and inhaled before giving me the most adorable smile and throwing them in the air. "These are to symbolise me, I do believe."

"Who else? You are my petal." I put so simply.

A slow smile crept upon her face and in the candlelight, I saw a hint of red about her cheeks as she shyly turned away to conceal her embarrassment.

Approaching from behind, I stroked my hand across her back as I swerved toward the room's corner and the device atop the cabinet. Having already pre-wound the instrument, I placed the needle on the vinyl and pressed the starter.

The scratching noise made her jump. "Oh, what is that? Is that really a…" Edvard Grieg's Morning Mood began and she clasped together her hands beneath her fine jaw. "Oh, Erica, you make me so happy. I do recall seeing one of those strange phonograph devices at the Scarborough Fayre last summer. It was the most wonderful thing. Whoever thought one could replay sound using a cranking device and revolving cylinder with grooves spread about the surface. Oh, how I begged him to teach me how it worked. He did of course." Of course, he did and it was her love of learning, not unlike myself in my youth, that I dearly loved about her.

"It's most wonderful indeed, just so long as the sound coming from it is not total garbage."

She hit me playfully on the arm. "How could you say such things?"

"Stick around in my time and you'll find out for yourself."

She ignored my judgement and glided toward what was in fact not a phonograph but a gramophone. I didn't have the heart to correct her and couldn't help smiling as I watched her raise, lower, raise and lower the needle, fascinated as she was with the ability to create music from a sheet of vinyl containing tiny grooves.

Once she'd restarted the classical piece of music for the seventh or eighth time, she pulled herself away, settling her gaze on me and it was no small flutter I felt in the pit of my stomach. She knew how I drooled over her and was kind enough never to mention it, but there was more than merely the look of admiration for me in *her* eyes. No, there was something more there too. Dare I even think it, that there was the merest flicker of attraction?

I could never compare to Tilly, but then, if she were to hold out for someone who could, she'd be waiting the rest of her life. And granted, I was fifteen years her senior, but when you had status and money, age would never count against you. And sure, ten years of bad living, which included an excess of fine dining, exercise consisting merely of pottering about my abode whilst drunk on an abundance of the finest Scotch straight from the Isle of Skye, well, it was all bound to take its toll on my appearance eventually. But Tilly had overlooked Elspeth's mediocre looks, so why not mine? I'd created her that way, you see. She was the perfect angel and if I'd never truly know what possessed her to find me attractive, as long as she did, that was all that mattered. A romantic, perhaps I no longer was, but then most people hadn't been let down like I had. Besides, the right to be romanticised had to be earned, not expected.

Not that Tilly expected, nor seemed to want anything other than, well, me. And as she stepped closer, placed her hands around the back of my Victorian prom dress and unfastened the top button, I tried to hide my surprise, as well as delight.

"You always have that same intense look in your eyes," she whispered in my ear as I wondered just who was seducing who. "Relax, Erica, you've done so much for me. Now I would like to do something for you."

Well, what could I do, other than oblige?

She moved her fingers down my back, in a vain effort at reaching the next button, and although I loved nothing more than the sensation of being enveloped in her hold, her not being able to reach around was somewhat cause for embarrassment. I exhaled and pulled in my belly to the point it almost hurt and was much relieved to feel the sudden slackening of material across my bare back, and that I hadn't given myself a hernia in the process. However, knowing there were another five buttons remaining and that I was unlikely to be any slimmer the further down she ventured, it was time for plan B.

I coughed and found myself looking at the floorboards. "Um, maybe it would be easier if I lifted it over my head."

"I've always had short arms," she stepped back, bless her, and said nothing in condescension, as I made a mental note to order some new dresses.

My vision blacked out and there was the smell of friction as I pulled the prom dress over my head before discarding it to the floor and then I found myself only in my white lingerie, stood before another woman, for the first time in…gosh, I had no idea. My hands automatically gravitated to my solar plexus as I made a self-conscious half turn to the side while looking down to the rug, where the green and red swirly patterns provided much comfort.

She knew, she just knew and took two strides toward me, reaching out for my hands. "Hey now, this is not the undauntable Erica I've come to know. Where is she?" It almost seemed like she honestly didn't care for my appearance and if anything, my sudden shrinking inside of myself only encouraged her.

I laughed and felt the tension leave. "You can read me better than any other person."

And with that, she pushed me onto the bed, where I landed with a slap and sank into the duvet. "I think you should not underestimate me."

My head span from finding myself unexpectedly supine. "Yeah, about that, sorry about doubting you and everything. It won't happen again."

She shook her head with displeasure and in one smooth motion slid herself between my thighs to bear down upon me. "Erica, now who's talking gibberish?" Her thigh absolutely pressed against my opening and before ten seconds ago, I'd have believed it to be accidental. Now...? "I think that you should cease talking altogether. Did you not initiate the phonograph for that very reason?"

To create mood and shut her up, yes, but I wasn't to know she'd turn out to be a vixen in no need of such aids. "Yea... yes, ma'am," I hissed, seething with exhilaration, and no small amount of fear.

She pulled back but remained positioned between my knees, which were hanging off the end of the bed while quivering somewhat and she glanced at my quite tame panties as one corner of her mouth curled up slightly, yet most deliciously. That was when I became aware I was more than a little damp down there. Indeed, I was dripping.

Through her dress, she teased me with her knee, gently brushing. Oh, it was most frustrating, "I see, I excite you, Erica?"

My mind fogged and could think of nothing to say, other than an incoherent groan as I willed her to press harder.

"Are you pushing against me?" She asked with disgust and with that, she was on top of me again. "Wicked girl." Her face was next to mine, her hot breath in my ear and I shuddered from the unexpected wet warmth and sounds of the ocean as she took my lobe in her mouth before releasing it with a bite, heavenly painful.

Who taught her all this? Because it wasn't me. Not that I cared in the moment as I mentally prepared for the experience of a lifetime.

She positioned herself on her elbows and simmered down atop of me with a look of such intensity and fire I wasn't sure if I'd be kissed or killed. Luckily, it was the former as she pressed her lips against mine, her tongue entering my mouth immediately as it clashed against mine with force. I closed my eyes and with the help of Morning Mood was transported to a field of daffodils, the sun rising behind the horizon. She pulled away, taking my lip some distance with her, a hint of blood tasting on my palate.

As she stood, backing away, I manoeuvred myself up to protest when my bra fell away. "Bloody hell, how did you do that?"

She shot me another angry glare. "Who said you could move? On your back, now!"

A nearby candle flickered as I obeyed, discarding my bra to the floor and subconsciously bringing my arms into my chest as I collapsed back to the mattress.

"That's better, now, you will not move again, unless I

give you permission to do so," the temptress ordered as I groaned in frustration at her still fully clothed form. "You wish to see me undress, Erica?"

"Yes!" I blurted out from my supine position.

Grieg finished and she paused, looking into blankness as the next track began. It was Edward Elgar's Nimrod, my all-time favourite piece of classical music and, being composed in 1899, was not one Tilly would be familiar with.

She closed her eyes and concentrated on the music and even from where I lay I could see tears welling in her eyes as a row of candles flickered by the far wall, casting shapes against the ceiling. A rose petal fell from her hair as she was, like me, transported to some utopia that would never exist. She seemed torn between remaining in character while savaging me and returning to the sweet Tilly I always knew.

Instead, she did something quite different and tucked her thumbs underneath the halter straps of her dress, pulling them smoothly away from her shoulders and letting go.

I felt the breeze hit my legs as the dress collapsed to the floor, revealing Tilly, my Tilly, in her essence.

It was as though some mysterious force chanced my angering her again, as my body sat up of its own accord, anything to get closer, although I sensed my legs would buckle should they attempt to stand, so instead I remained sat and gawped like a horny teenager seeing breasts for the first time.

The little siren had foregone the need for underwear, having clearly premeditated my seduction and as my pulse quickened to some insane intensity, my throat dried, sweat clammed on my hands, my knee trembled even more than ever and my glassy eyes scrutinised her body from foot to head, I was vaguely aware of her enjoying my torture.

Her legs were long, slender and sculpted leading to shapely hips that widened beyond what seemed natural, but only just. Short golden curls covered her pubic area below an abdomen that was flat and supple. She possessed the perky breasts of a healthy twenty-one-year-old, large, round and perfectly symmetrical with small areolas and nipples already erect from the room's chill. As expected, her skin was pale and spotless, with neither blemish nor freckle. The perfect body of youth, and one who kept her physique toned with riding and exercise. I'd created her this way, but even I could not have prepared myself for seeing her in person, up close and exposed.

Then something struck me. It was just a minor detail but it did register because I was seeing her naked for the first time. Where was the shell I'd seen on both other occasions? Had it somehow fallen away with her dress? Or had she, for whatever reason, chosen not to wear it this day?

"You've gone very quiet, Erica," she swivelled on her heel and ran a hand through her hair, the sideward view making something leap inside my belly; the heavy globes and the way they nestled against her ribs, but it was her pert backside, begging for my clutch, that almost sent me over the edge right then and there. "Oh, I see I have offended you." She placed a hand playfully over her mouth. "Maybe you'd prefer it if I were to dress?"

I sprang from the bed. "Don't you bloody dare."

"And I told you not to move!" The girl's breasts barely moved as she shoved me back to the bed, my heart fluttering from the drop and, I had to admit, being dominated.

"You are freakishly strong for such a…"

"Quiet!"

The angle of the bed cut her legs from my line of sight but I had the most incredible view of her hips swaying as she took two steps closer. Oh, God, she was coming closer, and then she was nestling herself between my shivering thighs. With her knee, she spread my legs further apart and positioned herself closer as I distinctly felt something drip from my opening. She glanced two fingers over the moisture, my body bucking from the sensation of her unexpected light touch before she placed her fingers inside her mouth to enjoy my juices. She made a humming sound as apprehension began to take hold of me. What was this girl capable of?

"You want me to stop or carry on?"

I took a second to gather my wits. "Carry, um, please, carry on. Don't stop. Ouch…"

She'd slapped my thigh. "What did I tell you?"

I hitched a breath as she slowly lowered herself over me, bringing her body beyond my head. There was never a better opportunity to clasp two handfuls of firm Victorian backside since her hips were level with my sternum, but then she drew herself back down and two large perky breasts were dragging slowly over my face. I almost exploded as my lips took their full weight and I managed to snag a nipple for all of a fraction of a second. She was captivating yet frustrating altogether.

Another bead of juice dribbled down my outer walls as she brought her lips to mine and I thought I'd pass out from the force of her kiss. Our tongues danced together as her hand cupped my breast and squeezed. She sucked on my lip as her thigh pressed against my clit and I ran my hands down the smooth skin of her back, to her buttocks where I took a firm hold and moulded the hard flesh in my grasp. She moaned something from her chest, her breasts crushing against my own, my heart pounding so hard it hurt, her scent so intense my senses were on fire. She raised her hips a touch and removed her knee as I felt her hand move down between our bodies as she released her lips from mine. I was thankful for the opportunity to breathe again and shuddered as a million nerve endings on my neck felt her kisses. Then my entire body juddered as her fingers pressed against my clit and began making circular motions with an impossible ease, I was so moist. I heaved and bucked as two fingers entered inside me and I pushed myself down against her fingers. She obliged by searching deeper before pulling out and sliding in again. She continued working me as she gazed down, her face close to mine with fire in her eyes, until she passed from clarity to almost a blur. My skin reddened at every pore as she slid down my body, running her hands tenderly over me.

I felt forlorn at her leaving but then her mouth clasped around my bundle of nerves, sucking, pulling, nibbling. Her tongue pressed hard against my clit and my back arched so hard it almost hurt. Her fingers reentered me and went to work on my inner wall.

"Fuck, fuck, fuck," I screamed, bucking again and grabbing two fistfuls of sheets as I gushed like no time I could ever recall. My hips left the bed entirely as I felt her mouth still held tight around my most intimate area and something inside of me exploded again. A fog fell over my vision, the ceiling span, my skin tingled and I began to shiver as my hips came to rest back on the bed.

I took a large intake of breath and wiped my forehead as I held out a hand for her to join me.

She came level and regarded me with a wicked expression, "I think you enjoyed that," she said, stroking my hair.

I was too exhausted to even think of a reply and responded with a mere nod. "I…I…"

She giggled and brushed my cheek with the outsides of her fingers. "Hush, my sweet."

I opened out my arms and she rolled into them as I lost

myself in her presence. There was so much more I wanted; both for me and for her, but for a long time, we simply lay together, holding each other, gently kissing, again and again, making conversation about everything and nothing.

"What was it like?" I asked sometime later, stroking her golden locks.

"Victorian England?" She had the uncanny knack of knowing and her face came alive. "It's wonderful. Oh, Erica, there's just so much opportunity for everyone. Half of Whitby has relocated to Newcastle for employment in the cotton mill or coal mine, an occupation is just so easy to come by and there are teaching or nursing situations for the ladies, and we can visit London, of all places, on the railway. Oh, it's huge and dirty and awful and all the men lust over you, but it's wonderful as well and did I tell you there's a building made entirely of iron and glass, would you believe, it's named the Crystal Palace but I much prefer Torquay in Devonshire, oh but there was a grisly murder there, which was the talk of society, and they caught the wretch and tried to hang him but the gallows wouldn't work, so they gave him life imprisonment instead and now all the people are saying he was innocent all along, oh Erica, and the theatre," she was seizing my arm by this point, "and literature; Treasure Island, Sherlock Holmes, Huckleberry Finn, oh I could go on, and t'was just the other week when the circus came to Whitby and the whole town was there and Caney the Clown made me laugh so hard. If only you could see it, Erica." She pulled back, leaving ten tiny red finger imprints on my forearm, "oh but I see I tire you?"

I shook my head. "No, no, not at all. I find you fascinating."

She blushed and turned away. "Erica, please."

I knew it all, obviously, but to hear it from Tilly, to

experience her enthusiasm and love of life was truly something. Even the dull, monotonous and downright awful she could find an interest in and make it sound beautiful. I caressed her shoulder and she turned back to me. "Tilly... growing up, when did you realise you liked girls?" Again, I knew the answer, but I was fishing for something, for anything, although I wasn't quite sure what.

She hesitated and I knew she was choosing her words carefully. "It wasn't that I liked girls. It was more that I *loved*," she paused and looked away, "one particular girl."

I clenched a fist, my nails digging into my palm as I held my eyes closed tight. I decided it was too painful to continue along those lines, so I asked her something else, something about her that even I didn't know, something of which I'd always been curious. "I know everything about you, Tilly, except for one very big thing."

"You have the desire to know what happened afterwards." She spoke as a matter of fact. Yet again, she knew, she just knew.

I swallowed and nodded, hoping for the best yet preparing for the worst. "After you both reconciled on the beach and ran away together, the story ends, happily ever after, kind of. But please," now I grabbed her arm and squeezed, "tell me, what became of you both?"

She placed her hand over mine. "Why, that's all in the imagination, silly. Whatever you decide happens, happens."

I exhaled and leaned back against the headrest. For some reason, that explanation wasn't good enough for me. Of course, I'd often wondered what happened to the two of them afterwards, but then the same could be applicable for every story ever told. It's always just assumed, at least in most cases, that the characters would be all right. But with my story, there was never any certainty about it, because of the enormity of what they'd done and what they'd inevitably continue to face, for the rest of their lives. They couldn't stay in Whitby, that much was obvious, but wherever they ended up, and I didn't know where, they'd face continuing hardships as two young girls in love in the Victorian world.

Just as a lump formed in my throat, the clock struck six, scaring the utter shite out of me.

Tilly shot me a look of panic and sprang from the bed, and my arms, "I must leave." She stooped to gather her dress from the floor.

It felt wrong, just so wrong, like a part of me was walking out which, of course, is what was about to happen. "No, please stay. You must stay." I pleaded, pushing myself from the bed and approaching her as she pulled the dress over her head. "Please." I took her hand after she'd threaded it through the halter strap. "Please, there's so much we have to discuss. I never got to…you know…"

She smiled and even looked a little frustrated herself at missing out on what I knew she understood, that I needed to ravage her like she'd done me. I needed to smell her, taste her, experience her, to be one with her. She took both my hands and kissed me on the lips. "Patience, my sweet."

I stamped my foot on the ground. "No! You always do this. You always leave just as I'm getting settled. And what is it with six o' bloody clock anyway? Why?" She reached with a foot toward her boot that lay close by and I gently pulled her by the hand. "Please, Tilly, you don't understand how loud I could make you scream, if only you'd stay. You think you're good with your tongue? Oh, babe, you don't know nothing, honey. I could make you pass out and regain consciousness only to pass out again." I wiggled my hips so she knew I meant it.

She slipped her boot on hands free, quite a skill. "I will be back. You know I will. When have I ever broken a promise?"

That wasn't good enough. "No, that's not good enough I'm afraid." And I told her so, before watching in dismay as she slipped the other boot on, pulled away from my hand and checked her hair in the mirror. "Look, please, at least think about this. I could read to you some more. I know how much you love reading and, um, the story is about you, after all." I pleaded, knowing how pathetic I sounded, but I didn't care.

She moved away from the mirror and pulled me into a tight embrace. "I will return tonight."

I threw down her arms. "Well, at least stay for breakfast. Look at you…you may well be perfect now, but if you don't eat you'll wither away. It would destroy me. So please. I have bacon, eggs, ham, toast, the best coffee you'll ever taste, not that Victorian piss you drink."

My lover ignored my tantrum, in fact, I swore she even enjoyed it because it proved I wanted her and she planted her hands on my shoulders. "Patience my sweet, we shall be together again and it shall be all the better for having waited." She kissed me warmly on the cheek as though that was final before walking to the door in her usual silent way and waited for me to see her out.

"At least a cup of tea?" I asked, only half joking having been soothed somewhat by her guarantees of returning. I believed it, which made her leaving easier to handle.

We descended the stairs, I opened the door and she faced me, cupped my jaw in her hands and kissed me gently but passionately before stepping away and without another word, disappeared into the mist as the first signs of daylight emerged over the city.

There was nothing to do but return to the bedroom from where I collapsed on the bed. Her sweet aroma still lingered on the sheets and I found myself giggling uncontrollably, kicking my legs and screaming with delirium yet conversely, I was so far beyond the point of exhaustion that I would easily sleep through the entire day before her return and I knew that for her, I'd change into some nocturnal creature of the night and gladly.

I closed my eyes, my tired body gradually began to shut down and I reflected that it was probably for the best she hadn't stayed any longer. "Too tired to perform…need sleep…must sleep…"

Knock, knock, knock, knock, knock.

My eyes opened with a start and my entire body stiffened.

Knock, knock, knock, knock, knock.

I checked the clock on the wall. "Six ten."

Whoever it was refusing to let me sleep, there was one person it wasn't - Tilly.

In fact, something, some feeling in my bones told me I already knew who it might be, who even now was banging on my door like a loanshark come to collect his debts.

Knock, knock, knock, knock, knock.

I staggered from the bed, found some much needed adrenaline, flung open the bedroom door, stomped past Percy and bounded down the steps.

The poker was already propped too temptingly in position and I knew there was a reason I'd kept it there, so I grasped its handle before wrenching open the door.

I'd guessed correctly and felt the forces of my body crushing my heart from within.

"What the fuck do you want!" I yelled, brandishing the iron object above my head.

Elspeth's eyes bulged as she backed away, turned and ran in no particular direction, still wearing that stupid maid uniform.

I ran out into the cold and in the process, very nearly bashed my head hard against the door, but I bounded into the courtyard and pursued her for as far as my lack of physical fitness would allow, which even pumped on adrenaline wasn't very far.

"That's it…run…" I screamed so loud my voice came out in rasps, "you little jezebel. You will not take her from me!"

8

ELSPETH

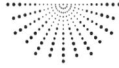

I laid on the bed, trembling with some appalling concoction of rage and fear.

Oh, I was angry, all right, that Elspeth would show up unannounced at my home, *my* home, and all for some self-serving reason no doubt. "The sheer cheek of the girl," I spat through gritted teeth as I rolled over and shut my eyes, "interrupting my sleep…must be on top form tonight…how dare she."

I rolled over and readjusted the pillows. "What the bloody hell did she want anyway?" Maybe I should have heard her out rather than chase her straight out of town.

"No!" It was obvious what she wanted. She wanted what I wanted. "But you'll not have her." *I* was with Tilly now.

I shuffled again and brought my hands to rest below my face. They were shaking.

I threw off the covers and slapped the mattress several times. "Useless." How could I sleep with so much unresolved business flying around in my head?

Admitting defeat, I stepped out of bed and plodded

toward the window, peeled back the curtains and surveyed the courtyard below. A thick layer of frost was covering the grass beside the minster as a breeze swept a swathe of leaves along the street.

I showered and dressed, ensuring to wrap up warm with a thick overcoat, scarf and gloves before heading outside and locking the door behind me. A typical gloomy day in England, except this kind of cold was quite rare even for November. I had no wish to remain outside for long, but luckily that wouldn't turn out to be an issue.

I only made it as far as Dean's Park, a beautiful public garden that enclosed the north side of the minster, before I found what I was looking for.

Elspeth was sitting alone on the first bench beyond the gate, evidently having not run very far. I must be losing my touch.

There were other people walking through the park with their dogs and I chuckled at the sight of a Yorkshire Terrier wearing a coat, it was that kind of morning. But other than that it was quiet, save perhaps for the crunching of frost beneath my boots as I approached the girl who sat facing forward and seemed not to notice my advance.

As I neared, naturally I began to examine her and I could now be certain it was the same girl I'd seen twice previously. For how long had she been stalking me throughout the city? She wore that damned housekeeper's uniform, which I could now see had a large tear in the fabric around the cuff, possibly from when Daversham had been enjoying himself. The repair bill would come out of her wages, no doubt. But, it was strange, because I'd never written about any tear in the story. Were these two characters beginning to take on a life of their own? Or had she simply shredded her best work clothes whilst running away from a certain poker wielding maniac?

With a deliberately loud and menacing exhalation, I took the seat beside her, which faced the northern wall of the minster, and I spent the next few seconds marvelling at the stained glass windows, taking my time, sending the message that *I was in control* - And always would be. Well, apart from my losing it earlier.

I glanced at her from the corner of my eye and saw, across the gap between us, that she was shivering most violently. Was that the cold or my doing? Or perhaps I thought too highly of myself. She sniffled and wiped her nose with the inside of her forearm. I also wondered if I detected the faintest hint of a sob.

I waited for the adorable little Yorkshire Terrier to pass with his owner and then, whilst looking forward at the minster, gave her my words. "I, um…I need to know you won't cause me any problems." I spoke in as deep and as calm a voice as I could, steam gushing from my mouth as I did.

She slowly turned her white bonneted head to face me. Red blotches were set beneath her eyes, which had puffed up like a child's after he'd spent three days crying over a rattle. Doubtless, she was undergoing all kinds of trauma to which I may or may not be able to relate. In fact, at closer inspection, her eyes were bloodshot and the skin around the upper portion of her cheeks was flaking. Could tears really do that?

But there was something else about her. It was almost as though something just wasn't there, like something was missing. Either that or her heart and soul had been ripped out. She sniffed again and wiped her nose with a handkerchief. "I…won't," she half heaved, half rasped before turning back to face the splendid building in front, which had suddenly taken on a whole new beauty for me.

Yes, it was the second largest building of its type in all

Europe, second only to Cologne, except I much preferred York Minster for obvious reasons. The stained glass windows were arguably the finest in all the world and consisted of at least two million individual pieces. Best of all, there were Roman foundations from previous structures visible from the crypt below and I made a mental note to enjoy another visit very soon. Yes, it was a beautiful day.

I nodded, slapped my thighs and stood, satisfied that would be the end of it, and I'd made the first two steps toward the park gate when something made me stop and turn back.

"That was your cue to leave," you jezebel, "so if you wouldn't mind making yourself scarce, I'd appreciate it. Perhaps you could go to Whitby or back to whichever dimension you came from," or better yet, the bottom of the Ouse. Tilly wouldn't be calling around for many hours yet, but there was no chance I was taking the risk with this, not with Elspeth, no way. Nope, she absolutely had to go. "So shoo," I demanded as she sat there like a sulking child and I made the universal sign for *get away from me* with my hands, baring teeth, ensuring to leave just enough hard edge in my voice and manner that she got the message.

Finally, she stood just as a chilly gust bit across the park and she clutched herself against the breeze, hobbling on unstable and doubtless freezing cold legs in the direction of Stonegate. As long as she was gone, that's all that mattered and good riddance.

It was funny, but after arriving home and despite still being physically exhausted, I underwent a huge hunger pang. So, I cranked up the heating, pulled off the overcoat and boots, heated some oil in a pan and threw in several rashers of bacon, sausages, two eggs, tomatoes and mushrooms. I'd start my diet some other day because nothing in the world beat the full English breakfast and I readied two slices of bread to chuck in the pan just as soon as the bacon was cooked. That way the fried bread would be covered in delicious juices, I pondered, not totally unlike the dripping that Tilly would know all about. I boiled some water and shovelled four teaspoonfuls of Hacienda la Esmeralda, only the world's finest coffee imported from Panama, into the cafetière, poured in the water and allowed it to work its magic.

Two minutes later and I took a seat at the kitchen table, sipped the black gold with five added teaspoons of sugar and piled a forkful of bacon with segment of fried bread down my mouth. Another four minutes and it was vanquished. "If that won't send me to sleep then nothing will."

I dragged myself back to the bedroom to finally sleep, uninterrupted, for the rest of the day. It was whilst closing the curtains that I saw her and no small quantity of egg almost returned back the way it went in.

"That fucking simpleton." My hands clenched hard with a fistful of curtain in each and one of the hooks pulled out from the rail.

There she was, only sat outside on the courtyard bench that directly faced my front door, as though she didn't have a care in the entire bloody world. She held her legs together, her hands buried between, and seemed to be to-ing and fro-ing in a feeble effort at keeping herself warm. Pigeons approached her and pecked at the grass nearby.

Fighting back the bile in my throat, I instead decided to be more constructive, or to at least think up a constructive use for the poker. But no, it was daylight and tourists were already loitering as they always did. Again, I'd have to play nice.

The moment I stepped outside, the horrific chill reminded

me I'd forgotten my overcoat, not that it mattered though because this would only take a minute.

"You, missy, told me you wouldn't give me any problems," I shouted, stomping across the courtyard, making a beeline for the troublesome mite. She looked up, startled by my sudden appearance. "Well? What do you call this?" Considering everything, I was being exceptionally restrained. More so than the jezebel deserved.

Because she was seated, her housekeeper's dress had hitched up her legs to reveal the tiny black platform shoes she was wearing. She'd be freezing in those, they offered zero protection against the cold and as she stood, I noticed her feet were turned inwards in some bizarre symptom of, I don't know, perhaps the early onset of hypothermia. Not that it was my problem. Indeed, she'd brought this on herself. And neither did I feel for her sobbing as she wandered around the side of the minster, pinching up her shoulders and clutching herself.

I waited for two freezing cold minutes, about as much as I could tolerate, to ensure she didn't sneak back to reclaim the bench. Finally, satisfied, I strode back inside and applied the locks, pleased to be back in the warmth.

That girl had cost me nearly two hours of lost sleep but at least now it was over and she'd pissed off back into the abyss. I hoped that with everything going on I'd be able to fall effortlessly into a deep sleep, only to awaken with minutes to spare before my Tilly's arrival. Just to make sure, I heated some milk in a pan and brought down the hot chocolate from the shelf. The resultant delicious concoction tasted all the better for it being freezing outside and while I took sips from the mug I also busied myself with the odd job that needed completing about the house before the evening's planned lovemaking. The cushions and pillows were fluffed, bedsheets changed, flowers watered and gramophone cranked. It was whilst inserting a new candle into the holder on the window ledge when my hand involuntarily clenched and I heard the snap as both parts of the now broken candle fell to the floor.

For a whole minute, my glare burned a hole through her as I willed the wretch to ignite into a ball of flame and effervesce into nothingness, but perhaps the poker really would be more practical. "She's really gone and done it this time." I spat the words as she sat on the exact same spot to commence staring into nothingness.

One thing was becoming abundantly clear, that she might not leave easily and would, therefore, need dealing with.

I thread my hand through my hair, closed it, squeezed and pulled, shutting my eyes as the pain soothed me. And then I hit upon an idea.

I donned my overcoat, scarf and gloves before checking myself in the mirror. "Calm yourself. Do not, I repeat, do not allow her to provoke you."

Once my impending rage was checked, I descended the steps, opened the door and walked into the cold.

She looked up after I'd covered half the distance and, like a mouse caught by a cat in the middle of the floor, sprang to move.

"Hold on," I called, hurrying to catch up, just as a chill cut across the courtyard and made me shiver. "You must be catching your death out here?" Had she really been meaning to wait until midnight? The genuine lunatic.

She slowed, perhaps soothed by my non-threatening words and tonality and I eased my arm inside of hers before continuing to walk around the side of the minster in the direction of High Petergate.

"My dear, you are freezing cold," I gave her a reassuring

pat and noticed the stiffness of her legs, "let's get warm, shall we, and have a nice cup of tea and a chat."

There's an overused saying that was nevertheless entirely appropriate...

Keep your friends close and your enemies closer.

9

RIVAL

*A*fter taking our seats in Reeds Tea Rooms, I reached across the table to feel Elspeth's cheek with the backs of my fingers. "You poor thing, so cold."

She sat opposite, shivering, her frail hands clutched together where the cloth of her uniform bunched at the crotch. Her skin had gone beyond the point of being pink to take on a blue tint and it wasn't lost on me that during the two minutes we'd been seated, she'd barely made eye contact. That, I thought, could only be a good thing. Intimidate the girl and she was less likely to cause problems.

"Your dear father must be worried out of his mind," I shook my head and made a tutting sound. "How do you expect him to grind all that wheat and haul around all those heavy sacks whilst you're giving him such cause for a heart attack? The mill's no place to be unless you have your full wits about you, what with all that heavy machinery buzzing and whizzing around, and the poor man must be out of his mind. But don't you fret, we'll see you on a nice warm bus," or horse and carriage, "back to Whitby."

She adjusted herself on the seat and made a strange coughing noise that may or may not have been due to her present ill health and perhaps impending hypothermia. She was about to speak when the waitress arrived.

"What can I get you?" She asked me, poised with notepad.

"Two pots of tea, please. Earl Grey, if you have it." I took the liberty of ordering for us both, given I knew Elspeth's drink of choice.

The waitress dipped a brow. "Of course, we have Earl Grey, but one large pot is the same as two regular sized ones and will cost a little less."

"Sure, whatever you think." It was beside the bloody point.

Elspeth brought my attention back to her with a high-pitched voice. "I can't go back to Whitby."

My closed fist found itself slammed into the table, the napkin dispenser shuffling a half inch to the side. I waited for the nosey couple on the next table to look away before continuing in a whisper. "Well, it's already done. There's a taxi coming to collect you in an hour. So we'll have this cosy chat and then you're going home and I'm not arguing with you." Of course, there was no taxi, yet, but there would be.

I leaned back and breathed, silently chastising myself for having lost it. *That is not the way to get her to like you, Erica.*

She nodded and her eyes widened in fright. It was obvious she was terrified of me, which gave me a strange kind of power kick, not at all totally unenjoyable but was not a part of the bloody plan and if I didn't get a grip over my emotions then there'd be far-reaching consequences for my future happiness.

"Y…yes," she finally agreed.

"Good." It was a relief, but then she'd already said she wouldn't cause me any problems, yet here she was, sitting in one of my favourite haunts, a mere twelve hours before the impending arrival of my love.

"Your tea." The waitress approached with a tray and set upon the table the teapot, which was no larger than what I had at home, for all she'd said, followed by a single teacup and saucer.

I gawked at her over my shoulder. "And we'll have the other cup whenever you're ready, sweetheart." I glanced at Elspeth, shaking my head and rolling my eyes for her benefit and was rewarded by the raising of the smallest smile. It wouldn't harm to show her I had a warm side, after all, and I waited until the waitress had slinked away before saying, "she must expect us to share the cup or something." I poured the tea in the cup and pushed the saucer in her direction. "Drink, my dear. You need it more than I do."

She slowly raised the saucer and took the cup handle in her fingers, before bringing it to her discoloured lips and taking a feminine sip, the liquid quivering as she did. She made a sweet sipping sound, replaced the cup on the saucer and lay it to rest on the table. "You're being very kind to me, Miss Gough."

I reached over and patted her sweet little hand. "Don't mention it and please, call me Erica."

"Oh, very well then." She took another sip and gave a shy smile.

I leaned back and studied her - Well, why not? She was my creation, wasn't she? I'd never bothered trying to sketch Elspeth, like I had many an hour with Tilly, though she did indeed look more or less as my imagination had always cast her. She had brown hair tied into an intricate bun that pushed up the top of her bonnet, the long brown strands that escaped hung limp and lifeless showing how she was in bad need of some professional treatment; shampooing, trimming and styling, and that was just for starters. Her father worked in the mill, after all, so doubtless money for the daughter's beauty regime was scarce. Her skin was pale but clear and healthy with only the occasional freckle around the bridge of the nose. Her lips were thin and narrow and might have looked reasonable if not almost blue. She possessed small, brown and warm eyes, which were probably her best feature, giving her something of a ratty appearance overall. Attractive if you were into that kind of thing but nothing like Tilly when it came to looks, or personality, for that matter, and certainly not brains. And although I knew she'd acquired a trim body from regular long walks along the beach and in the countryside, her true qualities came from other areas. No, Elspeth's real attraction was in her caring nature, which obviously had won over Tilly. She could also be truly hilarious, on the rare occasion she wasn't in a sulk or being accosted by one of the local likely lads around Whitby. She'd earned, quite cruelly, the name of *Jezebel*, on account of refusing to succumb to their advances, which was rather ironic really, but that's fiction. The girl had made me a millionaire five times over by the time I turned eighteen, and since the movie the money had never stopped, so who was I to criticise?

After a silence stretching several minutes, in which time she became gradually more uncomfortable, I leaned forward and patted her again on the hand, which was slowly beginning to take in some warmth.

The truth was that I was straining to remember my research from twenty years before, precise dates that would ring true for Elspeth - I had her best interests at heart you see, kind of.

"We need to have a serious conversation now, my dear." I tried to be stern whilst remaining at least a little friendly, which isn't at all easy for me to pull off and I wasn't sure how I sounded to her.

She set the saucer on the table and straightened her posture, again making that coughing sound. "Oh, ok. Please do tell."

"Now, Elspeth, as I'm sure you already know, although they may have abolished the death penalty for male homosexuality twenty two years ago, you'd be foolish to think the times of unenlightenment were over." The death penalty for sodomy was in fact abolished in 1861 and with maths not being my strong suit, I had to be on the top of my game if I wanted to sound convincing, and I paid very close attention to her, for any signs of what she was thinking. "You may have heard about a little something called the Labouchere Amendment?"

She made the strange coughing sound again, this time it seemed to come from lower down in her chest and after giving the question about five seconds of thought, she shook her head. "Well, they're debating something in parliament, but that's as much as I'm at liberty to know. My father natters around the dinner table about Sir Daversham and the state of the mill and things, and only ever makes the occasional reference to the goings-on outside of Whitby. In fact, I do declare, but I may have heard something at the hotel, with reference to Parliament, which is in London, I think."

Awe, the sweet simpleton; so naive and innocent. "That's great that you know all these things, honey." I gave my best sympathetic smile as the waitress placed down another cup and saucer before walking away. I poured some tea, stirred in five spoonfuls of sugar and slurped. After that, it was time to bring out the serious facial expression. I rubbed a hand over my face and turned down my mouth, doing my very best to look somewhat pained. "Elspeth, my sweet dear, you're a mere two years away from the Labouchere Amendment to the Criminal Law Act. In 1885 they will punish acts of homosexuality by imprisonment."

She gasped, "oh, my gosh, how terrible."

"Isn't it, Elspeth, isn't it." I tilted my head and softened my eyes for her benefit. "You're a sweet and innocent little creature and I fear you may not survive long in prison. Life can be very harsh in a Victorian gaol, what with all those murderers lurking around every corner, and nobody wants that for you." Like I said, I had her best interests at heart.

Though the fact was that the Labouchere Amendment made no reference at all to lesbianism, only to gay men, but Elspeth didn't need to know that.

The legend was that when the Prime Minister presented a summary of the amendment to Queen Victoria and she saw how it made references to this phenomenon called 'lesbianism,' she simply refused to believe that such a thing even existed, that women could in no way be attracted to each other, so she advised that such references be dropped, as it was all a huge waste of time, money and paperwork.

It kind of makes you wonder about the lives of our monarchs, but all thanks to her, we lesbians have had it relatively easy in comparison to our male counterparts, at least in the UK.

No, it was one of those things the prudes of Victorian England preferred to pretend did not exist and they certainly didn't speak of it, for fear of women discovering its actual existence and unlike men, women could certainly live in a relationship with each other, just so long as they kept it to themselves.

It had been *that* very thing which was the entire charm and appeal behind *A Petal And A Thorn* and why, if I chose not to, I would never need to work another day in my life. Both characters were in love, despite being completely unaware as to the existence of lesbianism. Neither had a clue what was happening to them, neither knew what to do about it and they both thought they were going to hell, but carried on regardless.

I touched her hand again, much warmth having returned and decided I'd have her on her way shortly. The further the better. "No, prison won't do for you at all, my dear. Are you aware of Oscar Wilde?"

After a short pause, she shook her head. Clearly, she was milling over something in her sweet little mind. "Um, no."

"No? You girls never discuss him at the hotel, aye? Now there's a surprise. Well, he'll be one such person to be imprisoned under the new laws." It never harmed to give concrete examples for added emphasis, though I'd be careful not to overdo it, especially given it looked like I was getting through to her. "You really should consider that nice Daversham lad. He's quite taken by you, isn't he, and he's the heir to a number of mills and rather a large country pile, as you know." She lowered her eyes and scowled into her tea but I continued undaunted regardless. "Your father would be so proud and you'd save him from the need of having to break his back, until his dying day, in that bloody mill, grinding all that wheat. It's no way to live, I tell you. Just think about him, Elspeth, just think about him."

She sniffed and nodded. "Thank you, once again, for all you've done for me, Miss…um, Erica."

"No, no, thank you. I'm glad we've had this little chat."

Satisfied she'd recovered enough, I paid the bill and we left the cafe. Walking was easier for her now but it was only a short way along High Petergate and under the Bootham Bar, one of the city wall's gatehouses, which brought us out the other side and off the pedestrian area, onto the main road.

I was curious, so to distract her from flinching at the fast moving vehicles, and just for a fun comparison, I asked her, "Elspeth, what's it like living in Victorian England?"

She shrugged, "I don't understand."

"How's life, my dear?"

"Oh, um, well, it's alright, I suppose…"

I held up a palm for her to stop. "You know what, it's ok." I think I understood all I needed and I thrust out my arm, thankful for the convenient timing, just as a taxi drove by and it stopped with only the tiniest screech.

"Come here," I opened out my arms and after a small hesitation, she shuffled forward to accept my embrace. I gave her a squeeze and inhaled a mouthful of what had to be wood polish, whilst ignoring the gawks from onlookers, who'd clearly never seen a girl in Victorian garb before, which was saying something considering this was York. "Now you take care and stay warm." I gave her a final pat on the back, thankful to finally be sending the troubled girl away.

She grimaced at the taxi and stepped away from it.

"Whoops, how silly, please, let me just…" I opened the back door and after a few seconds of dithering, she clambered inside. I closed it after her and poked my head through the opened passenger side window at the front. "To Whitby, all the way please and don't stop."

The driver glowered into the back seat, to me, again to the back then shifted toward the window, away from me, whilst tugging on his earlobe. His mouth plunged open, which he then covered with his hand. Then I remembered.

"Oops, sorry, I'm all over the place today. Here…" I brought a hundred pounds from my bag and handed it to the man, who took it in a lame grip whilst giving me, well, how can I put it, an odd look.

As the taxi screeched away, I waved to Elspeth and headed home to sleep.

10

A CUP OF TEA

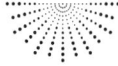

*I*t was the knocking that roused me but it required several salvos before my half-conscious mind made the connection. "Oh, damn, Tilly."

Throwing back the covers, my tired body arose slowly, which was about as fast as I could manage in my panic.

Bloody hell, but I'd at least wanted to take a shower and apply some makeup before her arrival, I thought, whilst simultaneously donning my red gown and flinging open the door. The former, we could do together, so it wasn't all bad.

Stumbling beyond Percy pecking at his seed, I shook off the gargantuan folly of oversleeping as the excitement began flooding through every nerve in my body.

Tilly was here!

I picked up speed, almost slipped down the stairs, unlocked the door and yanked it open.

My head jerked back, which was about all the natural response I could muster from the unwelcome sight before me.

"W…wh…what the bloody hell are you doing here?" I demanded of the jezebel who even now, was loitering in my

128

threshold without a care for anything, certainly not for my fraying nerves.

"Good morning, Erica," she absolutely said, with the hint of a smile as though she was arriving for a day of dusting, "I trust you slept well?"

"W…what?" Really, what? I scratched my head and thrust my face out beyond the threshold and she quickly stepped back.

It was daylight, that much was clear, and at least two groups of tourists were already photographing the east side of the minster. One or two individuals were also taking pictures in my direction.

I grabbed her arm, pulled her inside and slammed the door.

"Oh, good gosh, Erica. What on earth has got into you?" She backed away as far as the tiny confines at the bottom of my stairs would permit.

I wiped the sleep from my eyes, still not quite believing who'd returned to torment me. "What time is it?"

"Time?" She shrugged her scrawny shoulders and continued to look uncomfortable.

I almost spat into her face, "I overslept," but instead I just grit my teeth and jabbed a finger up the steps. "Go!"

She didn't argue nor delay and blundered up the stairs causing a major tremor when she creaked over that second step. Tilly, she most certainly was not.

Percy made the kind of squawk usually reserved for when he was hungry, except he already had a full dish of nibbles. "I trust your judgement, my lovely," I told the bird, "and I know, I know, don't you mind that one. We'll see what she wants and then send her away…again." I reassured him, assuming the jezebel overheard and not caring overly much either way.

She had, as it transpired, and now stood in the living room with a hand covering her mouth.

"Just take a seat, missy, and I'll be right with you."

I prepared a pot of tea in the kitchen and then carried the tray into the other room where Elspeth waited.

Despite her, up until now, perky mood, she still looked like crap. Indeed, if anything, the red blotches beneath her eyes were of a deeper colour, the skin even sorer than yesterday. Despite her mood, these things couldn't be hidden, not from me. She still wore her work outfit, which was beginning to take on a stale stench. Did she still even work at the hotel? Clearly, she was in need of a good kick up the backside, as well as some beauty treatment. Worst of all, she dumped herself down on the divan, in the same spot usually reserved for Tilly.

I made a shifting motion with my hand. "You couldn't just…"

"Just what?" Oh, she just didn't get it.

"Shift over a bit."

She looked to her left, back to me and squinted. "But whatever for…oh, never mind." She scooted down, having evidently been cowed by my angry expression.

"Thank you," I set down the tray and poured two cups of tea, adding milk and my regular five heaps before handing her the other the way she liked it.

She accepted the cup and saucer and took a sip before returning the cup with a rattle of my fine china and making that demented coughing sound again.

I'd taken the chair opposite and now leaned back, glaring at her without saying a word, crossed one leg over the other and bounced my foot about rhythmically in some forlorn effort at tormenting her.

"Oh, it's ten in the morning, by the by."

She acknowledged my attempt at small talk by tilting her chin up, "ah," before taking another sip of Earl Grey and retreating back into herself. Was *this* why she called round?

Again, it was my obsession with Victorian England and taking it too bloody far, which was the reason I was glaring into Elspeth's bland face rather than gazing into Tilly's. I'd tried, oh how I'd tried, to purchase a Victorian alarm clock but those things were far too scarce to be found anywhere other than a museum and I wasn't about to go soiling my abode with a piece of modern Chinese rubbish. How would *that* look on my cabinet beside the gramophone and kerosene lamp? The main problem, however, was that in 2015, the lofty position of town 'Waker Upper' was now pretty much redundant and should I ever have gone through with paying one of the local teenagers to tap on my bedroom window with a cane at the pre-assigned time every morning, it'd only come to the attention of the local papers, which was at odds with the lifestyle I'd chosen for myself. That of a hermit. Of course, the other thing was that there was seldom any reason to get up in the morning anyway and though I usually awoke at a regular time, all thanks to the trucks that continuously rumbled by at the end of the street, there were always the occasions, usually whisky induced, when I'd rise deep into the afternoon. And there was never a thing I could do about it.

I thought again about Tilly, the fun I'd missed out on last night, and how the poor girl must have been banging silly on my door to no avail. "And all because of you," I snarled at the daft maid.

She coughed. "Um, excuse me?"

I didn't answer, which made her even more uncomfortable and she responded by staring blankly around the room, taking in minute details and pretending to be interested. Except, I knew her, and that her mind was far from interested in my fixtures and fabrics but on one thing and one thing only.

But she couldn't have it! I'd make damned sure about that.

That she was intimidated by me was absolutely clear, as she bloody well should have been, and I wondered how she planned on occupying her hands once she'd finished her tea. I drained my cup and saw how hers was still half full, doubtless because she was savouring it for that very purpose.

For some reason, my mind flashed back to school, to the time I encouraged the other kids to rebel against the dress code by coming to class wearing baseball caps and how the Head Mistress, Mrs Baines, had called me into her office. She'd done the exact same springy thing with her foot that I was doing now, whilst staring me down and trying to make me feel like an insignificant insect.

I mean really, I've always been a few dykes short of a feminist movement, but playing host to my own fictional characters after they called round for afternoon tea really was taking things to a whole new level.

What would Mrs Baines think of me now?

But it was time to ditch the old plan of being nice to Elspeth, after all, she'd just cost me a night with Tilly. "I'm extremely disappointed in you." I increased the pace of foot flapping and gave her an almighty scowl, doing my very best to torment her. "I knew you were needy and gullible and oftentimes stupid but even I never had you down as a selfish bitch."

Elspeth gasped out loud but still couldn't bring herself to meet my eye. "Oh, please, the vulgar language, Erica. I have never heard such bad usage of English and you an author, of all things."

Now, I wasn't quite sure what to make of that. It surprised me so much I could only sit in shock. Being reprimanded was a strange contradiction coming from her, but she'd been truly smited by my 'vulgar' language. And now I'd been told off by them both. Rather odd.

Finally, I found my voice. "You're already giving *me* more lip than you ever dared give her mother. Don't think I haven't noticed." And don't think I hadn't noticed that I wasn't saying a certain person's name. "But," and I held out the palms of my hands, "what are you doing here? I sent you back to Whitby."

She sipped more tea with a wobbly hand. "Well, it's like this…I thought about what you said and on deliberation, I'm in acceptance of the potential for consequences. But I can't just turn off my feelings and I'd be willing to suffer imprisonment and loss of liberty and reputation…for her."

Had I really cowed her as much as she'd ruffled me? Because thus far she'd also not dared raise the subject of the elephant in my presence, that I'd yet to hear this simple fool utter Tilly's name either. Though, clearly, I'd not carried out the job of intimidating her anywhere near enough, considering she was presently wearing out the material on my Victorian red velvet and ornately carved oakwood divan that had once belonged to Rudyard Kipling, sipping tea in my front room, of all things - *And* giving me lip. In fact, I was beginning to see more of Elspeth than Tilly, which was the complete opposite of what I wanted but I'd soon put a bloody stop to that. And that thieving taxi driver took a hundred quid from me. I slammed my teacup against the saucer, startling her.

"I'm not talking about *you* and the loss of *your* liberty. Is that all you care about, yourself? Have you stopped for one minute to consider that poor girl and *her* future? Now,

Elspeth…no, don't interject…now, she is of considerably better breeding than you and although she may have shown you charity in the past by continuing to be your friend through all these years, the day was always bound to arrive when her superior station would allow her the chance of acquiring a husband with means." Even though I hated saying all this and it had once been the very thing I'd fought against, there was no way around it. No, it had to be done, and I tried putting it in language she'd understand but all I got in return was a look of total confusion. It truly was like talking to a child. A change of tack was required. "I didn't want to have to say this, I wanted to spare your feelings by not giving you the brutal facts of the matter but the thing is, Elspeth, that by continuing down this road, it's not just your own liberty you're putting at risk, but also that of the person you *claim* to love."

That got her and I took both pleasure and relief in the quite audible wheeze as she covered her mouth and turned an even whiter shade of pale. "Oh, my gosh, I never thought about that." Her hand went almost limp and some tea spilt over the side to catch on the saucer. She'd appeared haggard right from the moment of her arrival, as though she'd foregone sleep, food and self-care for several days and nights but now it was like she'd aged a year in a minute.

"Indeed," I shifted my chair nearer, closing the large gap between us over the floor and softened my voice. "Elspeth, dear, when we love someone, sometimes we have to make difficult sacrifices. Sometimes we have to do what's right for *them*, even if it hurts. And I know it hurts, dear, but look at it this way…at least nobody you claim to care for will have to share a Victorian prison cell with a convicted killer. And it's not just her, you see, it's also your father's feelings you have to think about. He loves you dearly and you wouldn't wish to cause a scandal, would you? Whitby's a very small place, after all. Why, everybody knows the business and intimate goings-on of everybody else. And have you thought about the consequences for your father's situation by continuing to spurn the advances of the dashing Daversham? He will one day inherit the mill, I'm sure you're aware, and then what? Should your father lose his job he shall struggle to find another with a blackened family name. And all because of you, my sweet."

Harsh I was being, sure, but she'd cost me a night with Tilly. Not only that, but she'd cost me many more if I didn't put paid to these silly visits. I couldn't allow that to happen.

She was deep in contemplation and remained there for several minutes. Finally, she nodded, sniffed and breathed deeply. "You're right. Yes, of course, you're right." She scratched her neck and I half stood, about to move her on, when she piped up again. "Oh, but what if we were to keep everything to ourselves?" She shuffled, uncomfortable in her prudish Victorian way to be talking about the subject.

I paused halfway to standing whilst my legs held the strain of my bulk and I glared at her. "What? Keep it to yourselves? And how would you manage that exactly? You live in a tiny four-roomed shack with five sisters. And am I not right to assume that you're well acquainted with the girl's mother, yes?"

She hesitated then nodded her agreement. "Yes, of course, you're right. I'm sorry."

I straightened my now fatigued pegs, wiped a bead from my forehead and motioned with a hand to the door. "This way, madam."

"Oh." She stood, patted down her housekeeper's attire and stepped in the direction of my pointy finger, down the stairs and starting up again a rarely quiet exotic bird, the noise of which I'd now have to endure for at least the next thirty minutes.

I grabbed my bag on the way down and when we were both by the door, I handed over the extortionate taxi funds.

She turned slowly back to face me and my now almost prodding hands, her eyes passing over the familiar poker and, most worrying of all, looked me in the eyes. "Thank you for all you've done for me. I don't know how I'd survive without you, Erica."

I gestured to the wad of banknotes in her gloved mitt. "Just make sure he takes you all the way this time." Ignoring her discomfort within the cramped space, I reached around and pulled open the door. "Whitby's not a bad place, you know," even for a philistine, "why, you won't know it, but in another seven years, a certain unknown author will take one look at Whitby bay and then become inspired to write one of the most famous stories of all time. More famous than my own even."

Her face became animated for the first time in our two meetings and I couldn't help but notice something in her eyes and mouth, a glimmer of attractiveness. "Oh, how delightful, what is it?"

I scoffed, "would you read it if I told you?"

Her eyebrows, in much need of a tweezing, pinched together as she backed defensively out the door.

I shook my head in dismay. "No, I didn't think you would. You ignoramus!" Then I dropped the bomb. "Tilly would."

She froze at that - Her face - How *delightful* indeed.

"Goodbye, Elspeth," I slammed the door and headed upstairs for a shower, shouting over my shoulder, "Dracula."

11

BETROTHED

*S*tamping down the landing and somewhat dishevelling himself in the process, Rupert panted to Lady Wild. "Ma'am, I heard the bell."

The signalling system Lady Wild had established was once again proving its indispensable worth. Young Alfred, he with the sharpest eyes, was stationed on the balcony overlooking the dirt track that meandered through the fields approaching Burley House. Young Alfred would ring the bell, which would then alert Steven, whose bell, in turn, would signal to Rupert that the expected guest was even now approaching on horseback.

"Thank you, Rupert, you may settle the moisture upon your forehead and assume your position." Lady Wild then assembled the servants into their afore rehearsed spots by the door; two lines, four deep, menservants on one side, women on t'other. "Ninety-five-second warning," reminded she to they, thankful the system had been tried and tested for the occasion, afore stepping between the lines and appraising them.

"Marsha, chin up a tad more. Rupert, there's still a bead

of sweat above your eye, wipe it off. Clare, you call that a straight line? Step forward one half of an inch. Stephen, what are you doing here? Why do you think I had you on lookout? Get out of my sight." Satisfied, Lady Wild waited beside Groves at the head of the two lines and faced the door, daring not to search about the reception hall for dust or smudge, just in case she should find any.

The clipping of horse hooves against cobbles augmented on the outside, while on the in, the only sounds were that of the grandfather clock's swinging pendulum and the heavy breathing of the bloody butler.

With a look fit to scare Spring-heeled Jack himself, Lady Wild chastised Groves and from then the only sounds were that of the clock.

Boots struck stone as though an athletic and virile gentleman had just swung from a horse. A pause, followed by oak dampened voices through the door and then hooves struck up again as the stable boy led the horse away. Another pause, followed by a masculine clearing of throat through wood.

Finally, the bell above the door dinged and Groves took his cue, striding forward, his glove donned hand pulling the door to.

"Sir," with a bow of head, he gestured for the gentleman to enter.

The gentleman tipped his tile and stepped over the threshold.

"May I take your hat and coat, sir?"

The man ignored the assembly at first as his curious eyes naturally contemplated the enormity of the reception hall. "You may." He removed the hat and loosened his arms, allowing Groves manoeuvrability for the task and the coat was taken off to reveal the buttoned-up weskit beneath.

Groves folded the garment over his arm afore disappearing into a side room and then Lady Wild was pacing between the servants to greet the gentleman. "Mr Rushworth, how very pleasant to see you again."

Rushworth bowed his head and kissed the back of her hand.

"I trust the ride was a smooth one?" Enquired she.

"As smooth as a good horse through rain-sodden fields will allow, ma'am."

"Quite, Mr Rushworth, quite." She gestured toward the grand staircase, "we may start with the tour, should you so desire it? Unless, of course, you'd first wish to attend the other matters at hand?"

Rushworth rubbed his hands together. "Ma'am, the *other matters* have kept me waiting for nigh on nine months," his eyes softened as he stepped closer, "and, if I may be so bold, but after having been acquainted with her lady mother, I dare say that should I be kept waiting a moment longer, I'd be fit to burst."

Her Ladyship positively purred and contemplated how the grandchildren might possibly turn out. "Well then, sir, let's not waste another minute." She barked to the servants, "about your duties, do."

The study door opened, Lady Wild peeked her head inside and snapped at Grace, who was standing back to the wall. "Cover the damned table legs at once." The meeting was of the utmost consequence and did the fool wish for their most esteemed guest to become sexually excited by the curves of the furniture? It was sufficient to fizzle the mind of any man. "We'll be having words later, miss."

The mother quickly scrutinised the daughter, who was standing in the afore agreed upon position. Everything still in order there, thank goodness.

Grace adjusted the table cloth with haste, the surface of which lay furnished with tea and cakes. Finally, the most esteemed guest was permitted entrance.

Rushworth stepped inside and immediately feasted his eyes upon the girl.

"Mr Rushworth," glowed Lady Wild, "may I introduce to you my beautiful daughter, Miss Matilda Wild."

Rushworth shut his gaping jaw and took three giant strides toward her, thrusting out his hand and tilting forward at the hips to some obscene degree.

Tilly held out a dainty hand. "Charmed, I'm sure, Mr Rushworth."

"The…" coughed he, "the stories of your beauty, Miss Wild, do not do you near enough credit." He again cleared his throat and fixed his eyes on hers. "In fact, I dare say, everything I've heard has been a gross underestimation. Indeed, coming of age has far enhanced your beauty," he pressed his lips against the back of her hand and kissed her flesh.

"You are too kind, Mr Rushworth."

Lady Wild nodded to Grace, who then proceeded to prepare the refreshments. "How do you take your tea, sir?"

Tea was poured, scones and cream were passed around and small talk was made as Rushworth faced both Tilly and her mother across the table.

"You may rest assured, sir, that my daughter is fluent in both French and Latin. She plays the pianoforte and violin to the highest of standards and she sings, sir."

"Really?" He licked his lips and dried his palm on the handkerchief within his pocket. "I do hope to have the privilege of a hearing?" Twiddling the well trimmed-moustache upon his lip, he stole another glance at Tilly, which did not go unnoticed by the astute Lady Wild.

"Why buy the cow when you can have the milk for free?" Reproached she of Rushworth. "All in good time, sir, all in good time." She delicately selected a lemon drizzle square from a plate of French fancies. "You shall have the honour and the privilege of hearing Matilda's singing voice on your wedding night, I'm sure."

Rushworth nodded in acknowledgement afore returning his attention to the daughter. "It will be an arrangement most amicable, Miss Wild, I can assure you." Grinned he from his seated position, "I'm due to finish at Edinburgh at the end of the spring and after that, I'll be free to return to Whitby in order to practice. But I was thinking more along the lines of relocating to Edinburgh on a permanent basis." He managed to avert his lustful eyes from Tilly long enough to address this final point to the mother.

"Did you hear that, Matilda?" Lady Wild nudged her daughter with an elbow. "Edinburgh is *the* place to be if you're studying medicine."

"In the whole world, ma'am," added Rushworth, most helpfully, "and although I may only be the third of the Rushworth sons, you may rest assured I've been promised the funds with which to set myself up in residence."

She beamed at her future son-in-law, "I can assure you, the whole town has such pride that one of our own is making such a fine success of himself."

It would never have been any other way, for Mr Rushforth was born into means. One of seven sons issued from the owner of a mining company, he was a man in his mid-twenties, tall and well-groomed, somewhat dashing of demeanour with an all-around pleasant air and countenance. His cravat tucked into the filled out weskit above white shirt, his hair, parted to the side remained not ruffled from hat nor journey, and his close-shaven face, save for the immaculate bristles below his nose, betrayed no lines nor marks. He could have made any lady happy but somehow Lady Wild had secured his hand for her daughter, which had been quite a coup considering the competition.

He again twirled his moustache and studied Tilly's form, perched prim on the chair beyond the table and his reach. "Edinburgh society is all the rage and I do believe there are all kinds of clubs to join. Knitting, tea clubs, cookery and there's even a rather exclusive circle for the wives of doctors. I understand, Miss Wild, that you're a lover of literature? Well, none other than the likes of Robert Louis Stevenson can often be observed staggering about the alehouses." Laughed he to himself. "The man's tiresome and forever carts around some chap by the name of Doyle with his greasy Holmes manuscript, but nothing will ever come of him, I can assure you of that." He waved a dismissive hand, "not that I regularly patronise these places, you understand, ma'am."

Lady Wild sipped tea and flicked her eyes once to the left. "A June wedding, sir, would be most suitable, for it's the luckiest month of them all."

He nodded in acknowledgement, knowing it wise not to contradict the mother of the bride's plans as far as the delicate matters were concerned.

She took a small bite of sponge and swallowed. "Perhaps, therefore, it would not be unreasonable to expect my first grandchild by spring, sir."

He surveyed the girl and did not disagree, again acknowledging with a nod.

"I have the church of St Mary secured. All you need do, Mr Rushworth, is arrive on the day and do your bit." Shuffled Lady Wild in her seat afore turning to Tilly. "Which only leaves, Matilda, the question of bridesmaid."

Tilly shuddered to attention, "excuse me?"

Her mother shook her head. "Oh, really Matilda, I do wish you'd pay attention and agree, also, to allow your Latin tutor to hold your dress on the day. She's extremely fond of you and, I do declare, that if she misses out on this opportunity to dress up and put herself about the townsfolk, she may end up a spinster like your Aunt Dorothy."

"I've already chosen, mother," squeaked Tilly.

"Yes, and don't I know it. That jezebel who's the talk of the town." She shot a look of distaste in Rushworth's direction. "And this a church wedding. The reverend will be scandalised. Oh, well, we'll just have to make a larger donation. Really, Matilda, sometimes I truly despair."

"Mother, I keep telling you she's not a jez…"

"Ah, the reception, Mr Rushworth, are you a lamb or a beef man? I do hope the former, this is lamb country, after all."

※

"THERE'S something on your mind, something you're not telling me." Elspeth shuffled closer on the sand, but only an inch. "You always do that with your hair when you're nervous. You tuck it behind your ear only for it to fall out again when you next move your head."

Tilly buried her hands somewhere within the confines of her draped overskirt afore bringing them out again. "When is there ever not something on my mind?"

Elspeth fought the urge to pull her closer, to hold, to comfort her. "But this is different."

"You read me so well, my sweet." A sudden ambitious tide drifted to within a few yards of their feet and in the distance, seagulls landed in the shallows to pluck at stranded fish as daylight gradually seeped away from Whitby. Tilly muttered something, half prayer, half incoherence, anything to fight back the approaching sob. "Oh, but Elly, this is our special place and I always divulge all to you here."

"You always divulge all to me no matter where, but this is different, I've never afore seen you hold back like this." Elspeth dug her hand into the sand, uselessly shifting it around only for it to fall back where it had been. "But no matter, for I fear I already know what it might be."

Somewhere in the distance, horses' hooves rattled against stone.

Tilly dried her clammy hands with fistfuls of dress. "You know? Then pray tell."

"I fear I can not, yet I know all the same. Since the day you were born, this day was inevitable. Who am I to stand in your way? Or that of your mother."

"Who are *you*?" Heaved Tilly, "I feel positively sick. *Who are you* indeed."

They ignored the gull that flew over, almost between them, causing neither flinch nor cringe. The waves drew nearer, the rhythmical rushing sound as old as time bringing no peace.

Elspeth dug her nails through the cloth of her polish reeking housekeeper's dress and into her thigh. "I was wrong, I can hold on no more. You must divulge and I must hear it from your lips."

"Elly," tugged Tilly's chest as the tears streamed down her face like drops from a leaf in a thunderstorm, "I'm to be wed. I..." the need for a brown paper bag was overwhelming, "I..."

"Breathe, my sweet, you must breathe. But it is as I feared and expected all the same." Elspeth's arm lingered behind her friend's back, unsure whether it should carry out the action it desired, to hold, to comfort, to caress. "The gulls, I swear they're not afraid of us." She retracted her hand afore digging deeper into the sand with t'other.

"You feared?" Turned Tilly to her. "Pray tell, why you fear, do?" She reached for Elspeth's hand and clasped it. "Upon my soul, you must divulge why you fear so?"

Elspeth faced her friend, losing herself within the power of her green eyes. "I…I…fear because, I…"

A large gull cawed and flew so close the wind ruffled Tilly's golden curls, a fish dangling, most disgusting, from its beak. The girls screamed and separated with haste.

Tilly pressed a hand upon her heart afore settling herself. "Mother has set the wedding for June, at the church of St Mary." Clasped she of Elspeth's hand once more. "Please say you'll be my bridesmaid, do?"

Elspeth clawed a fistful of sand, imagining it was her remaining will to live and squeezed.

"Elly, you must. I swear t'was the one thing that gave me the most consternation, asking of you this one favour. How can I go through with such an endeavour without you close by?"

She allowed the sand to trickle through her fingers. "I cannot do it, my love, yet nor could I allow another in my stead. I will be there for you, for you only, and not for your mother, or…or for… Who is this…this *man* anyway?"

"His name's Mr, soon to be Dr Rushworth."

"Wait!" Elspeth held up a warning finger as panic overtook her.

"What is it, my sweet?"

Her face froze. "Upon your introduction, did this…this man kiss your cheek or your hand?"

Tilly tilted her head. "Why, Elly, I do declare you're unwell."

"Tilly?"

"Why on earth do you wish to know such things?"

Elspeth held a clenched fist to her aching heart. "Because…because, you may be…knapped," shrieked she the final word.

Tilly shook her head. "No silly, it's impossible to be knapped unless you're wed."

Elspeth's hand trembled upon her heart. "No, no…at the hotel, Miss Brown…she was no longer able to conceal her unborn child growing within and told all the maids that she became knapped after Master Atkinson kissed her on the cheek the night of the Annual Whitby Ball. Why, her father threatened him with disembowelment lest he agree to marry her, which he duly did."

Tilly's eye's widened in shock. "Oh, good gosh, Elly, but I thank God he only kissed me on the back of my hand. Mother would not allow otherwise." She held a hand over her mouth. "You don't think I'm knapped, do you, my sweet?"

Elspeth turned paler still while something else churned inside her head. "Wait, did you say *Rushworth*?"

"What? Um, oh yes."

"Rushworth? Rushworth? As in the jet mining family Rushworths?" Scowled Elspeth most foul upon the name.

"You are aware of them?" Nodded Tilly.

"I am aware of jet. Many a guest at the hotel wear jet jewellery whence in mourning. They shut themselves away, dress in black, talk to none other but their reflections and wear jet, a disgusting stone as black as your uncle's boot. I'm loathed to say it, but perhaps this is an omen for your impending union."

Tilly's mouth curled into a smile and Elspeth slapped her on the leg.

"And what is there to laugh about? Pray tell, you clout."

"My dear, Elly, but I do declare, you're not in the least

happy for me, are you? And yet you will not tell me why. Would not *Dr* Rushworth make a fine husband for a lady?" Bumped Tilly playfully against her shoulder.

"Are you happy for yourself? You cannot possibly love him after so short an acquaintance." Elspeth moved away from her friend's touch.

"We used to play as children. Well, he was several years older but would chase me around the allotments, call me names and tug my hair, if I recall. He's been in Scotland these years past."

"Men are all such strange creatures and you did not answer my question."

"Oh, Elly, of course I don't love him. How could I?" Croaked Tilly, after again clasping her friend's hand, staring intensely through her eyes as though imploring straight through to her mind.

Please know the truth about me, my one dear friend.

But divulge to Elspeth, Tilly could not, for fear of losing her forever. There was no apprehending the consequences of such unknowns, such wrongs, perhaps even to confine for all time her love to hell. That, Tilly could never do.

"But perhaps I could learn to love him?" Spoke Tilly, not seeing the increasing ambition of the Whitby tide, which rolled so close, it soddened the sand about their toes.

"Perhaps you might. Or perhaps you might not."

Tilly thumped both her thighs. "Well, what would you have me do instead? Oh, please do tell, Elly, you must." Implored she, shuffling so close the scent of polish mixed heavy with that of the sea. Whilst Tilly was having her future resolved, her love was busy toiling at the Bagdale Hall Hotel. "Elly, please, I implore you, tell me what to do."

Just say it and release me from this nightmare.

"What would you wish I told you what to do?"

"What?" Blinked Tilly.

"Oh, believe me, if only I had the courage to say it," Elspeth dared not even meet her eye but for a flicker.

"You must, I implore you so."

"What use is it in such a world as this? You'll relocate to an even larger abode, perhaps even to the country where you'll bear his children and drink tea with the wives of other doctors."

And I'll be all alone in this hell.

"And now you've gone quiet again." Elspeth threw a fistful of sand, which blew straight back in her face. "By Jove, I can be such a clout. And will you tell me why again you go mute." Rubbed she a finger in her eye. "Oh, how this sand stings me so."

"Allow me," Tilly lightly brushed the sand away with a finger. "How did you manage to get it so thoroughly in there?" Tilly licked her digit for moisture afore dabbing the sand from her eyelid, her pale flesh so soft to the touch and how Elspeth seemed joyed and frustrated, anxious yet pained all at once as she clasped her eyes shut and placed all her sense and being and feeling into experiencing the damp finger as it rubbed her skin.

Tilly prepared to announce a new revelation. With Elspeth's eyes closed it would spare her seeing the pain. "I'll be moving to Edinburgh, not the country."

Elspeth shuddered and t'was as though she lost body temperature afore the tears flushed out all remaining sand. If there was ever need for a brown paper bag, it was this moment. Heaved Elspeth, "you're leaving me? Then I will never see you again." It was all too much.

"But you'd be welcome in Edinburgh whenever you desired, my sweet." Tilly placed a hand upon Elspeth's arm. "And I do pray you visit often, for I'd be lost without you."

"Oh please, you'd forget about me in an instant." Elspeth Shook Tilly's hand away.

Tilly brought her hand back. "Oh, how your words stab at my heart. How could I ever forget you?"

Elspeth dried her face with a black sleeve afore placing her hand upon Tilly's. "But must you move so far away? Surely you could…you could…"

"…Yes? Surely I could what? Please divulge to me, do?" Tilly squeezed her friend's hand.

Elspeth closed her eyes, her chest heaved, seemingly counting in her head, she nodded afore opening her eyes and braced herself. The truth had to be told, and the time was now. "My love, could you not remain in Whitby and together we could…"

The tide swept over them, the freezing sea enveloping their legs.

"Oh, gosh, where did that come from?" Asked Tilly of her friend.

"Our time is over."

CHALLENGE

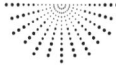

We said nothing as I ran my fingers repeatedly through Tilly's hair, experiencing the silky golden feel, its light flow, quality, smell and colour, which were all so perfect and alone was enough to send me over the edge. The clarity of my vision lost itself, phasing in and out, blurry one moment, indescribable the next only to again lose focus in her beauty. It was like she was a drug and I couldn't get enough.

She fixated on me but behind her eyes, I could never quite interpret what was truly there and too often I feared to find out, just in case the answer would destroy me, again.

She smiled as I lovingly brushed my hand over the side of her body, smooth but for the goosebumps as the candlelight shimmered from the slightest breeze. She shivered as the backs of my fingers grazed the depress of her waist where the nerves from her cool skin reacted to my warm touch. And then my touch turned hungry and I seized a buttock in a firm clasp.

She slapped my arm, "you are incorrigible."

My lips spread wide into a smile, "I can't help it. You bring out both the best and the worst in me."

For a while, she said nothing and it was as though she was thinking about what I'd just said. Tilly never was one for meaningless small talk, which suited me because I wasn't either. "I like it when you play with my hair," she said with barely an expression.

I took the hint and again lost my hand somewhere in her mane.

"You adore my hair, don't you."

I shrugged, "I made it like this for that very reason. I adore everything about you. To me, you're perfect in every way." A wave of peach washed over me as she propped herself up on an elbow.

"I'm perfect? Is that really so?"

"I think so."

She rolled onto her back and watched the ceiling as it performed its glimmering dance show courtesy of the candles. "Do I not moan and annoy and tease? Do I not miss the occasional note when I play Moonlight Sonata? Do I not get pimples in the heat and turn blue in the cold? Do I not toilet? Do I not leave you every morning?" There would be a point to this, I just had to work out what it was, what exactly she was getting at in her artistic Tilly way?

I tried to make a joke out of it. "Yes, but you always return in the evening."

She rolled back to face me and I felt the warmth of her breath as she spoke. "You only think this way because you love me so. With love, everything is perfection, even the things you hate because it's those things that together make the person you love. Perfection is subjective and could apply to anything, but only after you've given time to accept all its imperfections.

151

This is why *love at first sight* is a lie, unless perhaps, you're a man," she scorned. "You love me only because you've spent the last twenty years dreaming about me."

I shifted on the bed as I slowly realised the point she'd been trying to make. And although she hadn't said it, the insinuation was still there, that yes she was perfect to me, but what could I possibly be to her? Something compressed inside my chest, which affected my next words. "You're wise beyond your years."

"Ah, but am I twenty-one, or a hundred and fifty-three?"

I slapped her hard on the bare thigh.

"Ouch!"

"That was so very much not what I wanted to hear, you little minx," I tickled her armpits, "and you love to tease me."

She descended into a fit of hysterics, curling into a ball to shield herself from my mischievous fingers. "Oh…oh…no… please, you must…stop."

I eased up and we mirrored each other, propping ourselves onto our elbows with a hand behind our heads and my eyes drifted down to where her breast nestled against her ribs, her nipple erect in the coolness of the room.

"So," she began with a grin, "what else do you love about me?"

I took heart in her fishing for compliments. If I was nothing to her, she wouldn't care what I thought. "I love your loyalty and kindness, your bravery, your high sense of morality, your energy and love of all things."

She didn't smile after my kind words but held my eyes with something quite intense. "Tell me, Erica, these things you love about me, are they also things you aspire for in yourself?"

My chest compressed once more as again she made an insinuation that I'd need time to think over. And typical old me, I feared finding out, so chose instead not to ask straight up. I twirled a thick clump of golden hair around my finger as the silence continued. Finally, I cupped the breast that had been taunting me from so close.

"I also love this body," I hissed and applied pressure to her breast as I manoeuvred myself atop her.

She lay back as I straddled her hips, my spare hand joining her other breast and I pressed and squeezed, feasting in the sensation of their fullness even as they flattened out across her ribs.

She thrust up with her hips and I knew what she wanted, and I would not disappoint.

I lowered my mouth to hers and our lips connected, the taste of Earl Grey with its lemon infusion still sweet as our tongues collided in hot passion. My hand lay trapped between our chests and I had to place much of my weight on my free arm to slide it lower down her body until it reached her mound. I teased her slick outer lips with two fingers and she pulled her mouth away from mine and sighed sweetly into my ear.

"Please," she begged, thrusting up even harder with her hips, so I obliged, delving inside her with two eager fingers, her walls moist and tight around me.

"You love it when I fuck you, don't you," I panted as I took her ear in my mouth and she absolutely quivered beneath me.

I continued working inside her, sliding out before pushing back and always in time with her breathing.

Our bodies clammed together as her panting increased in intensity and I slid down her body, bringing my mouth over her swollen nipple. I circled it with my tongue, sucked, nibbled, tasted, experienced and then her body bucked beneath me.

"Erica," she heaved, her body seizing up as I felt her walls constrict around my fingers. She made a loud sigh as her body lost several degrees of warmth after her orgasm.

I brought my mouth away from her breast, a strand of saliva detaching with me. "We're just getting started," I licked my lips, not wishing to waste any of her taste.

I worked my kisses down her abdomen and pushed her knees further apart, exposing her glistening wetness to my eyes. I gently blew her clit and gazed up at her, female perfection as she lay back, hands grasping the bedposts, breasts rising and falling as she breathed and she looked back at me, eyes wild with fire.

In anticipation, saliva had built in my mouth. I swallowed before running my tongue once up the entire length of her outer walls.

"Ahhh…ummm," she groaned and encouraged, I continued, enveloping her entire bud with my tongue. I stroked her thighs as I went to work, teasing her inside my mouth, circling with my tongue, nibbling, playing and tasting a million hypersensitive nerve endings. She moaned and heaved before I again pushed two fingers inside her passage and continued kneading against her inner wall with ever increasing pressure, all as my tongue increased its hot pace around Tilly's delicious pearl.

She reached down and grabbed my hand that'd been stroking the sensitive flesh on the inside of her thigh and I felt her hips pressing against my mouth. She gave a sudden scream as her muscles tightened, a sudden gush of moisture unleashed against my fingers and like some starving fiend, I devoured her juices.

She pulled on my hand and I crawled beside her on the bed as we collapsed into each others' arms, our breathing heavy as the candles persisted with their flickering spectacle above. "I have been thoroughly ravaged by your wicked tongue," she rasped.

"I love you, Tilly, and I always have," I said in a moment of passion fuelled recklessness as my head came to rest on her chest.

Her hand, that'd been glancing across my arm froze and for too long she made no effort at responding as my body began to feel heavier with every passing second.

Finally, when I could no longer take her silence and the tears pricked at my eyes, I whispered, "I'm sorry, I shouldn't have said that." What had I been expecting anyway?

Her fingers recommenced their small circular caresses of my arm. "Tell me about Fiona," she asked in an authoritative voice.

I shifted, "wh…what?"

"You never speak of her."

I sat up and faced her. "Oh, honey, there's a reason for that."

She sat up too. "Please?" She stroked my jawline and spoke tenderly. "Don't our experiences make us the people we are?"

I exhaled and wondered how I could even begin to describe Fiona, given I'd never spoken about her to anyone and with good reason. I was over the bitch now, but it had taken many years, mostly living in solitary confinement, which in hindsight probably didn't help and it certainly hadn't made me happy.

"So, you want to know more about the person I am, huh?" Which kind of made sense, given I could still taste her juices on my lips.

"I want you to open up to me."

I pulled the covers over our bodies. "Where do I start?" I thought about it while we made ourselves comfortable, Tilly resting her head on my shoulder as I wrapped my arms around her midriff.

"Fiona and I grew up together," I laughed as I recalled a memory, "we used to share milk at playgroup. Then we attended primary school, middle school and secondary school as though we were conjoined. What can I say? She was my best, most trusted friend." I continued to explain how the two of us were inseparable despite my parents being professionals and hers being a bricklayer and admin assistant, despite the fact I lived in a three-hundred-year-old detached house in the most upmarket part of the city and she an end-terrace in Acomb. None of it mattered to us, even if our parents were uncomfortable with it; mine because it meant driving into a bad estate every time they collected me from her house; hers because they hated being looked down on, which my mother always did.

"She was a proper little redheaded stereotype, full of bounce and energy, fire and passion. She had deep green eyes that always captivated me, a toned body from swimming every morning of her life and an effortless manner that meant it was easy being around her, even for an uptight girl like me. Oh yeah, everybody loved her. Looking back, I should have seen the warning signs.

"It was when, for the first time in our lives, we were parted that things began to change. While I remained in York to study creative writing, she left for university in London to study music; she was good, played the guitar better than any eighteen-year-old you ever met, but it was all too much for us.

"It was during this period that I wrote *A Petal And A Thorn* and realised my true feelings for Fiona. It was all I could do to keep busy, to keep my mind off her, to stop myself from going insane. The days, weeks, months past, moping around the student house, crying, withering away, not knowing what she was doing, or who she was doing it with.

"I'm sure you can imagine my delight when three months after leaving, she arrived back in York for Christmas and broke the news that she wouldn't be returning to London. She'd been accepted as the lead guitarist in a band and quit university to become a full-time musician, touring and gigging.

"At the first opportunity, I endeavoured to ply her with wine and get her drunk so I could confess to her my true feelings, which I did that same night down at the student union bar."

"What happened next?" Tilly's voice was muffled against my chest.

I smiled at the recollection. "Turned out she was all in favour of some experimentation with her best friend. Only, what began as experimentation soon became a full-blown relationship.

"It was wonderful and because I now had large cheques coming in every month, we moved into a house overlooking the racecourse where we used to throw huge parties for the students and bet on the horses. Fun times. Inevitably, she'd tour with the band and leave for days or weeks at a time but she'd always return and our love never diminished.

"It was eight years into the relationship when everything changed." My voice cracked and I began taking deep breaths between sentences. "The band were touring Brazil when they had some sort of bust-up and announced they were breaking up. Apparently, Mike, the lead singer, had smashed a chair over the bassist's head," it occurred to me that even after all these years, I still couldn't bring myself to even think, let alone say, his name, "and looking back, it was only because of Mike that I ever discovered half of what had been happening for so many years."

Tilly tensed in my arms. "Oh, good gosh, what happened?"

"She'd been fucking the bassist is what happened. Always watch out for them, Tilly, they tend to linger at the back of the stage, unnoticed, all chilled out and easy going and because nobody ever notices them they take your women."

She twisted her head and looked at me with a confused expression.

"Of course, you sweet thing, you have no idea what a bassist is. All for the better." I could feel my body shivering and now I noticed that at some point during the last few minutes I'd turned my body slightly away from Tilly, whose head was now resting on my arm. My knees were also hitched in closer to my body.

"You said something had been happening for many years?" She enquired.

I breathed and made a strange humming sound. "Yep, pretty much. According to Mike, they'd been screwing each other ever since she joined up with them. And not just the bassist, but the drummer had his fill too at some point. And not just the drummer from the band," whose name I couldn't say either; drummer or band, "but also musicians from other bands they were touring with, which included some quite famous people."

"At first I refused to believe it when Mike called from Brazil and dropped the bomb and it took me days to find the courage to check her emails. Aye, it was all there, all right. And I spent a long time afterwards trying to piece together snippets of conversation, times of arrival and departure on certain dates, odd things she'd said and done and generally driving myself paranoid and insane, even more so than previously. Eventually, everything clicked into place. That they'd been in a relationship for a long time and if anybody was the 'piece on the side,' then it was I, the rich overly trusting best friend who was taken for a fool." I wiped at my eye, not a tear, for I was long cried out over her, but my skin was tingling in places from dredging everything back up. I could feel Tilly's breath on my flesh and the flick of her eyelashes on my collar bone as she blinked. "To the best of my knowledge, the bitch never returned from Brazil and neither did I ever hear from her again."

Tilly shot out a breath. "How awful."

I tightened my hold around her body. "Well, there you have it. Now you know why I don't trust people, why I don't like people, and why ever since I've kept the world at the distance it deserves." I hadn't meant to descend into self-pity because I was over it now, almost ten years later, but regardless, perhaps because I'd finally spoken about it or maybe it was owing to the fact Tilly had listened and cared, the tears now flowed and I sniffed and wiped away the drops that pooled on my face. "I used to be a better person, I promise you that I really was."

Tilly wiggled out from my arms, pushed herself up and rested against the headboard without saying a word. There she remained in deep thought and when I began to feel naked without her, I shifted positions to get a better look, only to find she was already watching me.

"What?" I asked, needing to know what was going through her mind.

She did one of the things that always melted me, the merest raising of a brow, but this was different. "You mean, you don't know?"

"I…I…what?" What was she getting at this time?

She pulled back the covers and stepped out from the bed

159

as I felt even more naked than ever. "It's time for me to go."
Her plump pale buttocks, so firm and perfect goaded me as
she stepped toward her dress that was folded over a chair.

I sat up and clutched the covers against my body. "But it's
not day yet." She never usually left me this early and the
panic manifested in my voice, more so because after pouring
out my heart and soul I felt quite vulnerable.

She pulled down her dress and straightened out the
creases before holding my eye from across the illuminated
room. "I should leave you with your thoughts."

Did she always have to be such a riddle?

13

CITY WALLS

I approached Micklegate Bar, the eight hundred-year-old, four-storey traditional entrance to the city for monarchs gone by, where the father, as well as many others, of King Richard III, had his head impaled on a spike and left to rot. There were no rotting heads around now though, as I ascended the steps to the city walls and began the two-mile walk around the medieval city's perimeter.

Tilly had left me with a puzzle and now, with aching brain, I needed time to solve it and what better way of doing so than to stroll around England's most beautiful city, take in the sites and the cold autumn air whilst massaging my head, figuratively speaking.

It had occurred, whilst pouring out my history, heart and soul to Tilly that there were some similarities between what had cruelly happened to me all those years ago and what I was doing to Elspeth now. In fact, I always knew what I was doing to Elspeth, the cruelty of it all, and could relate to the sheer brutal agonies of what she'd be living with this very moment - I just didn't care. I'd had it done to me, and maybe

I just wanted to correct the universe - It wasn't like my karma could get any worse.

But now, as I passed by a group of tourists on the wall, I couldn't help but wonder if that was exactly what Tilly had meant. That I'd opened up to explain the hurt that'd changed me so much as a person, without regard or sympathy for the girl I was now doing the same thing to. And to make it all so much worse, I was doing it to someone Tilly cared so much about. *Cared* being something of an understatement in this case.

The similarities certainly existed. Tilly and Elspeth had grown up best friends despite the odds, just as Fiona and I had. Both couples had needed many years to form their bonds before finally coming together. And, it now seemed, both couples had been severed by uncaring bastards.

"That was precisely what she meant by *leaving me with my thoughts,*" I conceded, instinctively looking away as I shifted past more tourists on the narrow wall.

I hunched my shoulders against the cold and hitched up my scarf as I felt a building nausea in my belly. Why would Tilly want me reflecting over Elspeth? Did she not love me as I did her? Would she ever love…

"Hello, Clara," her voice pulled me out from my reverie.

"What the bloody…are you stalking me?" I accused Gemma, wide-eyed and taking a step back, which was hardly a safe thing to do on the walls considering the side without the bastions dropped off steeply to the earthen slope below.

"Yes, of course, I am. Every day I wake up and think to myself, hmmm, what should I do today? I know, I'll stalk that Clara woman, she was so nice to me the other occasions we met, so what better way of spending my time?"

I made a show of rolling my eyes and tutted while trying my hardest not to laugh at her sarcastic candour. "Ok, you can knock off the mockery." I backed away against the stonework, allowing a man to pass and gently pulled Gemma by the arm to follow and I realised how immediately at ease she put me, which was quite remarkable considering our prior encounters. Though, maybe that was the reason, because things between us could hardly get worse.

She was wearing her usual tight pair of jeans with rips, obviously her style, but it was the tank top that drew my attention.

"Aren't you cold?" I enquired, running my eyes over her pink arms, red-inked tattoos and tiny hairs standing on end. Damn, but she looked good. "You work out, don't you," I said more as a matter of fact than a question.

She shrugged her bare shoulders, "I go running, I lift weights. It's fun and empowering. I also enjoy the occasional walk." She gestured ahead and we set off at a slower pace, I noticed in the direction *I'd* been heading, not her. "Oh, and for the record, I've just come from the gym, so although I may not be cold right now, I probably will be in a few minutes time."

I smiled, "sorry about accusing you of stalking."

She placed a hand on my well dressed shoulder and gaped in such an exaggerated way I saw two fillings down the left side of her mouth. "Clara? Is that really you? Apologising...I don't believe it. What has got into you?"

Something obviously had. "Thinking about it logically, it's a small city, we've probably walked past each other dozens, maybe even hundreds of times over the years. Only, we never recognised each other because, well, we had no reason to, did we."

"I've plenty reason to remember you now." She made a mock coughing noise with a hand held against her mouth. "Such great encounters we've had. But, you're right and we're both authors, we have our routines so it makes sense we'd hit each other eventually, right?" She held out her hand to me. "But, I accept your apology for accusing me of stalking you. It's still not an apology for insulting me and single-handedly destroying my book signing, but I guess it's a start." She was being perfectly nice about the whole thing, which was weird. If it were me I'd have long since launched her over one of the ramparts by now. Where were the girl's grudges?

Anyway, I took her hand, feeling the rough skin of calluses at the base of her fingers, probably from lifting weights at the gym, not that I had a clue about that. It was my money that empowered me, even if it had never made me happy.

But hello - Yep, definitely a dyke, I thought, as she held onto my hand for a period bordering on the uncomfortable, while giving me something of a cautious smile emanating from the eyes. Ok, I'd given her reason to despise me thus far.

"Did you, er, have any luck finding your mystery woman?" She casually asked after retracting her paw.

My eyes narrowed, "my mystery what?"

She interlinked her fingers in front of her belly and twirled her thumbs around each other. "The last time we met, the other month, you were chasing some woman from the ghost tour."

I held up a finger having recalled the unpleasant memory, "ah, yes, now I remember," how could I forget, "but she doesn't work for the ghost tour. No, the woman's nothing but a thorn in my arse."

She nodded, "I see. I thought she might have been an ex or something."

"Most certainly not," I jumped in, "and anyway, she's

164

gone now and good riddance." Then I asked her with an enquiring tone, "is it really that obvious?" I'd never gone out the way to look the part of lesbian, not even during the days of drink and gambling fuelled ladies nights we used to throw for the students. Privacy - Was always my primary concern.

"Well, the genre you write is kind of a giveaway and, um, you do have a Wikipedia page, love."

Aye, and countless articles and blog posts speculating about me no doubt. I exhaled and after a few seconds of contemplation nodded at the inevitability of it all. It was annoying, of course, especially considering the lengths I'd been to secure and maintain it; the lost court battles and a life of seclusion, although admittedly the latter was only partially for privacy reasons and mainly because I just despised most people. "Well, there goes my privacy," I shrugged, "I guess it's the age we live in." And in the moment there were two things that surprised me; how little I cared and that this girl had been reading into me. Perhaps it was that finally having found some happiness put everything else into perspective, or maybe my recent suicide bid was responsible for no longer giving a fuck about what I couldn't control.

We continued walking, for a while in silence, until I did something most unlike me. "How's your zombie career going?"

"Huh? Oh, it's up and down, hit and miss…you know. I just wish I was as talented as you," she said as though it was generally accepted I had talent, whatever that meant. I'd always believed my success had been less to do with my abilities and more to do with luck and that the release of *A Petal And A Thorn* happened to coincide with a sudden change in media support for 'the cause.' That I'd never managed to reproduce the same kind of success was testament to that theory and that quite possibly, I was a fraud, though, a bloody lucky one. Weren't the very worst people often the luckiest? Funny how things are.

I thought best to say something nice following her compliment and I half turned to face her as we walked, taking the opportunity to quickly examine her breasts, restricted and unmoving as they were within a sports bra. "You're very kind. Hmmm, let me think if there's anything I can say that might help." I tried to think up something positive while she gave me another puzzled look. "Oh yes, it's important to make your readers *feel*. As long as you can do that, you can be forgiven a lot." Yes, that would do. "I suppose it's harder to make emotion work with a zombie story, but not impossible."

She laughed and I felt her hand pat my back.

"What?"

"You're actually being nice and civil to me. Really, what happened? You must be getting laid." Was she fishing for information out of interest or just being nice like apparently, I was also being. If she had any sense it'd be the latter.

With all things considered, the girl was out of my league. Not because she was so attractive and I'd since lost my looks over the years of good living and alcohol abuse; I maintain that for any woman worth my time, my decaying looks should barely matter, alcohol abuse apart. No, Gemma was too good for me because she was a lovely, forgiving person while I was a grumpy, borderline evil cow with no soul or conscience. She'd said as much herself. Oh, sure, Tilly had managed to get past all of that but then Tilly was dicked in the nob, wasn't she. Not that I should be against making an actual friend in Gemma, my first in many years.

I playfully elbowed her. "You know what your main problem is? You're far too nice. Have you any idea how annoying you can be? You irritated me right from the first minute." Granted with the rope and everything, I'd been having a bad day, but I wouldn't tell her about that.

She held up her hands. "I've never been accused of being *too* nice before, but hey, I guess nobody's perfect, right?"

I came to a sudden stop. "What did you just say?" Clearly, she'd never met Tilly.

She stumbled on a loose cobble and pitched forward, only saving herself from hitting her face because of quick reactions, a good pair of running shoes and an eight hundred-year-old battlement. "Ouch, I'm such a dopey idiot," she brushed long strands of brown hair from her eyes before shielding her face from me.

I helped her straighten and settle herself and I stared, with a strange fascination as her skin, despite the cold, began to flush a deep red. Now I was close and paying attention, for the first time I also noticed her roots, a natural redhead, though why she had no desire to flaunt that, I could only imagine. Then I saw the two or three strands of grey above the ears, which might have explained the rest.

"Thanks, I'm such an idiot," she reinforced.

"I'll not disagree with you there," I stepped back as my arms fell to my sides.

She laughed, "back to form. That's the Clara I'm growing used to."

"Call me Erica. It's my real name." This time I held out my hand to her.

"Erica, aye? I had wondered. Can't say I've ever met a *Clara* before, even in York. It's a little too posh even for this place." She took my hand and this time her smile was wide, unguarded and real, even if one of her front two teeth did overlap the other. Like she said - Nobody's perfect. Well, apart from Tilly. "Though, thinking of you as *Erica* may take some getting used to after all this time," she beamed, still holding my hand. Yep, definitely a dyke.

Feeling a wave of self-consciousness, I pulled my hand away and placed them both in my pockets. "If it makes you feel worse, you're one of a privileged few to know it. Not even my publisher knows my real name."

"Worse, hey? It's interesting to know you can trust me after...well, everything." Any discomfort that might have followed her again bringing up our previous run-ins was cut short, albeit temporarily, as she continued. "I picked up a copy of *A Petal And A Thorn,*" there was a hint of embarrassment in her voice, "after our last meeting, how could I resist?" She playfully nudged me. "Like I said, I wish I had your talent. That final scene on the beach...I cried so hard." She continued rambling as I was reminded of Tilly and Elspeth reuniting on the sand and kissing before running away together and I kicked at a pebble that shot from the wall and rolled down the grass embankment. "But it's hard to work out who was the petal and who was the thorn. Both Tilly and Elspeth seemed like petals to me and were just so perfect for each other."

Something stabbed at my heart and I turned on her. "What the bloody hell do you mean by that?" I took both hands from my pockets and crossed them in front of my chest.

She leaned away. "Um, well, they are. They...they should have been together from the start but there were always things, fear, the unknown, society, selfish people keeping them apart. It was all just so cruel and unfair."

My blurry vision wandered over the wall and into some trees in the distance. "Selfish people? How do you mean selfish people?" I asked almost monotone.

She fiddled with the strap on her gym bag. "Well, you wrote the thing. It's just how I saw it, that's all. Really, Erica, there's no need to get all defensive. I'd have thought you'd be used to your critics by now and I've been nothing but complimentary about it." She knew I was expecting more of an answer and smiled as though that alone would act as a placatory gesture. "Let's see, now, um, well take Tilly's mother as one example. That bitch was far more interested in maintaining her status than in her daughter's happiness." She shrugged as my blurry vision found partial clarity on her reddened shoulders. "I guess those were the times, huh?"

"Yes, the times," I nodded, humouring her silly, yet somehow spot-on analysis whilst also feeling what could only be described as jealousy that another, probable lesbian, had even mentioned Tilly's name. Twice. How dare she? And not to mention the dredging up of Elspeth. *Perfect for each other*... Pfft.

There was silence as we passed through the York Museum Gardens with its various still standing Roman structures; a fort, parts of the original Roman walls and the Anglian Tower.

Although, in most part, she seemed to enjoy the silence as much as myself, I did detect the occasional nervous gesture. Her body had stiffened over the last minute, which might have been the cold and she scratched her arm for about the tenth time. "Listen," she finally broke the silence, "about my saying you had no conscience..."

I looked at her with a raised eyebrow. "Oh, that's totally true."

She again nudged me in the side. "No. After reading your book, I have to retract and apologise. I was clearly incorrect. You'd been wronged by the store and annoyed by my face, which is enough to make anybody see red, but it's obvious to me your conscience does not lie with insignificant matters of book signings, or cardboard cutouts of Kiera Knightly, but in more important things. Look, what I'm trying to say, Erica, is that you really *do* have a conscience and I'm truly sorry for what I said in the heat of the moment."

It was the second time she'd blundered through an apology but this time it didn't feel like a prerequisite to my own expected expression of regret for the events that happened in the bookshop, which she still wouldn't get. No, this apology was different and now she'd finished babbling I'd give her a different answer.

"Conscience?" I spotted the steps leading from the walls toward the minster and home. "Gemma, I could quite happily push my own mother into the Ouse."

I heard the gasp as her feet remained glued to the wall's cobbles and I shouted over my shoulder.

"And you're wrong. Elspeth's the thorn."

But thankfully, she was history.

14

REVELATION

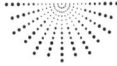

"*How* ow can we have a bloody wedding rehearsal without the bloody reverend present?" Rushworth clasped a handkerchief against his snout and the words came out somewhat muffled.

The constant hammering of nails into the beams from the labourers above enforced the need for Lady Wild to raise her voice. "Would you mind repeating that, sir?"

"Reverend Makepeace…where is the bloody man?" Shouted he, temporarily removing the kerchief, only for the raw odour of sewage to pervade his sinuses.

Her Ladyship fanned the air about her face most vigorously. "The reverend knows his business, sir, and requires neither instruction nor rehearsal." She looked away and bit her gums before hissing, "Matilda…the reverend? Any word?"

Tilly remained silent, played with her hair and continued staring blankly at the wall, its plaster stained green from leaf splattered rafter to stone cracked floor as the culprit lead gutter dangled precariously through the window, still dripping green sludge into the church.

Rushworth had overheard. "You mean, you don't know?"

"Ah, you heard that, I see, sir," conceded Lady Wild, taking a step closer to he. "It will all be fine, I'm rather sure of it." Again she bit her gums.

Tilly considered the Reverend Makepeace's service from this Sunday past and that he'd seemed entirely in good health at the time. Indeed, his sermon had been even more hearty and robust than any she could recall.

"Though you already know all this, I want to remind you that the Lord delivered his people out of Egypt, but later destroyed those who did not believe. And the angels who did not keep their positions of authority but abandoned their own home - these he has kept in darkness, bound with everlasting chains for judgment on the great Day. In a similar way, Sodom and Gomorrah and the surrounding towns gave themselves up to sexual immorality and perversion. They serve as an example of those who suffer the punishment of eternal fire." As rain had begun pattering against the slates above the congregations heads, he'd raised his hand, jabbing a finger t'ward the church roof and shouted the passages most animatedly and Tilly had shrunk hard back against the pew, feeling a most unladylike trickle of perspiration sliding down her back as he'd culminated the service with the final verse. "If a man lies with a man as one lies with a woman, both of them have done what is detestable. They must be put to death; their blood will be on their own heads."

Now, three days later, Rushworth awaited the cessation of the latest salvo of hammering from the rafters afore asking, "how bad is it, exactly?"

"Only as bad as a paralytic fit tends to be, *Doctor*. One might think you'd be fully aware of the severity of such an occurrence," said she with a face fit to cut kindling.

The doctor stepped forward. "The severity of a paralytic

fit differs from person to person. Again, I ask how bad is it exactly?"

"He can move neither the left side of his face nor body. Would you call that bad, *doctor*?" She wafted the stale air from her countenance. "He recognised me only whence I stood as close to he as I am now to you, sir, despite my having delivered him scones only a week afore the event." A light breeze, somewhat ironically relieving, blew in through the church's opened roof and Lady Wild inspired a welcome fresh breath of air.

"Could he understand you? Can the man see close enough to read a few passages perhaps?"

"He was a little slow, but then, he usually is. But his speech is slurred, on account of the left side of his face being a full inch lower down his head, doctor," recommended she, the fanning of air with her fan.

Rushworth held firm the cloth about his face, dismissing the lady's doubts with a flapping of t'other hand. "Fear not, ma'am, for my boys from Edinburgh shall ensure his well being, even if it means having to dress, toilet, feed, carry and force the words from his very mouth." He roamed his eyes upon Tilly's seated form, his loins positively aching in anticipation of the honeymoon. "For nothing shall prevent this ceremony from taking place; not gale, not the church roof being t'other side of the playing fields, not sludge rotting its very foundations and certainly not a stroke crippled reverend. Mark my words and fear not, Miss Wild, two days hence and we shall be wed."

Something peeped out from behind Tilly and then appeared the shrunken and sullen shape of Elspeth, clad in her usual filthy togs.

"Miss Dungworth," called out her friend's mother from across the battered church floor, "I see you finally grace us with your barely desired presence." She motioned for the working-class girl to come forth from behind Matilda. "Come, my dear, I'll not bite."

Elspeth stepped forward, crunching on broken slate fragments and flinching at the racket from above as she did.

"Now, you're late, Miss Dungworth. While you may keep your reasons, I trust you'll not be late on Friday?" She glared at her with steely eyes.

"I'm sorry, ma'am," gestured Elspeth at her uniform, "I've come straight from work and…"

"And you thought not to smarten up for the occasion of my daughter's wedding rehearsal."

Tilly stepped beside her friend. "Mother, she's here now, so why not leave her be?"

"Well, I hardly think things can get much worse. In fact, I do declare, an errant bridesmaid is the least of our problems right now," laughed Lady Wild, most uncharacteristically. "We've most likely exhausted all our bad luck, thank God," gestured she about the debris. "We only have the mayor and Arthur Pease due to attend, after all. He's the local MP, since you're most unlikely to know."

Elspeth kicked at the floor and shuffled on her feet, thinking best not to speak lest she incurs the madwoman's wrath.

That madwoman now studied her face and asked most insincerely, "who jilted you this time? No, never mind, I have no desire to know, but do make sharp and smarten up, your face if nothing else. Aren't you happy for your friend?"

"Of course, she is," interrupted Rushworth. "A little jealous, no doubt."

Elspeth straightened, "wh…what?"

He bounded toward Tilly, picked her up and spun her

around. "And in two days hence, I'll take you away from this place, forever, for our new life."

Lady Wild coughed, "Dr Rushworth, that is behaviour most inappropriate, sir. I'm sure you can keep your concupiscence to yourself until the honeymoon."

He placed her down and held up an apologetic hand. "I'm sorry, ma'am, I couldn't help myself," appraised he again, his fiancée's frame whilst biting his bottom lip, "ah yes, the honeymoon…"

"Honeymoon? Where's the honeymoon?" Asked Elspeth, a fleeting hand to her heart.

Lady Wild shook her head. "Why, it's at the Bagdale Hall Hotel, of course. Do they not tell you anything there? Three nights in Whitby afore three months on Loch Lomond."

"To get to know each other *properly,*" accented he the final word, acknowledging for the first time Elspeth's housekeeper's uniform by twiddling his moustache.

"Where the monster was sighted?" Enquired Elspeth, most alarmed.

"No silly, that's Loch Ness," corrected Tilly.

"But first the Bagdale Hall Hotel?" Squeaked Elspeth, turning three shades whiter.

"Huzzaaaah," yelped Rushworth, unknowingly pushing forth his loins whilst confirming Elspeth's worst nightmare.

"Oh, what has got into you now, Miss Dungworth?" Lady Wild awaited the burly menial atop the rafters to cease his latest infernal episode of hammering afore addressing Elspeth directly. "Let us pray you're not so down in the doldrums when you're lifting Matilda's train. It's your one job and you will not ruin the biggest day of her life just because Mr Daversham, or whoever, has jilted you. Do I make myself quite clear? Don't think I haven't been watching you closely, miss. Why, I do declare, but you have a face like an Easter

Island stone statue," turned she to Tilly, pasting on the smile as though the prior unpleasantness had not occurred, "and I'll want grandchildren, Matilda. I'm sure the doctor will show you the way of the world, the birds and the bees," flicked she with a smirk, an eye toward he.

"Oh, mother, whatever are you talking about?"

Her ladyship sniffed, "I do hope they can rid the place of this ungodly smell come Friday. And that dreadful MP, where's he to sit? Ah, yes that was it, Matilda, don't forget to have Grace pack your dresses afore Friday. You don't wish to be rushed come Monday."

"I hear you have a situation there?" Asked Rushworth of Elspeth.

"Um, where?"

He rolled his eyes with impatience and raised his voice. "At the bloody hotel. Where else? Were you not listening? That is the uniform of the hotel you wear, is it not? Yes, I thought so."

"Um…"

"How perfect, you can make extra certain the honeymoon suite is in splendid order for our arrival. And I'll require extra hot water, if you wouldn't mind, and a spare set of sheets."

Lady Wild, while Rushworth knew to nod in affirmation, commenced the discussion regarding which bible passages were to be read and by who, which hymns would be sung and who, in the event of a packed church, would have standing room only. It was agreed that in the event of a rainy day, which with their present luck should not be ruled out, the ceremony should take place regardless, even if the roof was not repaired in time, afore the impending reception that was to be held at the Whitby town hall, which had remained untouched by the gale of three nights ago. Aunt Agnes, who was only nine months into her period of mourning following the death of her late husband, would be last to enter the church and should be hidden amongst the lesser important guests somewhere at the back, so as not to cast negative aspersions over the couple. The usher should also, in the meantime, endeavour to ascertain whether any of the other guests were presently in a state of mourning so that they too could be shoved out of sight and did anybody have any doubts as to the ability of young Jimmy the butcher's boy, yet another working-class friend of Matilda's, to carry out the task without causing any unnecessary offence? Gifts of jet, courtesy of the Rushworth family, were to be distributed to the widows at the church entrance. These instructions were of the utmost consequence and Lady Wild would take it upon herself to make them extra clear to the usher on the morning of the ceremony.

During the discussion, Tilly and Elspeth sat quietly beside each other and whence Lady Wild was satisfied everybody knew their duties, the gathering was dismissed at which time the two girls travelled on foot to Elspeth's family lodgings, four rented rooms in a middle-terraced back to back house on Henrietta Street.

"Aye up, miss?" Asked Mr Dungworth of Tilly. "Make yersen at 'ome. Wiv got tripe an' boiled potato stew in't pan if yur 'ungry lass?" He shouted through to the kitchen, "yurl bring in't extra pot fur'lass, won't yur love."

Tilly pulled out a chair beside Elspeth at the table that constituted almost the entirety of the room and perched herself upon it. "Oh, that won't be necessary, Mr Dungworth, I'll eat upon my return home," said she, assuming a mill worker's earnings would not allow much throughout the week for the luxury of meat and what little there was ought better be spared for Elspeth's five younger sisters, who even now were each grinning back with twinkling eyes.

"Nonsense, love, 'ave yur seen yursen? Yur look like yur need a good meal down yur." Raised he his voice t'ward t'other room, "and bring out t' mutton, love. Can't 'ave 'er starvin' afore t' wedding, can wi?"

Elspeth fiddled with her platter and considered whether she could steal Tilly into the bedroom afore the meal's commencement, where she hoped to discuss matters most pressing. She silently cursed Rushworth a thousand times and once more for insisting upon escorting them both the entire way to Henrietta Street, leaving her but no opportunity for the discussion of said matters. She pinched her lips together and quietly cursed the presence of her father, Polly, Maggie, Alma, Edith and Beatrice, the latter five of whom still gazed admiringly at their beautiful guest clad in a dress most elegant. Elspeth cuffed the youngest, Beatrice, on the wrist for leering too close.

"Who is it what makes yur dresses?" Asked the seven-year-old.

Tilly leaned closer and pressed her nose against the child's. "I make them myself, dear."

Mr Dungworth, his back hunched from the weight of a million sacks of flour, shuffled across to the window and bashed it open as far as the rusty hinges and wooden frame, expanded by the summer deluges and heat, would allow. The smell of unventilated stale air and boiling stomach lining of cow wafting in from the kitchen gradually mixed with that of fish seeping in from outside.

"Are yur a real princess?" Asked Beatrice, leaning ever closer to her idol.

Tilly looked out the window at what she always loved about Elspeth's house, the view of fishing boats in the North Sea. "Oh, no, not a real one, my lovely."

Mr Dungworth took his seat at the head. "Aye, well, it'll

be a shame t' lose yur. Yuv bin a good friend t' mi daughter all these years past. She'll be a sore 'ead wi'out yur, sure enough."

For Tilly and Elspeth, there was something in hearing it from Mr Dungworth, so final, so definitive and so very real.

Mrs Dungworth served the tripe and boiled potato stew, with extra cuts of mutton. Two freshly baked bread loaves, the spoils of working in the industry, adorned the table centre while glasses of locally brewed beer or milk sat by each plate. Grace was said by Polly and then her father gave permission to devour the bounty.

Mr Dungworth spoke bitterly of Sir Daversham, who was again threatening to move his operation to Grimsby, ninety miles south where, he was sure, there was a large contingent of Irish who'd be willing to work for half the wage. Should he lose his situation, he doubted the likelihood of finding a new one with the local shipbuilders on account of his scoliosis, but he'd heard the Rushworth family were indeed taking on local people down at the jet mine, where, in the worst possible scenario, he might secure a situation driving carts.

It was conversation most familiar, as Tilly could tell from the general countenance around the table and something she'd be sorry to leave behind upon her relocating to the Scotch capital. Dinner was never quite so open and friendly at the Wild household, where she ate alone with her mother and a gaggle of servants who usually stood silently in waiting.

"Will yur teach me how t' make dresses? I'd like t' look like a princess too," twinkled Beatrice at Tilly, sans two front teeth.

Elspeth, not feeling hungry, forced her meal down, if only to accelerate the process but then Mr Dungworth, despite the lack of suitable furnishings, insisted on a game of *eye spy with my little eye.*

"It'll still be light out," said he, referring to it being the month of June and the fact that Tilly would still be able to walk home unaccompanied afterwards.

And whence every available utensil had been used and some had resorted to spying items outside the house, Elspeth insisted on taking Tilly upstairs for some 'ladies privacy,' and any sister who dared interrupt would be subject to a month's silent treatment.

Upon entering the bedroom and closing the door behind, Elspeth was most disconcerted to discover that, during the short walk upwards, Beatrice had somehow managed to sneak ahead and that even now, the form of her lump beneath the blanket of the bed she shared with Edith was most perceptible. Elspeth pulled back the sheet, revealing the mischievous younger sibling, who proceeded to attempt to hide her form in the crack beside the wall.

"Out!" Elspeth tapped her foot upon the floor, her patience sapping with every further interruption. T'was the reason they used the beach as their secret meeting place, alas what with the fiend Rushworth and his insistences on smothering his bride-to-be during her few remaining hours as an unwed lady, it could not have been so today. It was like the whole world had contrived to conspire against them this day, but Elspeth would have no more. "Out," said she once again.

The child ran to Tilly and threw her arms around her legs, burying her head against Tilly's belly. "I will miss yur princess."

"Oh, I…" comforted Tilly, her hands on the child's shoulders, "it's not goodbye forever." Tilly's sinuses filled with fluid as a glimmering sheen became her sight. But what could she do? Should scandal ensue then this child would be sans a roof above her head.

Elspeth allowed them their moment afore prodding Beatrice beyond the door and applying the lock. "Finally," turned she to her love as the tears flowed on cue. "I've been fit to burst these few hours past."

Tilly closed the gap but kept her distance. "Elly, I know what you're thinking. I saw it in your eyes then as I still see it now."

"You know me so well," heaved Elspeth as the bleak green painted walls seemed to enclose upon them, the three beds spun around her head and the design carved into the architrave where ceiling met wall created visual patterns in her mind.

"Oh, but you must be there for me. I need you. I can't go through with this without you." Tilly clenched her shaking hands into little fists. "I don't know what I'm doing, I don't know what will happen, I don't know this man."

Elspeth, in a world of haze teetered toward the window, steadied herself on the ledge and stared out at the spinning street below, at the men and children peddling their wares, Kenny the shoeshine as he spat upon an old man's boot afore rubbing over it with a cloth, Dick carrying a basket of coal for his mother's stove, horses dropping refuse over the cobbles as children ran to scoop it up in their wake, at the feral dogs begging for scraps.

Henrietta Street. Whitby. Home.

The only place Elspeth knew. But it would be forever changed without that one constant. Without that one person. Without that one companion who, against all the odds had remained her friend ever since that one day when, aged six, they discovered each other on the beach collecting seashells.

Now that friend was leaving, her love was being taken

away like some highly sought after possession of extreme value. And nothing would ever be the same again. How could Elspeth survive without her Tilly, the one person she loved more than life itself. It would be the finish of her because without Tilly there was nothing to help her breathe, nothing to give her purpose in life.

Her hands clenched around the wood chipped ledge as the outside disappeared into a blur and all that mattered were the next few minutes alone with her love, the moment she never dared bring about because of fear for the consequences of doing so. But now she no longer had a choice because, after this moment, she would never see Tilly again. It was time.

"I've always loved you," quivered her voice. "I've loved you unlike any other person in this life and I don't know if that's normal or if I'm bound for the madhouse for such impure thoughts, but I can't take it any longer. All I can think about is being with you and I know there's something wrong with me, but I don't care anymore because seeing you with someone else, to be taken away, will be the death of me. And sometimes I get the feeling you feel the exact same way and I can't believe I'm even saying all these things but it's either now or I must forever hold my peace and I know I'm going straight to hell, but I don't care…so there."

A small pool of transparent fluid had collected on the sill, her entire body shook, her blood flowed both hot and cold, the hairs stood up on her arms and sweat ran from every pore.

She dared not look back, to the face of disgust her love must surely hold.

And then Elspeth felt the hands upon her shoulders and she shivered as the hands drifted down to her waist and then Tilly was holding her close, the sides of their faces pressed together so tight.

Tilly, whose flesh was also cold, was also shaking and

crying and in some state of semi-conscious befuddlement. "Elly, my love. But I've always felt the same, ever since we swapped shells on the sand that fateful day." Her grip tightened about her love. "You're so brave for finally ending our misery," her wet cheek slid against Elspeth's.

Elspeth turned around in Tilly's arms and they faced each other, only their staggered breathing between them. Through dresses, they clutched the other's flesh, inhaled the air they shared, through their eyes saw into the other's soul, squeezed the other's arms hypersensitive with the increased flow of blood, adrenaline and some other chemical that came about but once in a lifetime. They stepped into each other and pulled, tugged, squeezed with their hands, anything to get closer; the smell, the touch. Once, for one fraction of a second, for one incredible moment sent from providence itself, their lips even brushed together but still, take it further they could not, because neither was quite sure how.

Then Elspeth recalled what Master Daversham had once tried do to her. Why she should come to think of that brute at a time like this she could not say but twas the night of the Annual Whitby Ball he'd slobbered his lips over her neck afore attempting the same with her lips. Mercifully, Tilly had arrived, an angel sent to save her innocence and Elspeth had wanted then, but had been too afraid, to try something similar with her saviour.

Elspeth, with her hands in Tilly's hair, gently pulled her closer. She saw the doubt in Tilly's eyes, but the trust and desire also. Tilly's lips parted, her eyes closed, she inhaled the air between them, the air that contained some unknown magical force and then their lips touched and time stopped, nothing else in the world existing but each other. It was so gentle. Elspeth, with her closed mouth pressing tenderly against Tilly's, Tilly who returned in kind gently hummed as they tasted the tears of each other.

They parted only when the need for air grew too overwhelming, as their blood flowed closer to the skin's surface, creating a tingling sensation, the same natural forces drawing blood away from their heads making them dizzy, but it was all so wonderful. It was like a bubble had enclosed the two, cutting off everything on the outside, entrapping them both on the in, that one moment in a person's life that is remembered unlike all others for it is engraved upon their souls.

Tilly sobbed into Elspeth's ear. "Oh, but why could you not have said something afore now? I'm due to wed two days hence."

A dark cloud enshrouded Elspeth's vision. "Please don't marry him. You can't, not after this, not after everything."

"But what else would you have me do? My whole life has been planned. Not that I care much for myself…my mother would disown me for one and I would be destitute should I refuse to marry the doctor but for you…" Tilly's hands slid away from her love, "it would be all the worse for you, your father, your sisters…the scandal, oh, I could never allow that."

"Oh, my dear father," shrieked Elspeth.

"He would be jinxed about the town and whence Sir Daversham moves the mill to Grimsby, he would struggle to secure a new situation in Whitby." His crooked back and inability to read and write would further restrict his prospects. An awful thought occurred to Tilly. "Your sisters, sweet Beatrice, what would become of them? Oh, they would lead a life of…of…pauperdom. Oh, how it doesn't bear thinking about," said she, releasing her grasp entirely and stepping away from temptation.

"You see," whimpered Elspeth, turning back to the window, "this is precisely why I love you so. You only ever put others afore your own happiness. But I dare say this is different because it will only inevitably lead to misery for us both," shrieked Elspeth, a sudden intake of high-pitched air into her lungs. "Oh, but you would be alone with him this Friday night." She cringed, her face a contortion of unbearable agony. "And all while I wait to attend to your husband's every whim, whatever they may be," said she, almost choking the words. "Why can't God just strike me down?"

"Don't talk like that," demanded Tilly, searching her mind for answers. "If only there was some other way, but I fear we're trapped and destined to live as society deems fit." Her arms hung limp by their sides. "Perhaps it is *we* who are in the wrong, my love?"

From the window, Elspeth whipped back on Tilly and shot her a glare of steel. "Does it feel wrong to you?"

Tilly looked down upon the floor afore whispering, "no, Elly, no it does not. But it doesn't change anything. I am still to be wed two days hence."

Elspeth shrunk back against the wall. "Oh, Tilly."

"That look again. You must. Please be there for me. I haven't the strength to go through with it without you close by."

"I'm sorry," Elspeth grabbed from the shelf a shell upon a piece of string afore handing it back to Tilly, "but I cannot."

"Then this is truly it, my love."

15

ENCOUNTER

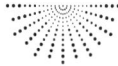

I slept until halfway through the afternoon, my body still feeling the after effects of an exhausting night of rolling, thrashing, slapping - somewhat pleasingly painful, biting, tugging, scratching, stabbing to a small degree, thrusting and whipping, involving all manner of tools, implements, accessories and apparatus.

My God, how I ached as I staggered down Stonegate with its varied tourist shops selling amongst other things; medieval weaponry, suits of armour and relics of centuries past. It was a beautiful day emphasised by the sun, uncharacteristically present for this time of year and tourists and locals alike smiled at me, of all people, as I made my way to nowhere in particular. It didn't matter because I was happy, for the first time in, well, ever.

Peering into the window of the antique centre, I browsed for something to purchase for Tilly, a small gesture to demonstrate how much she'd changed my entire outlook and I'd probably also buy some gifts for those other few people I still had anything to do with.

"Erica, good afternoon to you." It was the reflection of David Maher in the window that smiled back at me.

"And a very good afternoon to you too sir. And how, may I ask, fares your production of Dick Whittington?" I did not recognise either the tone of my voice or the actual words emitting from my mouth.

Maher took a step back and hesitated, seemingly unsure of me. "Dick Whittington? Oh, um, we fare well, thank you. Are you feeling quite alr…"

"David," I began, tapping him on the arm, "how goes everything with your new partner? We really should have a get together sometime and talk shop, yes?"

He squinted and I found annoyance in neither his fake tan, faked accent, fake mannerisms or waxed eyebrows. "Um, yes, yes, of course, we shall, yes. Well, when?"

"Whenever you want, David. Evenings aren't so great unless it's early on, but name the day and we'll do Betty's; breakfast, brunch or lunch." I gestured to the shop window. "I was searching for a gift. So I will leave you to your day, but it was nice seeing you again."

He nodded like a puppy. "It, um, was, Erica. And may I just say, you're looking exceptionally well."

"David, you may say it." It's amazing what getting laid can do for a girl.

He nodded again, scratched his chin of what little stubble he possessed and gave me rather an uncomfortable hug before continuing to stump down Stonegate, with an anxious glance or two over his shoulder.

After purchasing three or four trinkets, I continued to wander around town, and what would you know, after a few minutes, who else did I bump into but Glen Atkinson, AKA Hector Shackleton, the same man I once took to court over an issue of privacy. We were outside the Viking Centre and he swerved around a large group of tourists in a failed effort to avoid my person.

"Glen? Glen?" I blocked his path and he came to a reluctant stop. "Only the second time without your creepy child snatcher costume, hey?" I said with a playful tone, jabbing him in the ribs with an elbow.

He didn't appreciate my jibe. "This is me, Clara. This is how I look." He bent his neck around to look beyond me. "Now if you wouldn't mind, but I have things I need to do."

"Hold up, hold up," I shuffled and scratched the back of my neck. "If you'd like you can continue to run your little tour thing in your old spot, I won't mind." It'd make little difference anyway considering some grave stealing company had occupied the space the minute he was gone. Any conflict between the two might even prove mildly amusing.

His eyes narrowed. "Are you sure?"

I flapped a feeble hand. "Sure, why not."

"Well that's very kind of you, I'll have a think about it."

I jingled the bag from the antique shop and held it out toward him. "Well come on then, take your pick."

He glared at me uncertainly. "What is this?"

"It's one of those lucky dip things. Go on, have a go, it'll be fun." I jingled the bag again and rested its bottom on my opened hand.

He hesitated but then finally delved inside and I felt him feeling and moving the items about as he decided which item to take.

I counted to three then grabbed his hand while making a terrifying roaring noise.

He jumped back, yanking his arm with him, holding his hand like it had been bitten by a dog. The look on his face was too priceless. "You…you're quite certifiably insane."

I tutted and shook my head. "Oh, come on. You always did like a good scare. Now you know how it feels."

You know, I actually got a smile from the guy. "Yes," he conceded, which was a lot from him and he opened his hand to examine the prize, frowning. "It's a toy soldier."

"A genuine redcoat carved after the Crimean War." He glared at me so I answered him further. "It's Victorian."

"Ah," he nodded, "now it makes sense." He turned it over in his hand, unsure whether to be thankful or to hand it back.

"You can keep it. Or give it to your son?" I asked.

"I do have a son, yes."

"Well, there you go then. And you're correct."

"Excuse me?"

"I *am* quite certifiably insane."

I brushed past him and continued in the direction of The Shambles, weaving through the crowds of tourists and emerging in the narrow cobbled alleys, ginnels and passages of ancient York.

What else would I do on such a fine day? Coffee, more shopping, a tourist attraction, an alcoholic beverage or three? It was when I emerged in Coffee Yard and began looking through the window of the Barley Hall when I pondered the idea of combining a tourist attraction with alcohol. I'd often passed through the yard and glanced inside but never before had I been minded to consider actually donning medieval robes to drink real olde English ale, feast on a spit-roasted hog whilst watching a court jester prance about for my amusement - A real medieval-themed banquet.

Footsteps scuffed at the ground behind and then the silhouette of a girl emerged in the glass to my front. "I do declare, but the Barley Hall appears to be closed."

The voice. Too close, too familiar, too grating on my soul. I whipped around, the lump already building in my throat.

"You!"

I unknowingly clenched my hands into fists, she even looked down at them, but wasn't subdued or daunted in the slightest.

"Hello, Erica." If she'd looked like shit during our last meeting, now she was positively preparing to meet the grim reaper, and not one of those fake demons from the dungeons you occasionally saw scaring the kids around here. "Erica, we have to talk," the emaciated girl absolutely said.

I stepped away and my back pressed against the plate glass window while my heart pumped like a fiddler's elbow and I was, for a few seconds, unable to respond. Finally, I dug deep and found some semblance of my usual threatening mannerisms, the ones that for many years I'd used with success to repel the entire town.

"You, um, Elspeth, yes, indeed we *do* have to talk." I thrust my hands into my pockets so she wouldn't see how they trembled. And to think that up until now it'd been such a wonderful day. "Now, you just listen to me, missy, I've had just about enough of all these impromptu visits. You know full well I'm a very busy woman and I can't be having my schedule interrupted for…no, no, don't interrupt…I've had just about enough of…"

"…no, you must let me speak, Erica. Firstly, I'm well aware of…"

"…how dare you…"

"…if you please, would you just…"

I stepped forward and, mercifully, she stepped back, "…no, no, no," I shouted, "do not ever interrupt me, you little ingrate. If it wasn't for me, you wouldn't even exist, so why don't you just shut your trap." I held up a threatening finger, less than an inch from her cracked and almost blue lower lip.

She buttoned it though so obviously, despite everything, I

still scared the shit out of her. But now I had to quickly scan my rattled brain for something to say.

How should I handle this one? Her arriving out of nowhere had been so unexpected. The jezebel, by her mere appearance, had wrought a dark cloud over my day, week, month, year. And if I didn't deal with her, and quick, the situation could only deteriorate.

But what to do?

I could run her out of town. Again. But I'd already done that twice and yet here she was, once more, in my face, looking like she'd spent the past month chomping dirt whilst being eaten by the worms with her friends, the six hundred thousand beneath the city.

A part of me even thought to reintroduce her to Tilly, to see how the latter found her attractive now and be done with it. But no, I knew Tilly, and if any girl could get past all that, then it was her. I'd made her that way, dammit. Tilly would likely take her in, nurse the jezebel back to health and what then?

Bloody hell, but she was in a bad way. Pallid, gaunt and with the faintest smell of rot, like she was in the early stages of decomposing through lack of nutrition. The girl needed to eat, she needed a bath, she needed sleep and she needed some new bloody clothes. Her rags from the hotel were faded, torn and in places possessed large red stains as though she'd been self-harming but what creeped me out most were the eyes. It was like a switch had flicked inside her head and the eyes always gave it away. The red, grey bags beneath only added to the menace.

I'd taken this girl's life. I'd taken her everything. I'd taken her Tilly. Now she was at death's door and had come for me. And there's nothing more dangerous than a wounded animal backed into a corner, that is, apart from a spurned, jealous lesbian come for vengeance.

And now she was here, stood not three paces away and looking into my eyes like she never had before.

But after everything, I wasn't about to give up without a fight. Maybe my fears were exaggerated and I was imagining them. Perhaps I was envisioning things based on how I might act if I were her, and let's face it, if she were I, I'd be going unhinged on Miss Erica Gough. But considering everything, I still knew Elspeth's character and wasn't convinced she had it in her to stand up to someone like me, no matter how bad her present situation. After all, she'd allowed Tilly's mother to treat her like dirt her entire life.

I'd been silent for a while, after telling her to *shut it*, and now she looked at me in expectation. And despite her neglected appearance, there was something else there I'd never seen in her before. It was all in the eyes. But what was it? Defiance, scorn, composure?

No. This was different. This time she would not sit by and do nothing as I bundled her into a taxi and sent her fifty miles in the direction of the coast. This time she'd require a different approach.

I plastered on a rare smile, noting how doing so hurt my cheeks, and cautiously I threaded my arm inside her elbow and pulled her toward the ginnel that led to The Shambles. "This way my dear."

It was a relief she put up no resistance and her core body temperature was probably even lower than the time she'd spent hours sat outside in the frost. It was like those homeless people you see who, despite it being warm on a particular day, would still enshroud themselves in blankets as they hunch with their dogs inside a department store loading bay. They're still numb from the previous night, their bodies unable to generate heat due to a lack of nutrition and being out in the cold too long. But for all I knew, Elspeth was still living in Whitby, on Henrietta Street with her parents, or not.

"Where are we going?" She demanded with only the slightest slurring of speech, like a drunkard after downing his second.

"Um, why, we're going for a walk around York, of course, and should we happen to find a suitor," fat chance, "who should tickle your pickle or blow your skirt up then who would I be to stand in the way of true love, aye?"

She gave me a sideward scowl and I realised I should have left it at *tickle your pickle.*

"You're very kind, Erica, but I don't think I'm quite ready to…"

"…well don't be too hasty. You haven't even seen any of the fine specimens York has to offer yet." I exhaled, pulled her tighter in toward me and braved the rot. "I must say, you're being quite rude to my kinsmen, passing them up without so much as a glance. I'm doing my best here, you know."

She remained silent as we entered Parliament Street, the city's main shopping thoroughfare, which bustled with mid-afternoon shoppers, tourists and even the occasional smartly dressed and beautiful lady. Though considering I was attempting to find a match for Elspeth, and in her present state too, I had to be realistic. I thought about taking her down to Fibbers, to await the student dregs still leaving from last night, but in no way did I wish to be seen around that dive.

"How about her?" I pointed to a girl, mid-twenties, half her head shaved, bullring in the nose.

No response was forthcoming.

"Her?" This one was quite short and like Elspeth wore

torn clothes, unlike Elspeth the tears were intentional. Other than that, she possessed an empty menacing look in the eye, quite off-putting. "Well?"

"I don't think so," she released herself from my arm and stood tapping her foot.

I threw my arms up in exasperation, "look, I'm trying to help you here."

A man with a dog walked by and without knowing, my gaze followed after it. I must have also raised an eyebrow and was about to open my mouth when Elspeth saw me and turned away in disgust.

"Ok, maybe that's taking it a bit too far."

"You never did think much of me, did you." Could she not take a joke?

"On the contrary, you've made me stinking rich."

"And this is how you repay me?" She stepped away and half turned as though she was about to toddle off on her own, and I panicked at that.

I couldn't risk having Elspeth let loose in the city. It would be midnight in seven hours and I'd gladly spend the intervening time freezing in the cold of York if it meant preventing the two of them from having a chance meeting. Not that there'd be any *chance* about it. Elspeth, I knew, was set and fully intent on seeing Tilly and, since she'd succeeded in finding me five times now, as it turned out, she was bloody good at it - The stalking little bitch.

I opened out my arms, as though encompassing the hundreds of people who surround us and as I was beginning to lose hope, I asked in desperation. "Is there nobody you're interested in?" I don't know what I'd been trying to achieve, but then I was standing to lose a lot and I'd do anything to keep her. "No? Not interested? Well, all in your own time, I suppose." My voice changed tone as I made the mistake of getting too emotional. "Now listen here, it'll be hard getting over her but it really is best for all that you do. So see to it, missy."

No response from her.

"Shit!" Again, I threw up my hands and shook my head. "I tried dammit. I really did bloody try."

I was out of ideas. After everything, she was still here and nothing was resolved. I checked my watch and gritted my teeth whilst she stood there like a dumpling. Then, grabbing a clump of hair at the back of my head, I came up with the best solution to everything. In fact, I don't know why I hadn't thought of it before.

"Right, my dear, we're going for some alcohol."

16

BETTY'S

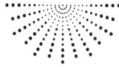

I dragged her by the arm to the only cafe a visitor to Yorkshire should see and I pointed out Betty's with its waiting crowd that gathered outside. "Look at that. Have you ever seen a cafe with a queue that stretches around the block?"

"No, I haven't." Her cold stiffened legs were laboured by my new found enthusiasm.

"It's always like this here." I led the way and headed straight for the front door, ignoring the queue, the back of which I couldn't even see, its irate tourists spitting insults at us in half a dozen languages. "Yeah, shut up. As if you wouldn't do the same in my position."

The manager smiled, "Miss Buckingham, good afternoon to you, let me find you a table."

I winked at Elspeth as we followed him toward an intimate table near the piano, its pianist playing some unfamiliar classical piece, which unsurprisingly was also lost on Elspeth.

It never mattered what time of the day it might be, Betty's was always crammed to full capacity and the atmosphere was typical of a beautiful Victorian themed cafe where everyone was happy, eating simple yet exquisite food while cosying up with loved ones. The chatter of a hundred conversations combined to create a din which would necessitate the raising of my voice to be heard. The tables were made of marble yet in the design, somehow they had managed not to overstep the boundaries into pretentiousness. The clientele were primarily tourists, of course, but as always there were patrons of all kinds; young families, elderly couples and everyone between.

"It's nice and warm in here," Elspeth peeped up, taking the seat with her back to the wall.

I removed my jacket and placed it behind the chair, receiving a menu from the waiter and taking my seat. The waiter said he'd return in a few minutes and, already knowing what I wanted, I gave the menu to Elspeth.

"Have you any idea what you'd like to eat?" I asked her, most motherly after about three minutes had past.

She made little tutting sounds as she scanned the writing, sitting quite prim and proper despite her present constitution. "Hmm," she squeaked as my patience dwindled, "I think… hmm…I will have the…hmm…I think I will have salad."

I snatched the menu back. "Are you fucking serious?" I clipped the menu with the back of my hand. "You're at Betty's and you want salad?" I scrutinised her emaciated form and gave her a scowl. "You don't want the bacon and raclette rösti? Or the Swiss Alpine macaroni? Or how about the haddock, salmon and prawn gratin? You want none of those things, just the fucking salad?" I threw down the menu in exasperated disgust, genuinely offended once it sank in.

She made a sweet coughing sound, "yes, salad will be quite sufficient, thank you."

"You do realise I'm paying, yes? Now's your chance to

finally do me some damage." I thumped the table. "Hurt me, damn you girl. I know you want to."

She giggled and my resolve melted. "Thank you, Erica."

I shook my head and waved the waiter back. "Yes, it'll be the Betty's Yorkshire sausages and the salad." I made a display of rolling my eyes for the waiter's benefit.

"Madam, would that be the side salad?"

"No, that would be the salad salad." He was about to interject but I cut him off by asking Elspeth, "and what would you like to drink, dear?" I glanced up at the waiter and winked, "this should be good."

She coughed, "I'll have some ale, please."

I shook my head and held a hand in front of her face as though doing so would shield the waiter from her idiotic words. "A bottle of pink champagne, please."

"Yes, madam."

The waiter left and I held an opened hand by my mouth like I was telling her confidentially, "trust me, there are some things in life you just have to try. Besides, your ale is watered down and most probably tastes like cat urine. Your opinions on alcohol are thus declared null and void."

She smiled and even held my eye for a brief moment before looking back down to fiddle with her empty glass - Back to her intimidated type, thankfully, so I guessed her little display at the Barley Hall was all for show. But it was incredible what a bit of heat and a smile could do for a girl because she already looked better, marginally, than when she'd cornered me in the empty courtyard. It was a relief to feel in control of the situation again, even if, right now, I still had no plan of action. Hopefully, something would come to me, it usually did.

"I feel the need to apologise for having such a dishevelled appearance at the dinner table," she squeaked, patting down her raggedy accoutrements fit for a purveyor of masochistic voyeurism and folding her hands in her lap. "I was raised to dress my best for dinner and to present a pleasant aspect and countenance. We, being myself and my sisters, may not have had much, but we were brought up correctly. I regret that this evening I've let down both myself and my mother and father."

Even *my* heart broke after that, almost. "Nonsense, you weren't to know your arch enemy would bring you out for dinner." Thinking about it, it did sound kind of weird.

"I don't think of you as my arch enemy, Erica."

I waited for her to expand on that but she didn't.

The champagne arrived and she watched with fascination as I popped the cork and I carefully filled both glasses whilst trying to think up a suitable toast. "To the Victorians," I raised mine, "without whom, none of us would even be here."

"To the Victorians," she agreed, clinking my glass and taking a small sip. Her eyes shot to life in a display I'd not ever seen from the girl, her usual drab brown eyes showcasing something that intrigued me. She took another, larger sip and discharged air from her nose. "Ooh, excuse me."

I smiled at the sight of her relaxing around me. "What do you think of the pink champagne?"

"It's most delicious."

We sat in silence for a while, which wasn't as uncomfortable as I might have thought. Luckily, the pianist was good and it gave us both an excuse not to be overly awkward with each other.

Considering everything I'd done to her and what she *would* do to me if only she could, we were hardly likely to ever hit it off. She studied the surroundings while taking sips of pink nectar, perhaps finding comfort in the familiarity of

Betty's Victorian modelling. But in truth, I couldn't very well read the girl like I'd learned to do quite easily with Tilly. I couldn't at all relate to Elspeth and at times wondered if she was planning on stabbing me with the fork that lay dangerously close to her twitchy hand. It was funny in a way, but Elspeth was likely to live long enough to see Betty's established in 1919, just as long as she didn't die of cholera in the meantime.

And that thought again made me think of both Tilly and Elspeth - What happened to them afterwards? Did they get cholera, end up in a Victorian workhouse or worse? Or did they, against all the odds, actually live long and happy lives during a time when society would have been against them every step of the way? As I had with Tilly, I considered asking Elspeth that same question which had always plagued me, but then thought better of it. I needed Elspeth to forget Tilly and so I wouldn't bring her up.

The food arrived and I rubbed my hands together. "Thank you, sir." I picked up the knife and fork, prepared to plunge into my bounty then became aware of the numpty grimacing at me from across the table. "Something the matter?"

She tilted her head. "Aren't we going to say grace?"

"Oh, for God's sake." I slammed down the cutlery and decided to humour her. "Go on then."

She emitted a quiet coughing noise from her chest, closed her eyes and held her hands together while muttering the words under her breath. I couldn't hear what the heck she was saying, but if I pretended I could, then surely that would count, right? Finally, she unclasped her hands and looked at me from across the table.

"Ready? May we eat now?"

"We may eat," she smiled, having given me permission.

I cut off a large chunk of outdoor reared and well-fed

pork and crammed it down my mouth along with a segment of grated potato, rösti style. An incomprehensible humming sound emitted from my throat as I sliced off another piece, "um, good."

Elspeth, meanwhile, was busy picking at the leaves on her plate, placing tiny bits in her mouth and chewing for ages. I dashed my plate with salt, she meanwhile sprinkled a small quantity into a pile on her plate's edge before proceeding to dip small cuts of tomato into it. I mentioned something about how great the local pig farmers were, while she spoke mostly about how tasty the champagne was, but only between mouthfuls. Oh, she'd make the perfect dinner guest, all right, if politeness over excitement was something you were after.

She took a cut of bread from the basket and scanned the tabletop. "Erica, do we have any dripping?"

I almost snorted rösti through my nose. "Here, have some of this." I pushed the butter toward her and she delicately scraped away at it with her knife before layering on a thin quantity.

She nibbled at the bread and emptied her glass and I called over the waiter to order another bottle, giving her a generous refill when it arrived.

I studied the waif, almost saddening to the eye as she sat like a frightened child, too scared to speak up lest she say the wrong thing, hunched shoulders despite her attempt at sitting straight, nibbling leaves that, considering her present state, would offer precious little nutrition. She took another sip and as she returned her glass to the table, my hand involuntarily slid toward hers before I consciously pulled it away.

"Elspeth," my voice almost cracked as she looked up, "here." I dumped a sausage on her plate, I had another remaining anyway, and she gave me an uncertain smile. "Trust me, you need it more than I do." I couldn't help but feel maternal toward her and I wondered how close she'd be to an eleven year-old-daughter I'd never be able to have.

"Thank you." She cut into the sausage and placed a small amount in her mouth along with some shredded lettuce.

"You're an exceptionally slow eater, you know that?"

She finished chewing, swallowed and spoke with a straight face, "taking one's time with eating gives one better health, greater wealth, longer life and more happiness. These are what we may obtain by eating slowly in a pleasant frame of mind, ensuring that we thoroughly masticate our food."

There was no way I could possibly respond to that bit of lunatic wisdom so instead, I silently acknowledged that she needed every bit of health, wealth, life and happiness she could get, so I'd let her have that one without challenge.

The couple at the next table, and not for the first time, frowned overtly in my direction, ensuring I was under no illusions as to their displeasure. That was when I noticed that at some point during the last ten minutes, they'd slid their table away from ours. In response, I repositioned my chair so they'd have to stare at my back, shielding Elspeth from their judgemental eyes in the process. Yeah, she was filthy but she was still a human being, dammit.

Incensed by the morons behind and wishing to lighten things up, I decided to have some fun. "Elspeth," I began, "I'm curious, what's your opinion on the third reform act?" I waited as she chewed and when she gave no response, asked another question. "How about the Schleswig-Holstein question? Do you have any thoughts about that?" No response. "No? Then tell me please, how do you feel about the rapid urban expansion taking place in towns across the country?"

She swallowed and took a very slow, deliberate sip of champagne before looking me in the eye and grinning.

Obviously, she was feeling the effects of the alcohol. "I refuse to discuss deep and abstruse principles at the dinner table, for doing so will impair my digestion."

For too long, all I could do was stare while wondering if I'd heard correctly. She, however, remained upright, never once altering her expression. It was too much, and I threw myself back into the chair, its front feet leaving the ground by several inches and the warmth spread through my body as I struggled to breathe through the hysterics. I wiped at a tear and had to stand so I could throw my arms around her, giving the girl a well deserved kiss on the cheek and then I required several minutes to compose myself, "our ancestors, everybody," I shouted with outstretched arms. "It's a wonder how your generation conquered the entire bloody world." Clearly, I was now feeling the alcoholic effects myself.

She giggled and took the liberty of refilling both our glasses.

"Mind you," I reflected, "it's not as though the common folk saw any of the spoils."

She tried to cover up the frayed material on her cuff by rolling up the sleeve, only to reveal some dried crusted crap on the underside. "Do you mind if I ask you something?"

That sounded ominous and I hesitated. "That depends. What?" Be careful now, girl.

She looked at me straight on. "Why have you given up? Or rather, why did you give up?"

My mouth parted slightly. She couldn't be referring to my suicide attempt. "How did you know about…"

"…It's the way you treat people, Erica, you have no care for anyone. You've just completely given up on people."

"Ah," I nodded and felt the relief wash through me, "now I get you. A number of reasons really. Disappointment, unhappiness, loneliness. Waking up and anticipating another day of the same, with no feeling, nothing." I gulped down some pink fluid. "Oh, I had high hopes as an idealistic teenager, sure, but they were all ground down by the day, by the person, and by every little disappointment. If you understand nothing else, then understand this; people are disappointing. And that's why I gave up."

She accidentally belched and covered her mouth. "Oh fiddlesticks, you have too high expectations of people. If you lived in Whitby in 1883 your expectations would be more natural." She hiccupped and didn't apologise and neither was she embarrassed. This girl was drunk and getting gobby. "If you saw the filth, the coal dust, the low levels of sanitation, people's teeth," she unfurled her sleeve, "the tears in people's clothing, the stink of times pre-deodorant, the stacking of coffins in the streets every time there's an outbreak of one thing or another, if you saw these things, then maybe you'd have more realistic expectations of people not being absolutely perfect." She sank her champagne and slammed down the glass, startling me. "Here and now, you all smell so fresh, mostly, and you *all* try to be so perfect with your expensive clothes and bags on credit and perfumes and…and careers, at least in comparison to us, and yet it's still not enough for you. People are still not happy. You want to be perfect and you expect everybody else to be the same or else you won't give them a chance, will you? And it's not as though *you're* perfect, Erica, is it? Why, you're the meanest person I've ever met, and I have to live with the whole town calling me Jezebel."

Her skin had turned a strange shade of pink but every single word of her spontaneous outburst hit me like darts to the eyeballs, it was just so unexpected coming from her. "Erica, how many people have you even given a chance? And how many times has the slightest fault caused you to dismiss them entirely?"

I held up a finger as my mouth opened to respond. But I couldn't. What could I possibly say to that? She had me.

Elspeth grinned in triumph and threw a hunk of bread at me. The Schleswig-Holstein question she knew absolutely nothing about, but nasty bitches, she was an authority on those. And she'd kept it quiet all this time - Bless.

"I do declare, I'm quite drunk," she belched again.

"You don't say."

Our eyes held across the table, her look was stern and determined, while I was at some pains to prevent myself actually smiling. Then the second balled up projectile of bread struck my forehead and bounced down my blouse. She began to giggle and that set me off again in kind.

It was ridiculous, but while we'd been here, I'd smiled and laughed harder than at any time I could recall. And this, the girl I took everything from, the same who'd take everything back again in an instant. My forehead was glistening with perspiration from excessive laughter. If only I could keep her, we could've been friends at least.

I studied her straggly form across the table, couldn't help but smile again at how ludicrous my life had become, and I stood, struggling to keep a straight face for long enough to drink a half glass of water before wiping my mouth with the serviette. "Would you excuse me for a moment, I'm just going to visit the bathroom."

She smiled back and I made my way between the tables. It was quite strange, but more than a few diners shifted their seats to allow for me more access space than was necessary. Ah Betty's, the most considerate of patrons, or maybe it was just good ole Yorkshire hospitality? Of course, perhaps my being happy was reason enough for good things to happen. They do say it's contagious.

I entered the bathroom and stared into my reflection; the teeth that were visible beneath the upturned upper lip, the creases at my eyes, the dimples on my cheeks, which in turn hurt from being stretched out like that, the unmistakable something in my eyes I'd not seen since my student days.

I ran the cold water, focused on the fluid as it splashed against the sink and coughed several times. I splashed some water against my face, then more. When I looked back up, the smile had gone down the plug with the water. I straightened my blouse collar and tightened its breast bow. I coughed again. "Easy does it, Erica."

I returned to the table and Elspeth, who'd been smiling when I left, was now sitting upright, hands in lap and with her eyes, she followed me expressionlessly all the way to the seat.

I threaded my arms back inside my jacket and grabbed my bag, opened my purse and left the money on the table. "Right, it's time we parted ways. Let's go." I made two steps before stopping to glance back and raising an eyebrow at the still seated girl. "Excuse me? Come! It's time you went on your way."

She remained seated and regarded me the same way she had at the Barley Hall. "No."

For a moment, I wondered if I'd heard her right. "Yes," I demanded, surprised at how calm I was remaining.

"No."

"Yes."

"No!"

"Yes, you must."

"No, I choose to stay."

I stepped closer but the resolve in her eyes only intensified. "Elspeth, you're leaving."

"I most certainly am not! I've come a long way." And you know what, she wasn't scared, which was the scary thing.

Panicking now, I rustled through my bag and brought out a wad of notes before throwing them to the table. "For your taxi. Take it!"

"I will not and you can't make me."

My hand trembled as I retrieved the money and returned it to my bag, shaking further as I applied the zip. "Elspeth, I..." but what to say?

She stood and slowly made her way around the table, maintaining a disturbing level and intensity of eye contact the entire way. For a moment, I even dared assume she was complying, but then she spoke.

"I know what you've done and I know what you're continuing to do. You're keeping me from my love. You're keeping me from Tilly. And you're keeping Tilly from me." Her words were slow and measured with only a hint of menace. Or maybe it was the use of *her name* twice, finally, that gave me one heck of a shiver all the way down my spine. "And you will no longer keep me away from her, my love, and what's more, I shall be waiting upon your door whence Tilly arrives, at the stroke of midnight, and it matters not how much you continue to threaten or manipulate or be mean to me, or how many times you send me back to Whitby, because I will always, always come back for Tilly, no matter how many times you send me away, and you can't keep me from her any longer, because *you* may have given up on the world, but I will continue coming back again and again and I will never give up on her, so there."

What had began as a well thought out and deliberate speech had degenerated into an emotionally driven tirade straight from the heart. She meant it. As if I didn't already know. Fuck, but the continued use of Tilly's name confirmed that. Tilly, Tilly, Tilly, bloody Tilly. It was like being back home with my parrot.

But what got me even more was that she, Elspeth of all people, the poor girl who'd shrunk back her whole life and taken crap from everybody, including Tilly's mother, had now given me this, that she had found the courage to speak to *me* in this way.

No, this was different.

She meant what she said. She would too show her unwanted self at my front door tonight at precisely the same time as Tilly's arrival.

How would *that* conversation go?

And then, I knew, it would all be over.

I could not allow that to happen.

But, as I gathered myself and dashed from the building, I knew, I still had one ace left up my sleeve.

I had to be quick.

The only problem was, that once it was done, it was done.

And there'd be no going back.

17

IN HOLY MATRIMONY

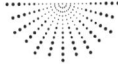

"*M*iss Wild, are yur quite ready, ma'am." Groves, unusually dapper in his church-going suit, waited upon Tilly.

It was only a short carriage ride from the town hall, where the family of the bride-to-be had prepared, over the bridge to the church of St Mary, where even now the groom awaited her entrance.

Through the partially opened window of the ground floor room, Tilly heard the intermittent clapping of hooves from the Quick Silver's four horses, its carriage painted with the crest of the Rushworth family. The horses' whinnies were dampened somewhat by the torrential downpour that'd accosted the big day.

"Ma'am? I asked if yur were quite ready?" Repeated Groves, taking a step closer and readjusting the white rose in the front pocket of his suit. A bolt of lightning stole his attention t'ward the gloomy skies outside. He frowned, turned back to Tilly and smiled. "Tis considered good luck ma'am. The thunderstorm, I mean," sneezed he into a kerchief afore replacing the fabric to the pocket whence it came. "Best be on us way, don't yur think?" Breathed he, loudly at the thought.

Tilly, ravishing in her dress, stared blankly into the mirror from her seated position and for an unknown'th time, tucked a cluster of perfect gold behind her ear.

"Not t' worry 'bout Miss Dungworth, ma'am. I understand yur Latin tutor'll be at the church t' lift yur train. Now, what's her name? If I could just…" breathed he, loud and nasally as he pondered this.

Tilly sighed but spoke quite calmly. "Her name's Miss Cartwright, Mr Groves. And yes, I'm sure she'll prove a sufficient…replacement."

Groves adjusted his cravat and then the links upon his cuffs afore producing a newspaper from somewhere about his person. Twas none other than the Whitby Gazette, which had forecasted fine weather, no less. "For the rain, ma'am."

Now, as they stood in the building's archway and peered out onto the cobbles as the rain bounced up in all directions, not five seconds dash away, the Quicksilver waited with its miserable coachman and horses. The town square lay bereft of trader, merchant and townsman, even the fruiterer had shut up shop for such a futile day's trade.

Poised with gazette in hand, Groves awaited a respite in the deluge to make the short bound t'ward the waiting cab, its obedient driver sat atop its front and feeling nature's full force.

The rain lessened for the briefest of moments and Groves held the rag aloft her veil as they dashed toward the coach's opened door. Tilly clambered inside followed by the drenched Groves.

"Oh, Mr Groves, you needn't have. Gallantry will only worsen your cold," said Tilly, more concerned for he than for her dampened golden curls or the white dress that had taken in water.

He snorted a heavy mucus filled breath and closed the door as the coach began to move. "Nonsense, Miss Wild, tis my job, nothing less. And if I may say so, miss, but yur look ever so beautiful as the day you was born, miss, and tis an honour for me t' give yur away," coughed he again into the kerchief, "and cheer up, miss, tis nothing but a happy day for us all."

Tilly stared blankly out the window as they rattled along the cobbles and the rain lashed across the carriage's flank.

"Aye, tis a happy day for us all. And, so I 'ear, they did manage t' fix the roof and I wager that smell did get rid of too, and if not then this rain'll do for the last of it." He took her hand afore giving it a squeeze. "Yur father would 'ave been proud too, miss, and although he can't be 'ere in person, I'm sure he'll be 'ere in spirit. Yes, real proud, he would."

The carriage stopped afore the swing bridge that spanned the River Esk, for having swung into motion it most certainly had and even now the traffic had built on both sides while they awaited the passing of a fishing vessel.

Groves slapped the roof with his newspaper. "Can't yur keep goin', sir?"

"Not unless you'd like the soon to be Mrs Rushworth to arrive at church having been submerged fully in the North Sea, sir," came the hoarse reply from without.

"Damn this," cursed Groves, "and we was already late on account of this bloody weather."

Tilly perked, "oh, but perhaps this is some *other* sort of omen, Mr Groves?"

"Nonsense, miss, I don't believe in omens."

"But, sir, didn't you just say the rain was good luck?"

"I, err, oh look, miss yur can sees the white bunting up on t'other side of the river."

Ten minutes later, the vessel had sailed through and the bridge was swung back into position.

"Don't yur worry, miss, we'll get yur married off yet. Not one more thing'll go wrong today," promised he as the coach clattered up the spiralling cobbled path on the east bank, bringing into view a panorama of the town below and across the other side of the river. "Look, there's where yur'll be staying t'night, tis nowt other than the Bagdale Hall Hotel," hacked he once more into his soiled kerchief afore tossing it out the window. "I should need another one of them the way things are going and I expect yur'll be 'aving words with Miss Dungwell whence you arrive there, aye? About 'er letting yur down so badly, right at the last minute an' all."

The hotel disappeared from view with the winding of the carriage as another strong gust thrashed against the window and the bunting, strung up high from shop to house, crisscrossed Church Street and flapped with the wind.

Under her breath, Tilly muttered in tongues and as the church emerged through the front window, began rocking back and forth where she sat.

"Nervous, aye, miss? Well ne'er mind, yur'll soon be beside the good doctor, he'll see yur right," blustered he, delving into his pocket for a kerchief and not finding one. "Soon, it'll all be over and yur'll be 'aving yur reception at t' town 'all, then off t' 'otel for you, miss."

"Bernard," caressed Tilly the shell about her neck, "can I tell you something?"

Groves jerked back his head. "Bern…erm, yes, miss, of course, yur can."

The coach drove parallel to the river bank and the beach

on the opposing side gradually came into view over the seafront guest houses.

"I don't think I can go through with this ceremony," hitched Tilly's breath within her throat.

Groves flapped a dismissive hand. "Don't yur worry, miss, tis a common occurrence. If my memory serves, my own wife needed dragging t' the ceremony 'erself," blew he his nose upon a sleeve. "Tis terrible weather for a cold, miss."

"Indeed, Mr Groves."

The surf came into view and Tilly leaned across Groves, forcing down the window afore thrusting her head out into the turbulence.

"What the bloody 'ell, lass! Yur'll ruin yur 'air. And this ain't no good for my cold neither. Do yur really wish t' walk down the aisle with a windswept 'ead?" The wind blew his white rose, the symbol of Yorkshire, clean out the window. "Oh, bloody 'ell. Now would yur look."

Tilly held open her eyes as best she could against the rain as the buildings ceased and her line of sight gave evidence to the solitary and feminine figure of someone so familiar.

Elspeth was standing, alone on the rain pattered and desolate sands, in the sea's shallows, her tiny frame precarious amidst the incoming tide as she faced terra incognito, abyss.

"Bring yursen in now, miss," pleaded Groves.

Tilly retook her seat as the water poured down her veiled countenance.

"Just look, yur've only gone an' messed yursen up now. What ever will I tell yur mother?" Panicked he, forlornly searching the cabin for something with which to dry the poor, unhinged girl.

The Quicksilver drew to a stop, two horses neighing at the

sight of so many people looking out from the sanctuary of the church's arch.

"Oh, we're 'ere, thank goodness for that, I think." He held out his elbow with a fine toothy grin. "Now, Miss Wild, if I may take yur arm so that I may walk yur down the aisle."

The coachman opened the door and set down the steps, the rain just as torrential as afore the trip commenced.

"No point bein' quick now is there and we've no further need of the bloody gazette neither. Oh look, they've lined the church path with white rose petals." Indeed, some of them hadn't even blown away.

Tilly delayed the elbow and commenced heaving as her wits dissolved from within, her courage effervesced into the breeze and her nails dug into the seat's edge.

Through a minute gap in the clouds, the sun shone a beam of strong June light that illuminated the carriage interior. Tilly screwed up her eyes but did neither shield them nor look away. It was so strange, for not one single square inch of Whitby had felt the sun all day.

And then, as soon as it had appeared, it was gone.

Tilly loosened her hands and turned to Groves, interrupting him afore he was able to speak. "Mr Groves, sir, I'm truly sorry, but you won't be walking me down the aisle on this day."

He took a step back. "What? What's this talk? Look, yur mother's waitin' in the archway."

Tilly held his glare, "I'm sorry, sir, and I'm sorry for my mother also. But I have to go." She pushed beyond the butler and stepped into the elements.

"What? This is crazy…Matilda…miss, it's your wedding."

Tilly hitched up her dress and strode across the lawn, turning back once. "Sir, I don't think I'll ever see you again.

Bernard…good luck…with my mother, I mean. And I wish you happiness in all things." Tilly took a deep intake of air, braced herself, faced the ridge and ran t'ward the steps carved into the cliff, her sodden wedding dress increasing in weight with every step of her heeled feet.

Voices called and shouted from behind, half masculine half feminine, all incensed, but stop to reconsider, to breathe, to think, Tilly did not. She took the first stone step that led down to the cove and paused only to remove the heels which laboured her so, throwing them into the bushes.

The stone hurt her feet but all she could do was continue as only now did the enormity of what she'd done begin to strike. She'd jilted Dr Rushworth, rejected him at the altar, actions which could only lead to scandal for her and shame upon her family. How could she ever return to society having abandoned a son of the mining Rushworths, who held such esteem in Whitby, and the whole of Yorkshire? She'd be banished from Whitby for the rest of her days.

But she'd had no choice. The reality of the matter was that, considering everything, it was a simple decision to make. All she'd lacked was the courage to follow it through and now, like afore when Elspeth had found such courage as Tilly had never known, now she would repay that courage in kind.

She emerged in the cove and turned onto the street, running along the narrow path on the river's edge that led t'ward the bridge. She didn't notice the openmouthed stares of the fishermen in their boats, as they gaped at the desperate girl fleeing in her wedding dress, at least not yet.

"Oh no," screeched she, clasping a hand to her pounding heart. For the bridge was again swinging outwards from its centre, as wide as it was cruel.

Knowing that awaiting the bridge to close again was in no

way an option, she clocked the face of the nearest small boatman, himself contemplating with caution the wild and sodden wench who now approached.

"Please sir, I must be about the other side, promptly, if you would be so kind," pointed she at the tethering afore stooping and taking it upon herself to unfasten the boat.

With disbelief, the man shook his head. "What in di bejeesis do ye think ye be doin' miss? Why, you're Rushworth's betrothed, ain't ye. Shouldn't ye be up yonder?" Pointed he upwards at the church atop the cliff with its well-dressed patrons presently shaking their fists down at none other than himself below. "Ye are, and ye should be. Oy must take ye back at once, lest my name be forever tarnished and oym rendered unable to ever return to this town."

Tilly threw the rope into the boat and sat down on the embankment prior to lowering herself inside, which she could not easily do without assistance. "Sir, I must be about the other side this minute, either with or without your aid."

"Oy shall not do it miss, and nor would ye in my position."

Tilly prepared to jump. "Fine, then I shall swim to the other side without your assistance and then the whole town shall know you refused help of a lady when she needed it most."

"Oh, for Petc's sake lass, won't ye see some sense, ah but ye really mean it so ye do." He took his hand of Tilly's afore helping her aboard. "Dis is most ludicrous behaviour miss. If only ye'd ha' chosen one of t'other boats. My brother in law relies on di Rushworths for his income, so he does." Nodded he to an oar, "well den, get stuck in lass and don't spare ye shoulder."

Tilly took ahold of the oar and pulled against the water. "This is most kind of you, Mr…?"

"Stoker, miss, Stoker and for di life of me, all oy wanted was to survey the place. Oy never 'spected dis miss. Dat's it, Chroyst, but ye be rowin' harder than oy even, so ye are. Don't tink oy'll ever returns here though. My blood pressure, ye see, tis enough to give ye a seizure, so it is. Women like ye, runnin' about like ye are and in weather such as dis. Tis a wonder ye've no' catched ye death. Ah, nearly der now, miss." Stoker dropped his oar afore tethering the boat to the western embankment. "Wish oy could say it was a pleasure miss. Maybe now, wit ye permission, oy may be back about my business?" He offered his clasped hands for a boost. "Put ye foot on dees, miss. Oh bejeesis, but yees no boots on oyther."

Tilly placed her foot in the nice man's hands. "You've been most kind, Mr Stoker," rose Tilly onto the surface above.

"Always was a sucker for a pretty face, so oy was. Ye take care now, strange miss. Oy'd tip me tile if oy 'ad one, so oy'll 'ave a tipple fur ye tonight instead."

Taking little heed for the preservation of her feet, Tilly ran along the promenade in the direction of the special place. The sails of boats flapped in the wind and two carts pulled by horses rumbled past but nothing else stirred, the weather having put paid to the day's trade. The ferocity of the rain would have stung, if only she had feeling of herself remaining, yet adrenaline continued to push her along, further and ever closer to her love.

Down a gentle decline and over a pile of downed wood from some forgotten project, around the corner and onto the sand. Tilly stopped; half for breath half to gather her wits.

Ahead, the forlorn figure stared out into emptiness, still standing in the shallows like she'd been there some time and not realised she was being slowly engulfed by the tide. There

Elspeth was, numb to the impending abyss. Another wave whipped about her knees, yet move one inch she did not.

"Elly!" Shouted Tilly, her voice drowned out by distance, rain and waves.

She could not wait another second and commenced running across the sea sodden sand and into the surf, her every step sinking before being wrenched out once more. The cold sea could make no further difference, not that she noticed the bitterness. Her veins flooded with chemicals unknown, and every second her love remained unaware of her presence was another second of pain for them both.

"Elly!" Called Tilly again and this time Elspeth twitched.

She slowly turned her head, her every muscle numb and unresponsive. There was recognition, in the eyes at least, even if her body could not acknowledge so. Then her mouth slowly moved. "T...i...l...l...y." Her face possessed a hundred questions and while pained, she tugged her feet free from the sand and prepared to meet her saviour head-on.

"Elly," cried Tilly, uncontrollable endless tears that merged with the sea.

"You...came? How is it so, my sweet?"

Tilly slowed her approach and walked the final paces, splashing, lifting her legs from the water that seemed to have calmed the last few seconds. Nothing existed in the world other than the sand, the sea, Tilly, Elspeth.

Tilly uselessly held up her dress, filthy with a hundred thousand grains of sand.

Elspeth's eye was drawn to it, at least one question answered, but how could she dwell on where she'd come from when all that mattered was where they were going.

Elspeth heaved and threw her arms about her love. "Oh, Tilly, what say you? Please tell me you came to heal my heart, do?" She braced herself for the reply that would forever change her life, her heart exploding with uncontrollable hope and agony both.

Tilly threw down Elspeth's arms and stepped back with a grimace afore snorting her contempt at the pitiful wretch in front. "Pfft, I came to tell you to stay away from me. I feel nothing for you and never have. My advice to you, you jezebel, is to leave me alone forever," gestured Tilly to the sea that surrounded them, "or better yet, perhaps you could do us both a kind turn and drown yourself."

Tilly turned back to the shore, hitched up her dress and without looking back, strolled into Whitby.

※

UNDER THE CANDLELIGHT'S GLOW, I scribbled out with ink the original ending and replaced it with the new one.

Tasting the bile in the back of my throat, I sighed, which gave way to a moan, so I sank another thimbleful of Scotch before refilling it and tossing the empty bottle to the floor behind.

I ran a clammy hand down the final page as teardrops spilt down the twenty-year-old paper. Then I shut the original leather-bound *A Petal And A Thorn* and retied the ribbon that held it together. Struggling out from my seat, I staggered toward the cabinet and reinserted the book home.

"Done," I croaked, locking the cabinet and placing the key inside the drawer. "No going back now."

And nor would there be.

My stomach twitched and I bounded for the room's corner, throwing up into the bin.

18

THE ETERNAL PEST

*K*nock, knock, knock.

I was already at the door waiting and opened it before the final beat from her sweet hand had finished ringing in my ears.

She breezed inside silently, without so much as a word, but giving the merest flicker of an eye as she moved past and glided up the stairs.

I poked my head out the opened door and scanned left and right, then again, examining the bench to the front where the eternal pest had sat on the first day of our acquaintance.

But she wasn't there. She promised she would be. But she wasn't.

I stepped out into the midnight cold, this time listening for any signs of her, but there were none, and neither was she lurking around by the minster like the expert stalker I knew her to be, or anywhere else.

Exhaling, I tried to lift my shoulders to present a more cutting figure before returning to Tilly. I'd thrown up, emptying the contents of my belly and the effects of the Scotch I'd taken had largely worn off since. My head hurt a little from the whisky, but I could tolerate that. In comparison to how crap I was feeling, for other reasons, it was nothing.

I entered the house, locked the door and clambered the steps. Percy greeted me with a squawk.

Tilly stood by the window, one hand parting the curtains from the centre as she peered out into the darkness. "Were you looking for someone, sweet Erica?"

My feet scuffed against the floorboards. "Someone? Like, who?" I dreaded asking.

"You tell me? I know but one person in this city." She released the curtain and angled around to face me. "Nobody in particular?"

"Nobody. It's just one of those nights, is all." I gestured behind with a hand. "Cup of Earl Grey tea? Just how you like it?"

She nodded and I plodded into the kitchen to boil the water. My eyes glassed over as I fixated on the steam that floated up from the spout and a minute later it began to whistle. I prepared the tray and carried it back to the living room, placing it on the table in front of the divan. I sat, patting the space beside me and Tilly sat down with her usual graceful and silent nature that I loved.

I poured tea into two cups, added the milk, five sugars to my own followed by two in Tilly's.

"Erica, you know I don't take sugar," she chided.

How could I get something like *that* wrong after all this time? "Whoops, silly me. I'm ever so sorry, let me get you another cup," I began to stand but she waved it away.

"It's of no real consequence. Two small teaspoons of sugar will hardly kill me. Why, it's not poison, in small quantities at least, and nor does it compare to a large quantity of strong liquor in one sitting, a rope tied to a beam or…dare I say…drowning in the likes of a bathtub, a river or…why…

even the sea." She stirred in the sugar and took her usual small sip without a sound. "How delightful to the taste…in small quantities."

I brought my own cup to my lips and took an extra long sip, shielding my face for as long as I could get away with. "Well, I hope I haven't spoiled your tea."

"My tea, no, Erica."

I hummed in affirmation.

"But, I do declare, you seem quite distant this evening, certainly not your usual puff and gaiety, Erica?" I almost fell off the seat with shock as she placed her hands neatly over her lap and stared blankly forward in the general direction of my book cabinet. In fact, she'd barely looked at me since her arrival.

She seemed different herself, but I wouldn't say that and neither would I ask who the bloody hell was teaching her new phrases. "I've, um, I've had a busy day."

I thought, for the hundredth time of Elspeth, her tired face, worn clothes and wild glaring eyes of our final meeting. How we'd shared several interesting and amusing moments and that, for a few instances during our merriment, despite everything I'd put her through, I'd seen flickers of happiness in her eyes. But I'd killed it and I couldn't be sure whether or not I'd killed her. But most shocking to me was that even the presence of Tilly was doing little to attenuate the feeling, what could only be described as, for the first time in my life, guilt.

Now she shuffled in her seat to face me. "Please, feel at liberty to divulge about your day."

I studied her face, for any signs she knew more than she was letting on. As it turned out, she'd make an excellent poker player. "Well, I've seen a couple of old acquaintances, drank coffee, bought a few things, um…" Elspeth's unkempt face filled my mind, her tears, her pain, "I drank some coffee at the coffee shop, see?" The last few words rasped out from my mouth.

She nodded, her face suddenly increasing in animation, encouraging me to continue, to elaborate, to *divulge*. "Go on. What else have you done today?"

I shook myself out from a semi-trance. "What else? Um, coffee, shops, coffee shops, old friends," I counted them off on my fingers and wondered how much the Scotch had frazzled my thinking, "oh, I saw David Maher," I flapped a dismissive hand, "but you wouldn't know him."

Elspeth again. The eternal pest, the lady of jezebel, interrupted my thinking processes whilst Tilly sat patiently awaiting more info, like I had any more to give, at least not anything that wouldn't incriminate me.

Tilly glanced at the grandfather clock before tipping her head back to stare at the ceiling.

"Oh, yes, a nice walk around the town." I tapped her on the elbow and she yawned. "You know how I struggle with my writing and how it helps with my thinking."

Elspeth again.

But where was she?

Didn't she say she'd come tonight?

No, she'd more than said, she promised and she meant it.

So why wasn't she here? Why wasn't she here to annoy me, to test me, to cost me another hundred quid in exorbitant taxi fares? Dammit, but why wasn't she here to take Tilly away and ruin my life?

My jaw quivered. "What have I done?" I wiped my eye with a sleeve. "Breathe, Erica, breath."

Tilly looked down from the ceiling and shuffled closer. "Erica? Are you alright?"

I inhaled a deep breath and gathered my composure. "Of

course," I confirmed to her suddenly very close face. God, but she was perfect in every way. Get a grip, you fool, or risk losing her forever. "I'm fine, I'm fine." I was about to suggest a few songs on the pianoforte before retiring to the bedroom when Tilly spoke.

"Are you quite sure you're not thinking of something...or somebody else?" She took ahold of my hand and I ran my thumb tenderly over her soft skin.

I shook my head and she dropped my hand like it was a used-up napkin before very slowly and very deliberately moving her body away to face the cabinet. This time there was no mistaking what she was looking at and I followed her line of sight toward a certain leather-bound book.

"Erica, might I suggest we finish reading the story?" She asked as though it was nothing.

Something ricocheted around my chest and I studied her extra carefully, for any telltale signs of knowledge I'd rather she not be privy to. "The story, but why?" I asked much louder than intended.

She blinked from my outburst but kept her composure. "Why? What do you mean *why*? Is it usual to read all the way to page two hundred and thirty-six only to then cease?"

Oh, God. I swallowed and searched my brain for an answer that wouldn't come. Why had I drunk so much bloody Talisker? That was it! I was done with that shit. Why had my usual quick thinking escaped me...

...and then again Elspeth fought her way back to the front of my mind; her scruffy hair, her boringness that I'd taken a strange liking to because you could never tell when she'd say or do something quite suddenly un-boring, her stupidity too and that in regard to her experiences, she wasn't quite as stupid as I'd first thought. But most of all it was her courage, that she returned again and again, despite being terrified, faced up to me, stared me down and had given me a piece of her not completely unenlightened mind. Despite all the obstacles she faced in life, and the extras I'd recently thrown in for added measure, she still came back, managed to smile and even be pleasant to my undeserving self. Where I'd given up on humanity many years ago, that poor girl never would - At least, not until I changed the story.

Oh, God, but what had I done?

And what had become of her?

"Are you quite alright?" Tilly asked with genuine concern, her hand squeezing my arm.

I tried to smile through the fluid that was building in my sinuses. Instead, I shook my head. "No, Tilly, I don't think I am."

Her grip tightened. "What is it? You must tell me?" She seemed to be encouraging me, almost like she knew everything already, but for some reason needed to hear it from me.

And then my mind flashed with images of poor Elspeth lying faced down in the sea on a cold autumn night with big fish taking chunks out of her, and the awful bile taste built stronger than ever in my throat.

Oh, how I'd do anything for Elspeth to knock on my door right this minute and expose me as the wicked, manipulating girlfriend stealer come borderline murderer that I was. She didn't deserve what I'd done to her, but I deserved everything that was coming to me.

I tried to stand from the divan and found an unexpected weakness in my legs, but using my hands I managed to steady myself.

Tilly looked up with an expression of expectation and worry, "Erica?"

I took hold of her hands and pulled her up, closed my

eyes and experienced her scent, for the final time. "Tilly, my darling, I must thank you for showing me love and warmth once again and for reminding me what it was to live. It was far more than I deserved." A single tear rolled down her cheek and I wiped it away with my thumb. "There's something important I have to do." I knew this was the end, even though I couldn't say it. Not that I needed to, she understood entirely.

"So, you're leaving me," she said, more as a statement of finality and acceptance than a question.

"No…yes, oh, God," my voice came out in short wisps as my beating heart threatened to smash through my chest, "please promise you'll still be here when I return?"

She grabbed my forearms and smiled most beautifully, from the mouth and eyes. "But if you leave then I no longer have any purpose here. You wish to do *what you have to do*, yet you also wish for me to be here upon your return. Erica, you must listen to my next words very carefully and make your decision because it is *you* who'll have to live with it."

I braced myself, already knowing what she'd say. "Go on."

"You can have either *me* or your redemption, but not both."

I pulled her close and brought her lips to mine in a powerful embrace mixed with our tears.

When I finally brought her back to arms' length, I recalled what she'd said to me the night she first appeared at my door, during a time when I was undergoing my darkest moment. "You once said *it was me you came for…*" I took a large gulp of air "and only now do I realise what you meant."

Except Tilly wasn't the only one who came for my redemption.

19

REDEMPTION

I'd grabbed a jacket, some gloves and my bag before running out the house, leaving Tilly inside with a door key to show herself out whenever she wished. I needed to be fast away and I didn't know how long I'd be.

Now, I clutched the jacket tight about my neck, wishing I'd also had the presence of mind to bring a scarf as I circled Clifford's Tower for the second time at nearly two in the morning.

The tower, during the ghost walk tour, had been the first place I saw Elspeth and I hoped, if she hadn't yet done anything stupid, I'd find her there. But neither did I believe she'd make it so easy as to be in the first place I checked.

The city's streets were as quiet as any city could be, illuminated by modern lighting, the occasional car, mostly police or taxi but also the odd ambulance to deal with drunkards collapsing outside bars. The latter Elspeth would have known in her time because some things never change, but I didn't know how she'd cope with motor vehicles whizzing past from all angles, and especially not in the state of mind I expected to find her in. How would the drunken, fascinated students view my innocent creation, found wandering the streets in her strange Victorian garb?

Clifford's Tower yielded no bedraggled housekeeper, so I crossed it off my mental list and next stomped to the bridge where I'd seen her the day after. Waiting for some considerable time, I eyed everybody who walked past and even spent several minutes peering over the rail into the Ouse for any strange shape that appeared in the water under this moonlit night with its rapidly falling fog. No, but the weather was about to make the task even harder.

Next, I headed to Dean's Park, beside the minster, the place where we first spoke, but the gates were locked. The fact I'd forgotten they locked the gates every evening was evidence to my present state of mind but regardless, I squinted through the gaps in the railing, searching for movement, while my hands shivered around the iron bars.

Finally, I hurried to the Ouse embankment by the museum gardens and scanned the path, as well as the river between Lendal Bridge all the way along to the ghost walk tour meeting point. It was the place I'd seen her standing dangerously close to the edge - Nothing.

It was no major surprise I hadn't found her in any of those places. But I had to be thorough. The most likely place I'd find her was next on the list.

I ascended the stone steps that led back to the bridge and flagged down a passing taxi. "To Whitby," I demanded as I closed the door after me.

"Whitby? That's fifty miles. I'll need the money upfront, love." He grimaced, twisting his head back between the seats to evaluate the dubious single female customer at this time of morning.

I thrust a hand into my bag and brought out more than

enough funds to cover his night shift. "And I'll need a lift back so consider yourself procured for the night."

He didn't argue and with the clear night roads we made the silent trip over the moors in a little over an hour, stopping on Whitby's North Promenade that faced out into the sea, its beach hidden to my sightline by the verge I'd have to descend via the steps that led toward the sand.

Grasping the door handle, I mentioned something to the driver about waiting an unspecified period of time whilst I took a walk along the beach. To my surprise, he barely even flinched.

"It's not the strangest thing I've been asked to do, love."

My belly churned with a mixture of fear for what I might find, or what I might not. Strangely, thoughts for my own well-being, a single lady taking a nighttime walk along the beach, hardly signified.

I crossed the road and from behind the wall, surveyed the beach below. The combination of street and moonlight enabled me to see directly in front almost as far as the incoming tide, low as it was at this hour. But both west and east, my bird's eye view was restricted by the increasingly heavy fog.

On my flank, the stairs built into the earth led down toward the sands, darker as it looked, now I was contemplating actually going down there.

I laughed and slapped the wall with my hands. "This is crazy." What ever was I thinking? Coming all the way to Whitby at this ridiculous hour to look for a deranged woman, who for all I knew was back in her own time, moving on with her life, probably putting herself about with some grieving jet wearing widow. She'd laugh for sure if she could see me now.

I shook my head and laughed again at my uncharacteristic

stupidity and foolish outburst of compassion - A trait I didn't possess and, as it turned out, for good reason - It caused me to lose my judgement. No, sorry Elspeth, but it was time to go home and tip the poor taxi driver extra for his trouble.

I was in the process of turning on my heel when something moved in the corner of my eye. A blur on the edge of visibility, between clarity and obscurity, clearness and fog, something definitely drifted across the sand toward the sea. It was the loose flapping of a dark dress in the wind that convinced me it was a certain forlorn and lost feminine figure. I fixated on the spot where slowly she moved as though possessed by some invisible force that'd taken over. And then she, or it, disappeared into the mist just as the tide surged over the imprints she'd left in the sand.

"Elspeth," I whispered, not certain but I had to be sure. And quick.

I ran for the gap in the wall that opened up to the stairs in the bank, grabbed the railing and bounded down, taking the final steps two at a time. My feet, sinking into sand announced I'd arrived on the beach where the light was significantly reduced in comparison to above, the fog at this level further restricting visibility.

Running across the soft sand proved exerting as I headed in the direction of the woman, wobbling with every flimsy step, the sound of rolling waves growing louder. The fog made it impossible to see more than a few steps in front but then I landed on harder sand, the waves having washed over it moments before. Unfortunately, any footprints had been erased by the same.

Stopping to catch my breath and to attempt to survey my surroundings, I assumed I'd reached close to the point where I first saw the moving shapes.

"Elspeth!" I shouted, then again and again, my voice only

half carrying over the crashing of the sea. I thrust my neck forward, squinting hard, carefully scanning every area of beach within the near vicinity. "Elspeth!" I called again.

And then I saw the shape. It was a dim form at first, but I hurried toward it and the outlines moved like the edges of a blur contorting.

The first wave lashed over my feet, the freeze alerting me to a new challenge. I swore but splashed onwards as I could now distinctly recognise arms, then legs, then a head. I was up to my knees in cold water, struggling with every step but onwards I pushed.

It was her!

There was no misinterpreting her outfit, hair and slender body. "Elspeth." Then I was upon her and she stopped as I grabbed ahold of her shoulders from behind. "Elspeth, you pudding."

One leg buckled from beneath her and I stooped to support the girl by propping her arm over my shoulder. The stench of something strong was thick on her breath. "Lea... leave me alone," she slurred, her entire body frozen. "You... you must let me d...d...d...do this."

With the bad light I could make out only minor details of her face and neither was I sure she recognised me, not that I cared in the moment, as the next wave enveloped my thighs. "We're going back, so step to it."

"You c...can't make me live." But she had no strength to fight against me, or unfortunately, to carry herself back to shore, which meant it'd be me carrying out the labour.

"We'll discuss it later," I pushed hard off the ground with my feet as the soles of my shoes sank into the sand below the water, which hardly made it any easier, but we made slow progress trudging toward the fog smudged lights atop the promenade in the distance.

She wiggled and shivered but didn't protest. "Why did you come?" Her voice lacked all semblance of verve. "Why must you torture me so? All I want is to sleep...to sleep forever...I just want the pain to end."

It broke my heart to hear it, which was a revelation in itself. Dammit, but I would not allow any harm to come to this girl.

We emerged from the sea tramping up the sodden sand and shaking from the cold. I had to wiggle out of my jacket whilst ensuring her arm didn't slip from my shoulder and I wrapped her in the thick garment, feeling the futility of her own clothes as they clung to her damp flesh. Her face was grim as expected; malnourished and sullen, discoloured to the point of being grey. She'd neglected herself for a long time and if the sea hadn't taken her tonight, she'd have found a way eventually. She had that look in the eyes, of a down and out destitute finally given up on the cruel world.

She became even more limp in my hold. "Take me back...please take me back."

I readjusted my grip around her emaciated body and with a heave of my legs, we were heading back. "Not tonight, miss."

Ascending the steps back to the promenade, she even contributed toward the effort by pulling on the railing and not fighting too hard against me, though knowing Elspeth, it was more out of politeness than the desire for self-sustainability. Even now, the girl could find again the sheer bloody minded, teeth gritting, stiff upper lip attitude of our people, even if she'd lost it for a while.

When I opened the taxi door, the driver, who'd reclined his seat and was lying back apparently asleep, awoke with a jolt.

"York," I said, helping Elspeth into the back where I

clambered in beside her and shut the door, "and some heating would be more than appreciated."

He made a double-take in the rearview mirror, then twisted in his seat to glare back at me. God alone knew how I must have looked. "Best I not even ask. Where in York?"

"Goodramgate, at the entrance to College Street." I pulled Elspeth closer into me and for some added warmth slipped her hands inside my gloves, which had been waiting, dry on the back seat. "And there's a surprise waiting when we get there, love."

The driver, who'd been changing gears, twisted back again and gave me a deranged look. "Um, no thanks, love."

"What?" I gave him an ugly face back. "What do you think you're…"

Elspeth interrupted, "a surprise? All I want is to sleep forever."

I turned back to her and my face softened. "Then you shall sleep in my bed and for as long as you wish."

The car veered left onto the rumble strip and the annoying jolts along with the reverberating noise stabbed painfully at my head. "You bloody fool, will you watch where you're going."

When we arrived, I paid the driver a little extra and he took the tip with a sympathetic smile. "Good luck, love."

"What do you mean *good luck*?" But the taxi was already pulling away leaving Elspeth and myself with the short walk through the pedestrianised area of the minster. "We're home now and you don't need to worry anymore. Everything'll be alright from now on, you'll see."

"Oh, what do you mean?" She asked with a faint voice.

"Patience, you'll see." It occurred to me, as I unlocked the door, that Tilly had most likely slipped out in the meantime, in which case - whoops.

And, after assisting Elspeth up the stairs, absorbing Percy's usual ear piercing screeches, I immediately knew Tilly was no longer around. I knew without having to look or call and is it turned out, so did Elspeth.

I guided her to the bedroom and sat her on the bed, all the while, for the first time, I was hit by the sinking feeling and realisation that I'd never again see Tilly. Must I, for the second time in my life, undergo the excruciating torture of loss, and all so I could look myself in the mirror and not despise what stared back at me. Would it really worth it?

It was a question I'd have the rest of my life to answer.

"Take your clothes off and get in the bed…no, no, for once, don't argue with me," I gestured over my shoulder to the door as I made to move, "and don't worry, I've seen better goodies on a charity store mannequin and that's why you need to eat. So I'll make you an Erica special; fried eggs, bacon, sausage, black pudding and I'll even save the fat dripping if it'll make you feel at home. Oh, and a hot cup of tea too, and I'm going to sit and watch while you consume every last bit. And then you're going to sleep."

She looked up from her perch on my bed, her face tired and glum and she spoke with a defeated voice. "Tilly was my surprise, wasn't she. But she's not here anymore."

No, she wasn't, and I swallowed as I tried to hold a calm voice. "Well, it's just as well really, considering how you look. You wouldn't want her seeing you like this…" she tried to interject but I cut her off, "…no, no, you wouldn't. And yes, I know she wouldn't care, but *you* really should. Don't you think it would hurt *her* if she saw you this way? And another thing, while we're on the subject; it's really never wise to pin your entire life and happiness on just one single thing, living or otherwise, is it. Have more about you girl, like Tilly does. Learn an instrument or a language or become good at a sport or something. Any one of us could get struck tomorrow by a...a horse and cart or something and you'll be making yourself more interesting to *her* but more importantly, you'll not be left so distraught and wrecked the next time she takes a fancy to someone new." I shook my head and almost regretted going into a rant but she needed to hear it. "Dear, dear, dear. Anyway..." I left the room. It wasn't easy for me either.

A few seconds later I poked my head back inside, she was taking the straps off her shoulders and looked at me with alarm before I said, "it's always the pretty ones. You ever notice that?"

20

WHITBY

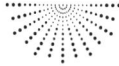

*O*ver the next few days and nights, Elspeth remained with me, leaving my sight only to undress or shower. I slept on the divan, which I'd dragged in from the living room. She ate as much fatty garbage, and the occasional Betty's delivered to the door, as I could force-feed her, drank tea, slept and recuperated. As it turned out, she snored like a steam-powered canal barge on the Leeds to Liverpool canal, which, in hindsight, might have explained why Tilly needed a rest from her. You see, I'm a sound sleeper, always have been, and not even my occasional whisky induced stupors have ever changed that.

"I do declare, but you do snore, worse even than my father." I hadn't known she was awake and I looked up from my desk in the corner where I'd been busy working. "Several times you have roused me with your obstructed respiratory passages." She was propped up on an elbow and I guessed she'd been watching me for a while.

I put my pen down. "So this is the thanks I get, huh?"

"What are you doing?" She tilted up her chin from the

other side of the room as though doing so might enable her sight to bend around corners. But her question surprised me.

"Um, nothing. Well, just noting down a few ideas…for the future. Not quite sure yet." I waved it away. "Anyway, how are you? Feeling stronger yet?"

She dropped one leg from the bed, then the other, and pushed herself into a sitting position. "I'm full of food and tea." She paused as I watched her. "And I'm wondering what's next?"

I slowly stood and moved across to the divan, shifted aside the duvet and patted the space beside me; part to see how easy she'd find the walk across the room after having been bedridden the last five days, part because it was about time we had *the* conversation.

She heaved herself up and needed a moment to steady herself but after that, she had no problems walking the short distance and approached the divan before taking the seat. "Ta-dah. You see, I'm not completely invalided."

"Good, you're doing very well."

"A sniffle and a rumbly tummy were never liable to be my death, Erica." There it was again, that stiff upper lip Englishness and I thought best not to mention she'd attempted suicide.

"You want to know what's next?" I glanced over toward my desk, to the half-filled sheet of paper and the screwed up balls of its predecessors in and around the bin. "Tell me, what *did* happen next?"

I needed *something*, not just because my career had died the minute I'd stopped writing about these two troublesome girls, but because I also needed to know for my own peace and harmony of mind. It had always troubled me, but now? How could I let Elspeth go now without knowing she and

Tilly would be all right? But if I was expecting something encouraging, I was to be left disappointed.

All she did was to look down into her frail hands, clasped in her lap, and didn't say a word.

It was agony, sheer bloody torture. And though I could hardly compare it to a mother with two missing children who remained unaware of their fates, on some levels, they were the children I'd never have, and I didn't know what their future would hold.

The tears gathered in my eyes so I stooped toward the table to take a large gulp of tea, ensuring I was composed again by the time I rejoined Elspeth. "It doesn't matter. Forget I asked."

We sat, drank tea and chatted as I studied her faculties and physical appearance, trying to determine whether she was well enough. Her complexion was all the better for having been in the warmth and with the amount of good food I'd plied her, it would be hard for anybody not to plump up a little. Most importantly, I was satisfied she wouldn't die from lacking the essentials of life which, save for oxygen, the plonker had been denying herself for an extended period of time. However, as we conversed about the advantages of riding a horse over the driving of motorised vehicles, and as I explained the new law which meant that women could now obtain their own property independent of their husbands, just so long as they were married and how this law would not apply to herself and Tilly for the said reason, I decided that with some tidying up, she'd be ready to move on - I'd miss her.

"Are you sure you're qualified to do this?" She cringed as the scissors lopped off a section of straggly brown hair.

I snipped at more loose ends and other bits I never liked. "Qualified? No. But reasonably competent?…Probably."

Snip, snip, snip. "In fact, it might be best if you shut your eyes while I go to work." I gently nudged her shoulder, "and let me get this straight; you trusted me with the red hair dye, but only now do you raise questions about my competency?"

She giggled, "hmm, that is rather strange, now that you mention it."

Nearly twenty years of being a failure had given me ample time to learn new skills, and she wasn't to know I'd taken courses in hair and beauty, even if I'd never stayed around long enough to receive the piece of paper that said I was allowed to do it.

"Now, you'll be a little ahead of your times with this look, but just a little. You'll be a revolutionary, but only a mild one, not too chancy." I gave her a soft elbow in the ribs. "What's more, a certain young lady will find you irresistible." She perked up at that as I held up her mane behind her head, unsure if I'd taken away too much. "Um, we're going for the Gibson Girl look. You're independent, sporty and simple." To show her, I wound up a loose-fitted bun at her crown. "See, it's effortless and graceful."

How I could blag it, but she seemed to like it. Either way, that she looked better than before could not be argued.

We moved onto nails, which I had a far superior proficiency at, and by the end of it, they were filed, smooth and glowing where they'd once been coarse, cracked and bloody awful.

During her bedridden stay, she'd been wearing a couple of nighties I'd lent her and I didn't tell her, but her little maid's outfit was now in the rubbish. Together, we selected a few of my Victorian dresses, from before my period of excessive weight gain and which I hoped one day to be able to wear again, and I watched as she tried them on. She was only a couple of inches shorter than myself, so I didn't envisage any major problems, with regards to height at least. I knew the minute I saw her in the dress I'd purchased when I was supposed to have been attending a former friend's wedding, that we'd found the right outfit.

It was an ivory coloured corset dress with only a slight train at the back and it had no straps, which emphasised her collar bones and neck, completely complimenting her slender features and I didn't think any of my former gay fashion friends could have picked out anything more suitable from a choice of a thousand. Once I'd given her matching heels, a part of me wondered why I'd always favoured Tilly.

I whistled and walked around her form as she scrutinised herself in the mirror. "Damn shame I really have to let you go."

"I do declare, but you can't wait to see the back of me," she turned sideways and I swore she was checking out her buttocks and the way they filled the tight little thing. "The heels though, it's all too much, don't you think? I shall return them, of course. The dress too."

I stepped toward the window and pretended to look outside. "Indeed, I cannot wait. And you can keep them." I spoke with a monotone voice.

After a second, I felt her warm hand on my arm and I turned to face her.

"Erica…"

I swallowed, "I know," I began fanning my face with futile hands. "Enough. Your dress, it's too loose. I have safety pins."

I commenced work pinning segments of the fabric together on the underside to give her a tighter fit and afterwards she looked like the dress had been tailored just for her.

I reviewed her again and brought a shaky hand to my

forehead and breathed before saying, "just your makeup now."

I plonked her down and went to work. Like any girl, I was seasoned with applying my own makeup but unpracticed with another. Primer, foundation and concealer where necessary. Eyebrows, a major plucking effort there, followed by eyeshadow, eyeliner and mascara. A bit of powder to soak up the excess oil. Finally, I picked out a shade of lipstick to match her new red hair.

The result: In a word - Stunning.

Remembering, I held up a finger before heading for a rummage through the wardrobe and bringing out the pièce de résistance.

Her eyes widened with delight and intense interest. "Oh, Erica, I can not," she placed a hand on her heart and almost looked offended, almost.

"You can and you bloody well are." I knew she wanted them, for it was not merely the ladies of my time who loved them.

"But…but…no…it's too much."

I held up the diamond and pearl necklace ensemble and motioned for her to turn around, which she did without dispute. She shivered when the cool gold touched her neck and gaped open-mouthed at her reflection in front.

"Erica, please, I really can't."

I connected the chain at the nape of her neck before standing beside her where we stared at our reflections. "You know, I've never once worn it. It was paid for by your misery and I want you to have the thing."

She nipped the principle jewel between finger and thumb, a twelve carat diamond in the shape of a pear, which had neatly tucked itself inside the wiring at the top of her corset. Admiring every one of its thirty-three jewels, she found herself unable to speak while I enjoyed, for the first time seeing her happy. That in itself was worth the price of the schmuck.

A tear fell from her eye and I was quick to reproach her. "Hey, now, don't you dare ruin your bloody makeup." I ran to fetch a tissue and gently dabbed below her eye.

She sniffed, "I will miss you."

"No you won't and you'd better bloody not," I had to turn away and in the moment I found myself needing to leave the room, which I did for several minutes to regain my composure.

When I returned, having splashed my face with cold water, it was mid-afternoon. "Well, if you're not ready now, you never will be."

She bounded toward me where I stood at the door. "I do declare, Erica, but I'm most nervous."

I tilted my head. "That's only natural, my love, and it's not a bad thing. Are you ready?"

She nodded and we headed downstairs to the door, stepped outside into the cool autumn air, where we connected arms, and meandered through a bunch of gawping tourists to the waiting taxi just off the pedestrian zone. We settled on the back seat and I told the driver where we wanted to go.

"Whitby?" He asked with a raised eyebrow.

"Forty-eight miles due northeast by north, would you require any further specifics?"

He ignored my smart-aleck remark and with brutal force, thrust the gears into first while I contemplated how it was that I'd never yet been kicked out of a taxi.

Elspeth and I held hands as we travelled over the moors in silence, the declining sun bringing on the twilight, which promised a Whitby tide between high and low.

We arrived in Whitby as the light dimmed, tourists

dispersed and employees had already returned home after a day of work, primarily in the tourism industries; hotels, museums and gift shops as the new crowd, those of the pubs, restaurants and bars, made their way to work. No longer was Whitby a place of fishing, jet mining or a hundred other occupations of the olden grind.

I told the driver to stop the taxi a mile to the west of North Promenade, the reason being that I wanted to spend a little more time with Elspeth before saying farewell forever. I paid the man and we watched him drive away. I didn't want him waiting around because I knew that after this was done, I'd want to stay around in the town just a little longer.

We walked along the seafront pavement while down below the sea made its boisterous progress, whipping up waves that dared thrash ever further up the sand. The occasional man or woman strolled the beach, throwing balls for dogs who obediently fetched them back.

Elspeth shivered, but whether from the cold or something else, I didn't know and wouldn't ask.

There was very little to say, for either of us. Sometimes you meet a person that under different circumstances could have been your greatest friend. Having to let Elspeth go so soon was a tragedy, but what choice was there?

She hitched up the dress as her little feet clipped against the concrete, strands of red hair gently blowing in the calm breeze and always, she kept a watch to her left, to the beach, scrutinising every person who walked or ran, stood or sat.

I took her arm in mine and silently pulled her closer into my side. My eyes began to sting, but I'd hold back the tears. I had to. The wave of heat that washed through my body made necessary the loosening of my jacket, which I unzipped for some relief.

The occasional car that drove past on our right now shone their headlights as the darkness increasingly won over.

We entered North Promenade, the town centre taking shape to the south and over the river mouth directly in front, atop the cliffs and set back, was the imposing eight hundred-year-old abbey, a favourite for Dracula stage plays and travelling Goths from around the world. And in front of that, situated almost on the cliff edge was the Church of St Mary.

Elspeth averted her eyes from those sites, always transfixed on the sands.

And then we arrived at the steps, built into the earth and leading directly below to the beach. I quickly scanned for the area I'd once identified as Tilly and Elspeth's special place; it was positioned a little over halfway toward the sea, directly in front of a huge mound of earth that jutted out into the sand. In the fading light, nobody was there.

For the first time, Elspeth turned her back to the sea to look at me, and she wiped at the streams of tears that refused to stop.

"Now don't you go setting me off with that," I embraced her in silence for what seemed like several minutes, pulling her in tight and feeling the huge lump in my throat. "Thank you," I whispered into her hair.

She pulled away. "What for?"

It took everything I had to save from exploding into tears, but I'd manage it, I was determined. "For saving me." It sounded so cliché, but it was the truth, she had saved my soul.

She clamped her lips together and began fanning at her face with her hands, taking deep breaths with eyes closed. If she'd wanted to respond then she was too overwhelmed to do so.

"Oh…" I remembered and delved into my bag, "a little something extra." I brought out the finishing touch and sprayed her liberally with Frédéric Malle Portrait of a Lady and upon smelling the fragrance, her eyes shined in an altogether different way.

I ran my hand down the bare flesh of her arm, my clenched jaw trembling just as, over her shoulder, movement on the beach drew my gaze.

She must have seen the look in my eyes because she whipped around and gasped. I had to support the girl as one leg almost buckled beneath her and she held a delicate hand to her heart. "Oh, gosh," her voice came out in a faint squeak, "this is really it."

I pressed my mouth against the side of her face and whispered, "just one favour, please…"

She nodded, "yes?"

"Please, just don't look back, only forwards, to your love, to your home." I kissed her cheek and gave her a gentle nudge toward the open steps. "Now, go to your lady." She paused at the top step and looked down, her chest heaving.

Below, Tilly stared out into the abyss, her sand spoiled wedding dress rising and falling with the breeze, her long and drenched golden curls making patterns in the distance, the sea finally closing in to swathe her bare feet.

Elspeth clung to the railing, her knuckles a pale shade of pink as she began her wobbly descent home.

I held onto the wall above as I watched the ending I'd denied them play out, only this time in reverse. Somewhere behind me an old horse and coach clattered along the road, carrying tourists probably, in a throwback to other times. Far off into the sea, a single small boat ribbed with the tide and seagulls cawed from somewhere to the west. The street lights hadn't yet turned on and the breath caught in my throat - It was a scene from my dreams, from the Victorian England I never thought to see. I took a deep intake of air and beneath the emerging stars, followed Elspeth with my gaze as she staggered toward her love.

All I could do was reflect on the events that had changed my life and entire way of thinking. I'd created Tilly as the perfect girl, but she wasn't. She had no imperfections for me to love. Maybe that's what comes from placing a girl on a pedestal before you've even come to know her, at least in person.

Yet for someone else, Tilly really *was* perfect and that's kind of the whole point. It was *they* who were perfect for each other. But things hadn't always been that way for them. They'd had to work at it for years before they even came together and without a doubt, they'd have to continue working at it for the rest of their lives, accepting each others' faults, quirks and bad habits. The thing is, they knew each others' imperfections and it made no difference. *That's* perfection.

Elspeth descended the final few steps of stone and then her feet felt the sand. Letting go of the rail, she continued in a straight line toward the girl who waited, staring into nothingness. A light breeze blew back Elspeth's hair and dress, giving her a surreal unearthly allure.

I was unaware of the whole world other than the impending reunion below as I wet my lips, the hairs on my arms stood on end and even my breathing commenced an irregular pattern. I leaned as far forward as the wall would allow without toppling over the top as Elspeth arrived to within a few short paces of happiness.

She stopped, hesitated and brought a hand to her heart.

The halting respite was too painful to watch and I willed her on. "Go, you're there, you're there."

Tilly, possibly sensing Elspeth's presence looked over her

shoulder, made a double-take, then turned fully around to face the newcomer.

Tilly's hand drifted toward her opened mouth, Elspeth's shoulders quaked, Tilly shook her head in disbelief, Elspeth opened out her arms.

Tilly fell into them and together, they crumpled to their knees in a tight embrace just as a gentle wave enclosed them before again receding. Their lips met in a passionate kiss, their hands lost in each others' hair. They pulled away, Tilly spoke words I'd never get to know, Elspeth nodded, they embraced again and then, just as the next gentle wave rolled over them...

...they were veiled by the dusk.

❄

I'D HELD myself together for Elspeth's benefit but now I couldn't help but break down against the wall.

Hyperventilating, I tipped out the contents of my bag over the ground, in search of a paper bag that wasn't there. Now, on my hands and knees I struggled for composure as two buses rumbled past, belching diesel from their exhausts, quickly followed by a flurry of cars tooting horns or shouting insults from opened windows whilst I struggled to remain conscious. My chest gave one final heave as my lungs battled to expire their excess oxygen and then...

...blackness.

EPILOGUE

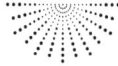

SIX MONTHS LATER

*E*ntering Georgina's Cafe on Low Petergate, I held open the door for my mother and placed a hand on her lower back as she tootled through. "There's a spare table by the wall on the left. Let's grab it," I spoke close to her ear, still getting used to the necessity of having to raise my voice so she could hear me. It was never like that.

I supported her by the arm as we approached the table, half noticing with the corner of my eye and ignoring the woman eyeballing me from the left.

Pulling out my mother's seat, I helped her down and read out the items on the menu as I stood over her.

"Erica, I can still scc."

She could still put the fear of God into me too. "What would you like? Latte, Americano, cappuccino?"

"Do they have a *normal* coffee?"

"Normal coffee, I'll see what I can do."

I headed toward the bar but was stopped halfway by a voice that came from behind a laptop screen.

"Erica?" It was Gemma who stood and ogled my figure.

"It is you, isn't it?" She nodded, "I wasn't sure. You look absolutely fantastic."

"Well, you know…" I thrust back my shoulders and stuck out my breasts, trying not to make it look too obvious, but revelling in the way she was probing me.

She opened out her palms and gaped. "I just can't believe how great you look." Her leering, as much as her words, were extra payment for all the hard work and sacrifice. "I mean, you look ten years younger."

"A good personal trainer and hill sprints, my love," though I wouldn't tell her the first three months had been literally hill *walks*. I'd also changed my diet and quit drinking, which were probably two of the hardest things I'd ever had to do but all that was only a few of the changes I'd recently made and an all-round better karma can do wonders for your appearance. Maybe it was all in the smile, which made meeting people a hundred times easier. No longer did I alienate every human being I came into contact with. There was truth in the old saying - For people to love you, you first have to learn to love yourself.

I glanced back over a shoulder to check on mother, who was busy berating a young couple at the next table so I decided there was no real rush to get back. I could talk to the charming young Gemma for a few minutes.

When I turned back to her, she was playing with her long dark hair. "Whoever your trainer is, you'll have to give me their number," she said while making an effort to sound nonchalant.

Couldn't she just take *my* number?

"So, what have you been doing?" She asked instead.

I pictured my two friends on the beach in Whitby as they embraced each other before disappearing forever. "I've been working on a sequel to *A Petal And A Thorn*. I, er, I just want to make sure they're both ok and live long and happy lives." I dismissed it by shaking my head and took two steps toward the bar. But something made me stop and return to the girl.

She watched my eyes, unsure, as I gave her svelte figure the same scrutiny she'd given me. The none biking biker chick attire worked well for her. She had her *look* and she stuck to it, and I admired the slight *I don't give a damn* attitude, even if she didn't go too far with it. Now she looked at me with even more caution and I thought I'd better state my case.

"Gemma, from what I already know, you're quite a bothersome woman and…no, no, please let me finish, I'm going somewhere with this, I promise you. You're an irritating woman, or at least that's what I had you for when we first met. I later discovered you're also quite clumsy," and beautiful, "but as you know, I'm not exactly perfect myself." A wide grin had stretched across her face and at that last remark, she laughed.

"You can say that again, hah," she bounced once on her toes and regarded me with a hint of expectation, probably because she'd guessed where I was attempting to take this.

Bloody hell, but my knees were shaking. "Anyway, I was wondering if you'd like to have a drink with me this evening?" I wouldn't say it'd be non-alcoholic on my part.

She grinned even wider but then tried to hide it, though there was no shielding the minuscules from me. "Of course, in fact, I was wondering what kept you so long."

I laughed and felt the tension wash away.

She glanced to her left. "You've changed."

"It's true, but say what you were going to." I couldn't help it, I was a woman, and we like to be complimented.

"Well, for one, you didn't push your mother into the Ouse."

I looked to my right as mother was still busy chastising the same young lady, apparently for the length of the summer dress she was wearing. "I guess there's always time."

"Well, I can see where you get it from." She brought out her phone and we exchanged numbers.

"I'll see you tonight," I confirmed and then ordered the drinks before returning to my mother.

She shuffled about in her seat and took several sips of coffee before finally mentioning it. "That woman you were speaking to…"

"…yes?"

She fiddled with her hands, "she looks lovely. Just right for you."

I leaned back in my chair and exchanged a look with Gemma across the noisy room. Then I smiled at mum. "Just right? How can you tell?" After everything I'd been through, the very notion was absurd. It took time and shared experiences for things to be *just right*.

She reached across the table and grabbed my wrists, taking my full attention. "I saw the way she looked at you when you were ordering the drinks."

I laughed. So that's what she was going on. "But mum, we hardly know each other. She can't be any more right for me than she is wrong. I'll give her a chance, which is as much as I can be expected to do for anybody."

"Well, aren't you just the romantic pragmatic," she said sarcastically whilst digging her nails into my wrists. "Be practical and shrewd all you want, but with love, sometimes you also need to wear your heart on your sleeve, let your guard down a little."

Bloody hell. There's no way of winning, is there?

Maybe when it comes to love, there's no right or wrong way. And you can contrive all you want but I'd only ever met

251

Gemma on numerous accidental encounters so obviously fate also wanted to get in there and play its own hand.

I thought again about Tilly and Elspeth and that, wherever they were, they more than most knew what was needed to make love work.

MESSAGE From The Author

I'd like to thank you for picking up this crazy book. I know it's quite different to my other stuff and to most in this genre, in fact, so I hope the change wasn't completely unwelcome.

During the story, I alluded to Erica writing the sequel to *A Petal And A Thorn*, which would resolve the unknown fates of Tilly and Elspeth. Indeed, during the writing of this book, I struck upon the idea of writing the actual story in its entirety, set in Victorian England.

What do you think, dear reader? Would it be something you'd be interested in? Would you like to know how life turns out for Tilly and Elspeth during a time when few people even knew about the existence of such things?

Whatever your opinion, please let me know in the form of a review on Amazon *wrings hands together with an evil grin.* I read all the reviews I get and I appreciate them all; good and bad.

Once again, thank you very much.

ALSO BY SALLY BRYAN

Novels

Trapped

Euro Tripped

Where Are You

Novellas

My Summer Romance

Printed in Great Britain
by Amazon